Pierre-Raymond closed Valerie's mouth with a kiss and put his hand up her skirt.

'*Ah oui!*' she murmured, her lips pressed hotly to his.

He turned her until her back was to the window, her feet apart to open her thighs for his caress.

Those passing in the street, if they glanced up, would see a woman flattened against the window – her dark hair, her thin black sweater, her full round bottom in a tight grey skirt. They would observe a man standing close to her, his hands hidden from view. And whatever he was doing to her, it made her whole body tremble and her beautiful bottom bump, bump, bump against the glass . . .

Amour Intime

Marie-Claire Villefranche

HEADLINE
DELTA

First published in 1995
by HEADLINE BOOK PUBLISHING

A HEADLINE DELTA paperback

10 9 8 7 6 5 4 3 2 1

ISBN 0 7472 5066 9

Typeset by CBS, Felixstowe, Suffolk

Printed and bound in Great Britain by
Cox & Wyman Ltd, Reading, Berks

HEADLINE BOOK PUBLISHING
A division of Hodder Headline PLC
338 Euston Road
London NW1 3BH

Amour Intime

Pierre-Raymond Finds Consolation

Liliane was half lying, half sprawling on the settee – a smile on her pretty face and her pullover up in her armpits to bare her breasts. She was an exquisite sight, a vision that heated a man's blood and made his nerves tingle in keenest anticipation of pleasure in store.

The settee she half lay on was the ugliest piece of furniture Pierre-Raymond had seen for a very long time. The frame was of blonde wood, perhaps beech, but the upholstery of the seat and back was a yellow and black imitation leopardskin.

Hideous, truly tasteless, Pierre-Raymond reflected. But then, the entire room was furnished in excruciating taste – which was evidently the choice of the idiot that Liliane lived with. How could she tolerate it? Pierre-Raymond wondered. Imagine sitting on this settee every day, it would drive one insane.

To make love on it was a deliberate act of defiance. Spitting in the face of grisly taste and cheap design. It made him feel quite heroic.

'*Chéri*?' Liliane said enquiringly, as if nudging him . . .

The look on her face was vague – almost as if she didn't know what happened next after a man had bared her breasts to stroke them. She sounded almost virginal, but it was years since a man had had her legs open the first time to teach her how it was done.

'What are you thinking?' she murmured.

She was aroused and ready to feel the weight of his body upon her. And hard flesh pushing up into her. Very ready.

She was wearing a thin white roll-top pullover, now rolled up to her chin. Her bra was unhooked and pushed up out of the way with the pullover, uncovering her breasts for Pierre-Raymond to play with. They were small pointed breasts, very appropriate to her slender, narrow-hipped figure.

Liliane was a pretty young woman, although in an unusual way. Her face was long and her chin pointed, her hair cut short, and brushed back, rich dark brown. It was a long time since Pierre-Raymond last undressed her and kissed her breasts – two years – but he had pleasing memories of her and her lovemaking.

There was one summer day in the country, he remembered, when he did it to her four times. It was in an apple-orchard and he'd had to carry her back to the car, she was too devastated to walk. On the return journey to Paris she suggested he stop the car in any quiet spot and did it to her again.

'We understand each other,' he said with his charming smile. Not that he had come to the apartment on the rue de Vaugirard today to make love to Liliane. She had been his girlfriend, but it was a long time ago and it hadn't been serious. With Pierre-Raymond it was never serious. He had come to see her because he was unhappy and he needed to talk to someone. He remembered how sympathetic a listener she had always been in the old days.

She touched her pointed little breasts with long fingers. She pushed her pullover further up under her armpits to display her charms to him. He stared thoughtfully at them.

'Be careful not to damage my gold chain,' she said, 'it was a present on my birthday. Let me take it off.'

The thin gold chain she was wearing round her neck had rolled up in the white pullover when he exposed her breasts and it was no longer visible. He shrugged and said it was secure – no harm would come to it. The momentary interruption did not please him because he had no wish to hear about birthday presents from her absent boyfriend.

Indeed, it seemed to him that this boyfriend's lack of taste, as revealed by his choice of the furnishings of the apartment, was having an insidious and bad effect on Liliane. Why else did she even remember her boyfriend at a time when her breasts were being kissed by Pierre-Raymond in person? She would never have behaved like that when she was *his* girlfriend.

With such abominable taste, what could this boyfriend of hers be like in bed? Pierre-Raymond wondered. Did he kiss her belly, did he suck her breasts till she was almost hysterical from the enormous sensations surging through her? Did he pour champagne into her bellybutton and lick it out?

To be accurate, Liliane had been Pierre-Raymond's employee at one time, not his girlfriend in the normal way. Everyone of any importance knew he was a leading portrait photographer, and for about a year Liliane had been his receptionist, his secretary, his book-keeper and his general assistant.

Naturally, on days when business was quiet, he undressed her in the studio and played with her.

It was Pierre-Raymond Becquet's confident belief – based upon years of experience – that he could reduce any woman to sobbing ecstasy. Several times, before they half fainted and begged him to stop, they could take no more . . . and they didn't always mean it when they said that.

'No, *chéri*, no more – you are killing me – ah yes, again, *mon amour*, do it again . . .'

He fondly remembered many babbling little cries of women with their arms around his neck and their legs apart.

Even Claudia, who had broken his heart, had sobbed and kicked in ecstatic spasms under him many a time. And begged him to do it to her again. And then again, her legs spread wide open on a bed. Or on her back on a sofa. Or on the floor. The thrills she found every time Pierre-Raymond lay on her belly and thrust his fifteen centimetres of stiff flesh into her – this made it virtually impossible for him to understand why she had deserted him.

When he found himself in urgent need of words of comfort and support, it was Liliane he phoned – of all the many, many women he had kissed and undressed and played with and ravaged. What a relief when she said he could call round that afternoon, Roland being away. Roland – that was the boy-friend she lived with, the man with impossible taste in furnishings.

Even so it was not easy to explain to Liliane that the reason for his desolation was another woman. A beautiful young woman. Liliane herself was beautiful, of course – Pierre-Raymond would never engage a plain receptionist. It was necessary for him to be surrounded by beautiful women, otherwise he would be unable to perform his artistic miracles of portrait photography.

'Desire is not only expressed horizontally,' he said. 'All my best work is an expression of desire. There is no better way to be in a permanent state of desire than to have desirable women available all day to admire and adore.'

He told everyone that. Some believed him. And he believed it himself.

For Pierre-Raymond, affairs with women were never serious. Now the impossible had happened. For once in his life it *had* become serious – absurdly serious. The truth was he was desperately in love with Claudia Deneuve – or at least he thought he was, which was much the same thing.

Claudia found him fascinating, she fell in love with him. And then after a month or two she decided that she wasn't. Everyone knows women have the right to change their minds for no reason, but when she told Pierre-Raymond she didn't love him any longer it was completely outside his comprehension. And when she said goodbye he was devastated.

He suffered agonies for three whole days and nights, alone at the beginning, and drunk and sick, until it became essential to talk to someone who would listen. Someone who could understand his heartbreak.

'Ah yes, how you have suffered, my poor darling,' the someone would say, smoothing his aching brow.

So here he was with Liliane Bonchamp on the imitation leopardskin settee, her little breasts bared beneath his roaming hands and their crimson points standing firmly to be caressed. And, if the truth is to be told, her skirt up around her thighs.

This hoisting of the skirt revealed to Pierre-Raymond's gaze an expanse of smooth pale skin above the top of her stockings. Her little white knickers had been eased over her hips and down her belly, far enough for a hint of brunette curls to show. Her body was familiar to him, he had taken it for his pleasure more times than he could remember when she used to work for him.

And to be candid, he adored Liliane's body. To kiss and

touch and lick and to do exquisite things to. Although to be truthful he adored many female bodies.

'Why?' Liliane was murmuring. 'Why, Pierre-Raymond?'

Perhaps she meant why had he half undressed her – why was he exciting her sexually with his clever fingers? And if that was what her words meant, it was a pointless question not worth an answer.

To give Pierre-Raymond his proper due, he had not come to her apartment for that, whatever she might think. He was so utterly disconsolate after his rejection by Claudia that he doubted if he would ever want to make love to any woman again.

'*Chérie*,' said Pierre-Raymond with a pale smile.

The word signified nothing at all, it was a pleasant noise to let her know he had heard her question.

No woman could compare with the beautiful Claudia. Of that he was completely convinced. Her smiles and her kisses – her round breasts and her elegant body. Those long legs of hers – and the way they wrapped themselves around his waist and held him close to her at the moment of ecstasy . . .

After knowing the best, no man of discernment settles for any less. Pierre-Raymond was a man of piercing discernment, all who knew him agreed on that. His experience of women was extensive, formidably extensive. He'd stripped so many women bare and lain on their smooth bellies that he truly understood the importance of love – he was a man who knew what he was talking about.

Claudia had spoiled him for other women, that was his belief, mournful though it was. For the rest of his life he feared that he would be celibate, demoralised and desolate.

It was summer and the long doors to Liliane's small balcony were open, but there was only the faintest of breezes. From outside came the sound of traffic along the busy rue de Vaugirard. Here on the ugly settee, Liliane was doing her best to console him. With her thin white pullover rolled up over her breasts and her grey skirt around her thighs.

Her face was a little flushed, her cheeks a delicate rose-pink. But the gentle heat of early summer had nothing to do with her condition; her pleasant colour came from Pierre-Raymond's long-fingered hands roaming over her naked breasts. He cupped them, he touched a fingertip to their crimson buds, he kissed them.

'Do shut up about this stupid Claudia,' Liliane nearly said – but she remained silent.

Her legs stirred uneasily on the fake leopardskin cushions, then moved as far apart as the little white knickers around her slender thighs allowed. She reached out to put a fingertip upon Pierre-Raymond's mouth. He smiled fondly at her and his tongue slipped out to lick her finger.

He pursed his lips and drew her finger into his mouth to suck it. She smiled back at him as her hand dropped to his thigh.

He continued to talk, as if nothing remarkable was happening. He'd been talking without drawing breath for half an hour, ever since he'd set foot in Liliane's apartment.

Talking of himself, his misery, his broken heart, his despair and despondency, his shattered emotions. And so on, a monologue of gloom.

Yet when Liliane's hand touched his thigh and her slow-moving fingertips explored carefully, what should she find but Pierre-Raymond's male part standing stiff inside his trousers? And to the tap-tap-tap of her finger through the fine woollen material that unseen but large part throbbed noticeably.

7

'My poor Pierre-Raymond,' she said, 'you are troubled – is it to be wondered at after all you have endured?'

She had not the least idea who this Claudia might be. Someone who had entered his life after she left his employment, so much was evident. She had no interest in Claudia, not even to ask if she was young, middle-aged, blonde, brunette, red-head, slender or plump. It was boring, this tale Pierre-Raymond was telling.

'Life has become a nightmare,' he informed Liliane.

'If there was only some way to console you,' she murmured.

He was so distracted, she thought, she could handle him until he was so aroused that he'd spurt inside his trousers before he realised what she was doing to him. That would stop his dreary moaning about Claudia – and it would be amusing to see the look on his face when his belly clenched in a climactic spasm and he knew too late that he had been secretly manipulated. Comical, in fact.

'No one can help me,' he said tragically, and his stiff flesh bounded under the touch of her hand.

This was emphatically not what he had come to Liliane's apartment for, that was very clear in his troubled heart and mind. He had not the least desire for this affair of bared breasts and brown curls between long pale thighs.

To slide his belly on to Liliane's belly and thrust up inside her – that was the last thing on his mind. To think about doing it with anyone else was a mockery of his great and undying love for Claudia Deneuve. This was an eternal and sacred love, and a memory he could never demean, a trust he could never break.

How then did it come about that in only half an hour with Liliane, he and she were together on a settee? Her breasts bare and his hands on them? If neither he nor she intended any of this, why was it happening?

The answer was remarkably simple. Because of his ardent nature and his life-long habits, Pierre-Raymond was incapable of being alone with any woman between the ages of sixteen and sixty without making sexual overtures. Married or unmarried, plain or pretty, virgin or tart, it made very little difference to him.

Pierre-Raymond adored women. He never passed up any opportunity to show this in the most practical way he understood, which was to slip down their knickers and ease them on to their backs.

He was thirty-four and his reaction to being alone with a woman was so automatic by now that while he was telling Liliane his miseries at being rejected by the woman he loved to distraction, he had fondled her breasts without thinking what he was doing.

'Women adore me,' he said to anyone who asked why he did what he did, and he would shrug and smile.

Naturally, he adored Liliane's spiky little breasts. He found it charming, the manner in which their points pushed themselves against the thin pullover so that they showed through clearly. While he was describing his sleepless nights and walking about the streets of Paris till dawn, his hands slid up into the pullover. Her little white bra came undone almost by itself and his fingers were stroking her bare warm flesh.

There were tears of grief in Pierre-Raymond's eyes as he told Liliane his life was finished – he hardly noticed himself that he was pulling her skirt up and had his hand between her thighs to clasp her between them. Perhaps he was unaware of the moment when he slipped her knickers down, not to her knees but halfway down her long slim thighs to show her brunette curls.

He did all this unconsciously. For him it was like unwrapping an expensive box of chocolates. Undo the ribbon and the wrapper, then take off the lid. This happened without much in the way of real inclination to taste a bon-bon, just to see what selection was inside the box.

To stroke a pretty woman's breasts during conversation was an ordinary part of Pierre-Raymond's routine, done without thought – and so was pulling her knickers down. Perhaps subconsciously he desired what was taking place. Certainly his experience told him that women are unlikely to say *non* with their knickers down their legs and their *belle-chose* revealed to the man concerned. As was Liliane's at this moment.

'But this is too much!' she remarked.

Her tone was complacent – she didn't seem to be protesting or objecting because he was casually feeling her *joujou*. Her words were a sympathetic comment on his emotional disaster.

'But yes,' he agreed, 'it is intolerable, a catastrophe.'

In spite of his exorbitant experience with women, in spite of the hundreds of soft warm bellies he had lain on, Pierre-Raymond was as complete an idiot about women as every other man. It was his simple belief that he was irresistibly attractive to women, that they murmured and sighed in delight when he caressed their breasts. That they lay down and opened their legs because to be loved by him was the supreme moment of their lives.

It goes without saying that women have reasons and motives of their own in these matters – sexual pleasure may not always be uppermost in a woman's mind when a man kisses her breasts. Liliane Bonchamp – who had worked for Pierre-

Raymond previously and had also helped him pass the time when there were no sitters to be photographed – she had more than one motive in her mind.

In fact, if Pierre-Raymond could have seen into her head and observed her most secret thoughts while he was playing with her pretty little breasts, he would have been very surprised.

The situation on the imitation leopardskin settee was absurd and Liliane was bored to distraction by this sad tale of heartbreak and spurned love. When Pierre-Raymond's hands began their slow exploration of her body, she knew it had no significance. It was a part of his ordinary behaviour.

When she worked for him she had learnt that he was very expert with women's bodies. Furthermore, it was undeniable that he was good-looking and pleasing. Why not close her ears to his dreary tale, she asked herself, relax and let him give her the sexual pleasure he understood so well?

'Ah,' she murmured, 'ah, yes, Pierre-Raymond . . .'

'*Chérie*,' he murmured back.

But, women being women, her motive was not really that simple and uncomplicated. She was tired of her boyfriend, Roland, the man who paid for the leopardskin settee she was sprawling upon with her knickers down. Roland had become tedious to her – even his regular nightly performance in bed now failed to raise her to the peak of ecstasy it once had.

Roland was adequate, of course, when he lay on her belly and thrust away vigorously. But pretty young women expect more from a lover than mere adequacy – adequacy is for husbands. Time for a change, Liliane concluded, while she was still young enough and pretty enough to be selective.

The sudden appearance of Pierre-Raymond Becquet from her past couldn't have been better timed from Liliane's point of view. Roland was away for three days and here was Pierre-Raymond full of misery – and incapable of keeping his hands to himself. Just as he'd always been.

There were times when she thought of Pierre-Raymond not as a man with a length of stiff flesh sticking out in front but as a strong tireless *thing* dragging a man along behind it.

And it was truly tireless, the stiffness she could feel under her fingers as she caressed through the cloth of his trousers.

In the old days this *thing* had rubbed against every part of her slender and beautiful body, her breasts and her belly, her feet and her throat. She had even conducted conversations with it as she held it in her hand.

'You believe you can dominate me,' she addressed it more than once in those days, 'but you are my slave, not my master.'

Whatever the relationship might be, that long stiff *thing* had spurted its enthusiasm into her times without number – not only into her *joujou* but into every opening of her slender body.

Liliane had never been with another man who displayed half the energy and stamina of Pierre-Raymond when his *thing* was stiff – which was very often. And no other man ever displayed anything like his desire to vary the ways in which he did it to her.

Roland, for example, his imagination was very restricted – he simply wanted her on her back, night after night after night in bed with her legs apart. For him to lie on top and push it up her. Sometimes for a change she persuaded him to let her lie on top and spike herself on him, but he wasn't at all keen on it.

Pierre-Raymond, it had to be confessed, was in a class by himself. Liliane had fond memories of the time she worked for him. And as things stood at present in her life, she would be happy to exchange him for Roland.

On terms more favourable to herself, of course. There was no great advantage she could think of in being his employee again, available on dull afternoons to keep him amused. No, she wanted a different arrangement this time. She wanted to take Claudia's place. It seemed to her she had a chance – why else had he come to her with his ridiculous tale of a broken heart unless he had a real affection for her?

'Kiss me, *chéri*,' she sighed.

She arched her back to make her charming little breasts stand out more prominently.

It was fortunate for Pierre-Raymond that he had no suspicion of what Liliane was thinking. He kissed the tips of her breasts and rambled on about his miseries almost without interruption. He slid his hand up her skirt and felt her smooth bare thighs above her stockings. His fingers moved imperceptibly above the little knickers he had eased halfway down toward her knees.

Liliane sighed hopefully – it seemed that his monologue about Claudia was coming to an end at last.

He had long agile fingers. She remembered them well – and the ecstasies they had produced in her so often back in his studio on slow days. The first time he handled her was so casual that she'd been on the brink of orgasm before she realised just what he was doing to her.

At the time, she had been sitting at the small plain desk on which the studio accounting and correspondence was done – it was only her second day in the job. Pierre-Raymond was explaining how he kept track of the invoicing – he was facing her, perched on the edge of the desk. There arose a certain tension – perhaps even a magnetic pull, one might say – between their bodies.

Ah mon Dieu, she thought, amazed to find that she was becoming aroused just from being stared at by this fascinating man, *but it is absurd, to be affected so easily*!

At first his hand rested lightly on her shoulder, a gesture of encouragement it could almost be said. He was staring down the front of her blouse at her pointed little breasts which, as it happened, were hardly covered at all by her bra. Very soon after that it became obvious to Liliane there was a distinct bulge in the front of Pierre-Raymond's stylish trousers.

Aha, he is as excited as I am, she said to herself, *but a man becomes stiff so easily, it is not really flattering. A pair of stockings discarded on a bed where a woman has slept is enough to excite most men. As easily as if the woman was in the room and naked except for the stockings*.

He slid off the desk and turned to stand beside her, a finger tracing the lines of figures in the ledger open on the desk for her inspection. His hand moved itself down from her shoulder to under her arm, through her thin blouse his fingers just touched her breast. She heard herself sigh and tried to control it.

He showed her the view – they stood at the window, looking at the Seine below and the booksellers' stalls along the quay. She felt his hand on her bottom, he was stroking the cheeks with an appreciation that calmed her. He slid his hand under the hem of her skirt, up the back of her thighs.

'*Ah non,* Monsieur Becquet,' she said – or she started to say. By then his fingers were in her knickers and caressing her bottom. Deep down between the cheeks!

He said something about the view of Paris from the window

14

but she wasn't listening. His hand slid down her bottom, fingertips in the crease, until he was feeling between her thighs. It was impossible to speak – a persuasive feeling of pleasure thrilled through her whole body. He was so very casual about what he was doing to her and his manner of doing it was so very courteous that nobody could possibly take offence.

He was an attractive man, Pierre-Raymond, and Liliane was not married nor heavily involved at that time with a boyfriend. She let him fondle her between the legs, she slid her feet apart on the floor to open her thighs. Eventually, when she was right at the edge of orgasm, he guided her trembling steps to the chaise longue that was part of the furniture of his office.

Her body shook feverishly when he removed her blouse. And her knickers – and lifted her legs up in the air. She expected him to get down and lie on her, but he hooked her legs over his shoulders, leaned over and slid his stiff part into her.

She watched it going in, her belly shaking with sensation as the long hard part penetrated her, opening her, pushing up deep into her. His hands were on her bare breasts, kneading them. He looked into her eyes, he murmured her name while he slid in and out in a rhythm which brought on her orgasm almost at once.

Pierre-Raymond laughed and rolled her pointed little breasts, his thumbs flickered over the straining buds. He swung his hips easily and expertly back and forth, making her feel the thrust and domination of his hardness inside her. Then the orgasm took her again and her legs were thrashing on his shoulders, feet up in the air, her shoes kicked to the far corners of the office.

Her hands clawed at his lean belly and strong thighs. She

had ripped his shirt out of his open trousers and her nails raked down his belly to the root of the stiff male part that slid into her and out again – the part that impelled her into a third orgasm. Pierre-Raymond shrieked at the claw of her fingernails down his flesh and jolted his desire fiercely into her.

After that first time it was more or less a daily occurrence, Pierre-Raymond ravishing her body to astounding pleasures. With vivid delight she recalled those long hours when he played with her and practised his skills on her body. That part of her life was printed on her mind forever – recollections of overwhelming ecstasies. There could be no argument about it at all, Pierre-Raymond was a virtuoso of sexual pleasure.

It was never the same twice with him. Sometimes he had her on the desk, sitting with her legs apart – or on her back with her legs up on his shoulders. Other times he led her from her desk into the studio and took her on a high-backed Indonesian wicker chair. On her back, or on her knees with her arms on the chair-seat. Even standing with her back to the wall – Pierre-Raymond loved to do it different ways.

'You are magnificent,' she would murmur brokenly after he had given her a devastating series of orgasms and she was unable to stand on her feet for a while.

She stretched out a trembling hand to touch his softening wet part and hold it. 'You are insatiable, Pierre-Raymond . . .'

'But of course,' he would say with a smile, stroking her face and pleased by her words, 'of course, *chérie.*'

Liliane Has A Plan

Pierre-Raymond was totally faithless in his dealings with women – that went without saying. Liliane discovered this soon after she went to work at his studio. After he'd made love to her, of course. Less than a week with him was enough for her to realise that he was on terms of intimate friendship with all the women who came to have their pictures taken. He made love to them in the studio, in the office, anywhere he chose – or nearly all of them.

Liliane had another role in his enterprise besides being his receptionist/secretary/book-keeper/etc. It was to part her legs for Pierre-Raymond when he had no female client to play with in his studio. Half an hour with no entry in the appointment book and his hand was up Liliane's skirt and in her little knickers to feel her darling *joujou*. And not long after that he'd slide her knickers down her legs and have them off.

She accepted this subordinate status for a time – his conceit in believing that he was utterly irresistible to women was more amusing than exasperating. For a time. Self-delusion on such a scale was breathtaking. But a year proved enough for her, then she decided to move on.

Pierre-Raymond was sorry to lose her. He never understood why she wanted to leave. He made a grand effort, he took her

17

out to dinner, he took her to his apartment, he took her to bed. She'd never been in a bed with him before – as many times as he'd made love to her, it had always been at the studio.

He brought all his considerable skills into play. By morning he'd ravaged her so thoroughly she was half in love with him.

But even that wasn't enough to change her mind. She tried her best to explain it to him, but he never understood what she was saying.

He came to the conclusion that this tale of not wishing to be number thirty-six in his harem was an excuse. The true explanation was much simpler, he told himself, she'd met a man and was in love. That was the only way he could make sense of her resignation.

It had never happened to him personally – becoming so devoted to one person that it was impossible to contemplate making love to others. He had heard and read about it and knew it existed – and he was certain that's what had happened to Liliane.

He gave her a generous leaving bonus and they parted friends, though he was completely wrong about her motives. And now here they were together again two years later – on a leopardskin settee. In an apartment on the rue de Vaugirard she shared with another man, Roland Somebody.

And she was half lying on her back with her white pullover up under her arms and her knickers round her knees. His long stiff *thing* was sticking out of his trousers like a flagpole and he was sliding it into her. She drew her breath in sharply as she felt her *joujou* opened and filled by Pierre-Raymond's penetration.

He hadn't changed, she decided, that was obvious. But she had her own plans for him in future.

'*Chéri*,' she sighed, parting her legs as far as her underwear permitted. She was highly aroused and felt her willpower slide gently away on tremors of delicious sensation. But somewhere in the core of her being the intention to subjugate Pierre-Raymond and take Claudia's place in his life remained unaffected.

Naturally, she didn't believe his heartbreak was genuine. Her opinion was that he'd never been in love. Not once. Perhaps he was capable of great enthusiasm occasionally, but that was the extent of it. This long and dreary lament about Claudia was not convincing. It was necessary to bring it to a conclusion – and Liliane was certain she knew how.

For the last five minutes she had been holding his stiff part through the cloth of his trousers – squeezing it and rubbing it lightly. So far he seemed not to be aware of what she was doing to him, even though his stiffness was throbbing under the slow stroke of her thumb. Now she undid his trousers and put her hand right inside.

She felt under his shirt and into his underwear, touching and stroking, until her fingers found hard flesh and she grasped it firmly. The many times she had felt the strength and stiffness of it inside her! Felt it sliding purposefully in her warm wet slippery flesh, gentle and evocative, raising her by easy steps to a long quivering ecstasy.

And how many times had she felt it slam hard into her, churn her belly with ferocious sensation that made her shriek and sob for release from unbearable pleasure? The savage spurt of his desire into her! Into her mouth, as well as her belly. She had sucked Pierre-Raymond's throbbing hardness into her mouth often in the old days and had made him shake and whimper with excitement.

It was in his office one rainy afternoon, the first time that she did that to him. Because of the rain a client had phoned to cancel her appointment. Even with an umbrella and taking a taxi to the studio, she said, the dampness in the air would ruin her hair-do and the photograph would be very unflattering.

Pierre-Raymond was sitting on the edge of the desk. Without a word, only his usual charming smile, he opened his trousers and took out his male part, stiff and long. Liliane guessed what he wanted. She hitched up her skirt and knelt on the floor between his dangling legs, her face close to his upright flesh.

His hands rested lightly on her shoulders while she stared at his twitching stiffness. His knees closed in to grip her sides and she could hear his quick breathing.

'*Ah mon Dieu* – it's so big,' she sighed.

She opened her mouth and slipped the plum-purple head between her lips. She touched it with her tongue, tracing the shape and size of that silky and unhooded head. 'Ah, ah, ah,' Pierre-Raymond moaned. She sucked it in further and felt it slide against the wet roof of her mouth, then further.

Her little white teeth nipped the long shaft, her lips closed to hold it in place, her mouth was filled with warm hard flesh. She put a hand into his open trousers to cup his hairy pompoms – his knees in her armpits held her tight – while her tongue slid quickly over the naked head in her mouth. Pierre-Raymond panted and shook and his fingers dug into her shoulders through her light spring frock.

Half a minute later, no more, and he arched his back and cried out loudly as he spurted into her mouth.

'*Chérie, chérie, je t'adore*,' he was babbling wildly.

But here and now, on the imitation leopardskin settee in her apartment, she wasn't going to do that for him. Perhaps later –

it would depend. She knew that in another two minutes this long hard *thing* of his would be up inside her. He must know it too – although he was maintaining an air of indifference.

'Ah no,' Pierre-Raymond murmured sadly to the slow sliding of her long fingers on his stiff part, 'it is not possible.'

'But why not? What do you mean?'

'I can never allow myself those pleasures again,' he said in a voice that sounded as if the world was about to end. 'I'm too shocked by what has happened. It is impossible to consider love after the betrayal I have endured.'

Liliane knew he was talking complete nonsense but decided it was better not to say so – men could take offence so quickly if they imagined their masculinity was being laughed at. Leave him his idiotic illusion, it would make no difference now she'd got his hardness in her hand and was stroking up and down.

Even while he was protesting that he would never, never again give his heart and soul to a woman, however loving she might be – Liliane slid her legs further apart on the settee. Her pretty face was flushed pink from the touch of his clever fingers and she put a hand on his shoulder to pull him closer to her body.

Pierre-Raymond's attention was caught by the movement of her thighs. He glanced down thoughtfully at the gap between her knickers and her belly – as if he'd never seen a woman's *joujou* before in his life. He stopped chattering – that was a distinct improvement, Liliane said to herself. His fingers were combing through her fleece.

Liliane was dark brunette, but she had less body hair than is usual for brown-haired women. An upright strip of curls adorned her *bijou*, not the broad-topped triangle that is most frequent. When she was alone and naked before her mirror she felt

21

pleased by this arrangement of brunette curls between her slender legs. She kept her little fleece neatly clipped – to an even narrower strip than nature intended.

It was extremely arousing, this grooming by Pierre-Raymond's agile fingers. He made her curls stand up and bush out, so that her tuft seemed larger than it truly was – and against the pale skin of her belly the brown curls were rich and pleasing.

'Ah, life was so uncomplicated in those days,' he murmured, a mournful look on his face, 'when you were with me at the studio and we touched and kissed whenever the mood took us.'

As Liliane recalled from her year in his employ, it was a question of when the mood took *him*. Which was very often. In fact, she'd never in her life known a man who wanted to do it half as often as Pierre-Raymond. Her year as his employee had seemed one long unofficial honeymoon of being undressed and ravished to orgasm day after day. Working for him, she had no desire and no energy and no need for a boyfriend outside her job.

'Uncomplicated, yes,' she agreed with a little nod – although not meaning the same as he did, 'but time never stands still.'

'I adored you then,' he said, 'but you never believed me when I told you so. What a pity you left – if you had stayed with me I wouldn't be in this disastrous emotional condition – you were always so intelligent, so prudent. I respected you for it. With you there I would never have been drawn into this catastrophe.'

Liliane arched her eyebrows in amazement to hear herself made responsible for Pierre-Raymond's idiocies with another woman. A little sigh of exasperation almost escaped her but she was able to suppress it.

At the same time, it was interesting to hear him claim he had respected her for her good sense – it gave moral support to her plan to capture him. She raised her round little bottom off the settee to push her knickers further down her thighs.

Pierre-Raymond's mournful expression was vanishing. He leaned over to kiss the bare flesh of her belly, the tip of his tongue pressing into her dimple of a bellybutton. She sighed gently to feel him slip her knickers down to her ankles and over her feet – now she could part her legs wide enough for him to renew his acquaintance with the part of her he adored most ardently.

'Ah yes,' he said softly, staring at her soft pink peach, his fingertips caressing the fleshy lips, 'it seems so strange that we are together again after so much has happened.'

She set her shoulder blades comfortably against the imitation leopardskin back of the settee and spread her thighs widely. A series of sighs escaped Pierre-Raymond as he was unbuckling his black leather belt. He slipped out of the jacket of his striped grey suit, he loosened his bright blue tie.

The yellow and black upholstered settee was for two people to sit side by side. It was not long enough to lie full-length on, not for ordinary-sized grown-ups. Liliane was about to suggest they moved into the bedroom, to continue in horizontal comfort, when Pierre-Raymond went down on his knees on the floor between her parted thighs.

His long hard twitching part pointed at her *bijou* like a forefinger pointing the right direction. She took it in her hand to guide it where they both wanted it to be.

'Yes, it's just as I remember,' she sighed, 'stiff and strong and thick and ready day and night to perform its duty.'

'Always,' he murmured, 'always, *chérie*.'

The plum-purple head met the pouting lips between her legs in a thrilling manner – she drew breath sharply in anticipation of what was to come. Then a strong push by Pierre-Raymond took him into her. She let her breath out in a long sigh at feeling her hot flesh opened and stretched by his long sliding penetration.

Her arms were about his neck while she pressed her bare belly against him. His cheek was against hers – he couldn't see the secret smile on her pretty face. His broken heart was evidently healed by the urgent sensations in another part of his anatomy, a part located much lower down in the human body.

As for eternal and sacred love, it flew out of the window the instant Pierre-Raymond had another woman's knickers down. Which was precisely what Liliane had expected.

'You are adorable,' he gasped, sliding in and out of her warm moistness with an easy stroke, 'you understand me – what a fool I was to let you leave when you did!'

Naturally Liliane understood him – well enough to know he was merely babbling in the excitement of sexual delight. Words said in these moments had no validity or significance afterward.

'Ah you, you . . .' she breathed – she was very close to her own point of no return.

He had stirred her intensely by playing with her breasts from the first moment that he arrived at her apartment and launched into his tale of despair of lost love. Soon, very soon, Liliane was going to reach an ecstatic climax. She wanted it more than anything in the world at that moment.

But she was not a fool. Through the throbbing pleasure of her body she kept a grip on her hopes to reclaim Pierre-Raymond for herself. She wanted him to be at her command as he had been at Claudia's – if he could be believed about that situation.

In the matter of lovemaking, Pierre-Raymond could do it very slowly or he could do it very fast, according to his mood. That was something Liliane had learned when she worked for him.

If a client was due in five minutes time to be photographed but the mood was on him, he'd stand Liliane against the studio wall, knickers around her knees. Push smoothly up into her. And finish in ten or twelve hard strokes.

But when an hour without a sitter stretched ahead, he removed her knickers and put her on her back on the chaise longue, legs spread wide, and played delicately with her for what seemed an eternity, before he mounted her spasming belly.

When he was inside her, there was another eternity of teasing and slipping to and fro, in and out, up and down – till she was on the very edge of hysteria with ravening sexual sensation.

He was an expert, Pierre-Raymond – a virtuoso. Even if he had her in a hurry against a wall or bending forward with her hands upon the desk and her skirt up over her bare bottom, it might be quick, but he never failed to take her to complete orgasm.

In ten strokes? she thought through the blazing whirl of her sexual release. *This is not possible*! But it was – and he did, and she did.

On slow days at the studio, when there was an hour before the next sitter was due, then his delicate attentions to her pretty breasts and to her *jouet* were devastating. His agile tongue and fingers evoked tremendous waves of sensation in her – he could make her experience orgasm twice at least, three times even, before he lay over her belly and slid his stiff part in. Then he'd make her climax another two or three times before he jetted his passion into her.

A particular pleasure of slow days, though they were few, was Pierre-Raymond returning the favour she performed when he asked – letting him make use of her pretty mouth. He turned her chair round so that her back was to the desk, he removed her knickers and her skirt as well. She sat bare-bottomed on the chair with her feet well apart and Pierre-Raymond kneeling between them.

He stroked her *belle-chose* with his clever fingers, he opened the pretty pink lips, he caressed her little secret bud inside. When she began to tremble, he put his head between her legs and pushed his tongue into her. He did it slowly and carefully. She trembled more and sighed to feel his wet tongue caressing, his hot breath in her groin.

'Ah, Pierre-Raymond,' she moaned, 'one day you will murder me with pleasure – you will have to explain to the police why I am sitting in your office without my knickers, dead with a look of ecstasy on my face. Ah, yes, don't stop, *chéri*, don't stop . . .'

In a very short time, a minute perhaps, Liliane was much too deeply involved with her exquisite sensations to be able to say anything that made sense. The flicker of his tongue was sending tremors through her belly that caused her to shriek in delight. Her hands reached down to grasp Pierre-Raymond's ears and press his face closer in between her bare and quivering thighs.

That tongue of his, it probed her, it slid and rubbed against her secret bud. His thumbs were hooked in her, exposing her secret place to his deliciously tormenting tongue, torturing her with spasms of impossible pleasure. The glide of his tongue was threatening to destroy her sanity – she adored him, worshipped him, wanted him for herself.

He was holding the wet lips of her *joujou* wide open. She felt the dew of her intense arousal on those parted pink lips and on the insides of her splayed and shaking thighs . . . ah, her orgasm one second away! Her belly fluttered, she gasped and squirmed at the very instant of exploding into ecstasy.

'Pierre-Raymond,' she was moaning, 'make me . . .'

She clawed her fingernails into the dark curls of his head – her feet had come up off the floor and now flailed behind his back. As the orgasm began she screamed shrilly – his tongue darted in faster and his thumbs held her open ruthlessly as he exploited her climax to the limit of endurance.

She writhed and jerked to the stupendous sensations that shot through her. She screamed, 'No more, no more, yes, more, more,' and his urgent tongue lapped over her swollen bud relentlessly till her mind blacked out and she collapsed in the chair.

The memory of those days when he used his tongue was so vivid still in Liliane's mind that she was going to do everything she could to persuade him to do it before he left the apartment. He had to be in the right mood, which meant this foolish hankering after Claudia must be pushed out of his mind.

That shouldn't be too difficult now she had him on the settee and her knickers were off. And he was between her legs with his fifteen centimetres throbbing in her. She knew him well enough to be confident his mood would change for the better now.

'*Chéri*,' she whispered to him, clenching her belly muscles to squeeze his stiff male part, massaging it as if with her hand. She wondered which it would be, fast or slow, now his long hard part was inside her. She pressed her thighs apart on the yellow and black mock leopardskin cushions and held him close to her, his bare belly pressed close to her bare belly.

'*Je t'adore,* Lili,' he gabbled, stabbing into her with quick, sharp, nervous little jabs, '*je t'adore, chérie!*'

So it was to be fast and hard, this renewal of their intimate acquaintance! Liliane lay back, her limbs loose, her body open and welcoming – she surrendered herself to the surging waves of sensation. She was counting his strokes to discover exactly how fast he could be when he wanted to.

But the pleasure was too intense – at the count of nine her body jerked and a fierce little orgasm erased the possibility of any conscious thinking. A moment later Pierre-Raymond cried out and slammed in furiously as he spurted.

He had forced his hands under her bottom, between soft flesh and imitation leopardskin cushions. He gripped her cheeks hard – his fingernails pierced her flesh as he jerked and wailed and jetted his desire into her. She screamed softly because it was so brutally delicious.

'Ah, yes, yes, yes!' she sobbed. 'Don't stop, *chéri!*'

'*Je t'aime,* Lili, *je t'aime,*' Pierre-Raymond moaned.

When her senses returned she decided it had been as wonderful as ever but over too quickly to be truly satisfying. Fortunately, she knew what to do. After Pierre-Raymond regained his strength – which would take perhaps ten minutes, if he was as persistent in lovemaking as he used to be, she meant to take him into the bedroom. So that he could do it slowly and deliberately – as in the days when she worked for him and there was no haste.

'I have surprised myself,' he said, with a sigh of contentment.

'Really?' she said, not sure what he meant.

'I feared I could never truly adore a woman again. But I can, thanks to you, Liliane – my heart is whole again.'

'And another part of you is also working very well,' she said with a kiss on his cheek, 'come into the bedroom with me, so we can recall some of the pleasures of our past days together.'

It wasn't going to be just an hour's roll on the bed, Liliane promised herself. Another surprise awaited Pierre-Raymond when she had him naked and stiff again – she intended to keep him in bed with her for the rest of the day.

As she knew, it was easy enough to excite him with a touch of the fingers or a glimpse of open thighs. The tip of a breast in his ear, the clasp of his hand between her legs. Once she had him interested, he wouldn't want to hurry away.

When he needed a little rest, a moment or two's respite while he recovered his strength, Liliane was going to roll him on his back on the bed and kneel between his legs and take his hot and sticky stiffness in her hand. She could make it jump for joy by sliding her fingers up and down the swollen shaft, make it strain upwards, huge and shaking in her grasp. And tease him.

That's enough now, she'd say with a grin, staring down at his flushed face, *I'm going to stop now.*

Liliane – I implore you, he'd moan, his twitching part at it's maximum length and thickness, *don't stop now!*

Tell me that you adore me Pierre-Raymond or I shall stop this very instant.

I adore you, Lili – I was a fool to let you leave me.

Are you just saying that – or do you truly adore me?

She would have him gasping and desperate to be taken the

29

rest of the way, the jerking flesh in her massaging hand speaking of his frantic eagerness for her to continue – to take him so far that his desire would come fountaining up into the air.

She led him by the hand into the bedroom. He stared without a word at the bed, a construction of wood and gilded ironwork. It was impossible to know what style it was supposed to be, it had fake brocade curtains and long gold tassels arranged in a sort of open-sided tent. Could one really make love on so ridiculous a bed? Liliane's boyfriend had bought it to perform on – proof that he was an uneducated savage!

In seconds they were both naked on the bed together, his fifteen centimetres of hard flesh standing up boldly. He stared down at Liliane's slender body, naked and delectable – pointed little breasts, soft little belly with its recessed dimple, the narrow strip of brunette curls between her thighs. She had removed the gold chain from round her neck, he observed – she still had the gold ear-studs that were probably part of the same birthday present from her boyfriend.

She was staring at Pierre-Raymond's stiffness with a certain respect and admiration. *And why not*, he said to himself, *it is magnificent, every woman who sees it agrees on that.*

He was crouching over her and put his knee between her thighs, pressing them apart. She looked up into his face, aroused as highly as he was, breathless to feel the weight of his body on her. But he was stroking her, both his hands gliding on her belly, over her breasts, down between her open legs.

'Oh *chéri*,' she murmured, 'please, please . . .'

She rolled her body from side to side, not to escape from the touch of his clever hands, but because she was too aroused to lie still now. He caressed her belly and she gasped, his hands moved down between her legs and her body jerked wildly. He leaned over her to lick her breasts, she moaned. His mouth moved down her body slowly to kiss between her thighs.

He knelt upright between her spread legs. Liliane reached up and touched the dark curls on his chest and then the dark curls between his legs where his long thick part jutted up fiercely. She took it her hand and held it to feel how strong it was – she wanted it in her mouth, demanding her submission.

'But what you do to me is outrageous,' she told him.

Her legs moved wider apart, her bottom lifted off the bed in a gesture of invitation.

His belly was on hers and he was pushing into her and she was yielding and open to him. Her chin was up, her dark brown eyes wide open and looking into his. On her face was a half smile. If Pierre-Raymond had been in command of his senses just then he'd have recognised it as a knowing smile. He might have asked himself the reason for it. But he didn't.

The slide of his hard flesh inside her was driving him into a sexual frenzy very rapidly. His fingers were clenched tight on her shoulders, his loins rose and fell jerkily to drive himself into her. Liliane too was frantic with sensation – she was even more aroused than he was.

Her orgasm came suddenly – in quick little spasms that arched her back up off the bed and jammed her belly against his. Pierre-Raymond heard how she cried out in her delight, the push of her hot belly on his ravished his imagination and triggered his release. He stared into Liliane's eyes, their mouths met in a clinging kiss while he gushed his passion into her belly.

Yes, yes, yes, yes, Liliane was screaming silently inside her head, *I'm going to keep you here all night, Pierre-Raymond*.

After that, tomorrow morning when she brought him fresh

coffee in bed and kissed him awake, he would be drained of desire and pale and trembling. He would go down on his knees to lick her bare feet in delight and gratitude. And then one would see what one would see, Liliane told herself.

Back To Work

When he left Liliane's apartment finally – after many kisses and caresses on every part of her slim naked body, most sincere declarations of mutual adoration and ardent wishes they would soon be together again – Pierre-Raymond had a ravenous appetite.

Liliane had given him the usual breakfast of *café-au-lait* and soft roll with apricot preserve, but he required more than that to restore his energy. On the way to his studio he went into a brasserie he knew on the Boulevard Raspail and ordered himself a six-egg omelette. With cheese and ham – plenty of both. After that he had a small glass of cognac and smoked a cigarette. It was midday when he reached his studio on the Quai St Michel. He felt his stamina was much restored.

He'd been away for three days. Mademoiselle Charbonnet smiled at him when he came into the studio and said he looked a little pale and tired – was he certain he was fully recovered from his illness? Was it wise to return to work so soon?

She was his present receptionist, secretary, book-keeper, and she had the impression Pierre-Raymond had been ill – that being the convenient lie he had told her on the phone. It was not exactly a lie – on the morning after Claudia Deneuve told him she never wanted to see him again, he had woken up alone with a crippling headache and a stomach jumping like a frog in a cold pond. This must be the worst hangover he'd ever known, he thought sickly.

The thought of getting up and dressing and going to work made him retch. It was a dreadful effort to phone Mlle Charbonnet at the studio and tell her to cancel all appointments. 'It must be a summer flu,' he lied to her, 'a day or two in bed will cure it.'

In effect, he stayed in bed to sleep it off until about seven that evening, then hunger drove him out to a restaurant. He did not get drunk again, the memory of the hangover was too painful and too recent, but he had a glass or two to cheer himself up.

He was too miserable to work next day, but that was emotion, not alcohol. After lunch on the third day he remembered Liliane Bonchamp and went to see her. What a stroke of good fortune her boyfriend happened to be absent at exactly the right time! She had the right cure for what troubled Pierre-Raymond's heart and mind – and it was between her pretty thighs. He stayed with her all day and all the night too, feeling more and more cheerful.

Now here he was back at his studio on the Quai St Michel and Mlle Charbonnet was looking him over carefully.

'Are you sure you're better now?' she asked. 'Another day in bed might be more sensible. It's no problem to put the bookings off till next week.'

Pierre-Raymond liked Mlle Charbonnet. In fact, he liked every woman who ever worked for him, otherwise he'd never employ them at all. On this fine morning Mlle Charbonnet was wearing a thin black sleeveless pullover and when she jumped up from her chair as he came in her heavy round breasts bounced – that soft elastic bounce of desirable female flesh.

That was the point of choosing beautiful women as employees – to watch their bodies in motion. It gladdened the heart and it raised the spirit with every passing hour at work. Not that the spirit alone was raised – the male part raised its head inside one's underwear and took a keen interest. Which was positive proof that all was well.

Pierre-Raymond loved to be stiff and strong in his underwear – even when he was working, taking pictures, talking to clients on the phone, whatever. It was a theory of his – a firm belief – that he was at his best when his important part stood up stiff. No matter what the occasion, even if there was not the remotest intention of utilising this stiffness for its natural purpose.

In accordance with his theory, the target he aimed at was to be in a condition of hardness for two-thirds of his waking day. At least two-thirds. It was no great problem for him as he had a vivid and creative imagination. He could make himself stiff in his trousers by thinking of the woman he'd touched last – of how he'd handled her breasts and stroked between her thighs.

At the end of a long day, when he'd pleasured a client or two in addition to little games with his receptionist-secretary, if imagination proved inadequate, he need only slip his hand into his trouser pocket and stroke his cherished part with a fingertip and it would stand up hard and bold.

As for his sleeping hours, that was another matter. *Grandjean* down between Pierre-Raymond's thighs in his silk pyjamas had to make his own arrangements during the night. Presumably he did – Pierre-Raymond woke most mornings to find a satisfactory state of hardness. Often with memories of dreams in which he had done fascinating things to beautiful women. Remarkable things – even impossible things sometimes. And they were the most interesting of all to him.

The gentle bounce of Mlle Charbonnet's big breasts inside her pullover was precisely what was required to put a smile on his face and give him the impression all was well with the world.

He assured her that he had recovered from his mysterious flu. It would be unkind to tell her he'd acquired this slight air of fatigue on a leopardskin settee with Liliane Bonchamp. Then in bed with her. From four o'clock yesterday afternoon until after ten this morning.

'Strong black coffee?' she asked.

He nodded and she went to pour him a cup from the supply kept permanently hot over a spirit burner. Her bottom was plump, the cheeks wobbled deliciously under her skirt when she walked away from him to get the coffee.

'*Ah, c'est bon,*' he said, but very quietly to himself.

She had the sort of round fleshy bottom that made a man want to stand behind her and put his arms round her waist and rub his upright part against those superb cheeks. The good God had been very kind to men when he designed women's bodies as they were – Pierre-Raymond thanked Him cordially for it.

That plump bottom, for example, stretching the skirt tight when Valerie Charbonnet bent over, it was as near to perfection as anyone could ever hope to find in this very imperfect world. It compelled a man to think of holding handfuls of soft flesh – of sinking his teeth into warm springy cheeks . . .

It was out of the question to explain to Mlle Charbonnet the reason for his absence of three days. Pierre-Raymond was unable to reveal to her the humiliation of his rejection by beautiful but faithless Claudia. It would be too absurdly embarrassing to have an employee who knew about that.

To Liliane he could pour out his troubled soul – as indeed he had – and that was not all he poured out in her company, not by a long way. But she was different. She was a friend now that she no longer worked for him – at least, that was how he saw it.

There was another difference too. With Liliane he had established an intimacy as soon as she started to work for him. He handled her pointed little breasts ten times a day – slid a hand up her skirt to stroke her thighs every time he thought of it.

At least once a day he had her knickers off to slide into her warm softness and enjoy the ecstasy he needed. And dear Liliane adored him for it. Or so he fondly believed.

'There is no one like you, Pierre-Raymond,' she declared, not only when he pleasured her but many times during the day.

Naturally, he was in complete agreement with her on that. And it reassured him that she understood him and was devoted to him.

He was not on the same terms with Valerie Charbonnet. She was a year or two older than Liliane, she would be twenty-eight in two months time. She had a full face and a full figure, where Liliane was stylishly slender. Valerie could be described as *comfortable* or even as *well-fleshed*. But that was not the reason either.

To Pierre-Raymond it was not important, the question of young or middle-aged, thin or plump. He adored all women over the age of sixteen and missed no opportunity to demonstrate it. Naturally he bared Valerie's full round breasts and played with them almost from the day she started to work at the studio. Those beautiful big breasts were her best recommendation, he'd decided when he interviewed her for the job.

And very naturally he slipped her knickers down her plump and shapely thighs and had her on her back. Regularly. All that was part of the job and went without saying.

But he did not feel the same intimacy he had with Liliane. He attributed this to Valerie's lack of seriousness – there was an air of slight mockery about her. A gleam in her velvet brown eyes, the way the corner of her mouth turned up in a half-grin for no reason.

Even when Pierre-Raymond laid her on her back and rode her to a shattering orgasm – when he made her shriek and kick her legs up in the air in fantastic ecstasy – that look was on her face when she opened her eyes afterwards to stare at him and assure him he was superb.

He couldn't decide whether she meant what she said or whether she was enjoying a secret joke about him. It was disconcerting, it caused him to be slightly uneasy with her – even when he was on her belly and seconds from spurting into it.

There was another reason, more down-to-earth, why in the two years she had worked for him he had not achieved the same level of understanding and intimacy he had with Liliane. His business had achieved a great success, Pierre-Raymond Becquet had become the celebrated portrait photographer.

Half the well-to-do women and actresses of Paris came to his studio to have their photograph taken. Magazines wrote articles about him, newspapers noted his commissions in the gossip pages – a portrait with *Becquet* inscribed in his own handwriting in a bottom corner was equal to a work of art.

In consequence, there were so many clients these days that

he did not have as much time to devote to playing with Valerie as with Liliane. It was not only a question of time, there was the matter of the energy. On a busy day he would pleasure three or four women. He still bared Valerie's big soft breasts to handle and kiss when they were alone – that was his routine and not to be omitted.

He still slipped a hand up her skirt and between her generous thighs to stroke her. That was part of his nature and he did it without thinking. But he was not so prompt to have her knickers off and lie on her belly. He did that with her no more than two or three times a week – any less would have seemed a diminution of his prestige and prowess. Which was unthinkable.

Pierre-Raymond's studio had no windows – natural light was an obstruction to taking photographs intended to make women of forty – over made-up women trying to conceal the incipient little lines around their eyes and mouth and the skin of their neck – appear youthful and desirable.

That was what they paid him for – and for that he had become celebrated. So the studio windows were blocked in, a battery of lamps stood around to produce the effects Pierre-Raymond wanted and which he knew how to achieve.

The adjoining room, where he greeted his clients and offered them a glass of chilled champagne if they were important, that was furnished elegantly and it had proper windows through which the towers of Nôtre Dame cathedral could be seen.

And the Seine below, with the St Michel bridge, the pleasure boats packed with foreign tourists going up and down the river. And along the nearer bank, the line of second-hand bookstalls, where middle-aged men in spectacles and berets stood browsing.

Pierre-Raymond stood at the window, staring out at this

scene but hardly seeing it. Behind him Valerie sat at her desk typing rapidly. The coffee cup was in his hand, he had drunk two cups and was feeling more vigorous. His thoughts were of Liliane and the time he'd passed with her.

He was asking himself why he'd stayed with her all night. But he realised the first question that needed answering was why he had gone to Liliane at all. Why *her*, why not some other woman? To talk, to pour out his troubles into an ear he believed to be sympathetic. But why Liliane, after two years?

He could think of no satisfactory answer to that. And anyway, the memory of her bed drove the unresolved question out of his head. That bed, that astounding construction of wood and gilded ironwork with fake brocade curtains and tassels!

It was ridiculous to think of making love on that monstrosity of a bed, that was his first thought on seeing it – he was sure he would laugh too much to stay hard. If Liliane's boyfriend could perform on it, that proved he was a savage without style or taste.

In spite of Pierre-Raymond's contempt for the strange bed, the truth was that when Liliane stretched out naked underneath the absurd tent of brocade, he was hard as steel in the part of him that mattered most.

She was, after all, a most attractive woman with her pointed little breasts and long slender thighs. And that narrow upright strip of curls between. Because of his attentions to her on the leopardskin settee, the lips of her *jouet* were wet and open to welcome him again.

The bed may have been bizarre but Pierre-Raymond slid out of his clothes and took Liliane in his arms. Under those folds of imitation brocade he did deliciously interesting things to her, and she to him. From four in the afternoon until midnight when they fell asleep – with an hour or so break at eight while she prepared dinner and they drank a bottle of Beaujolais with it.

It was nearly ten when they woke up that morning. Before they left the bedroom Liliane surprised him. She was still naked and sitting on the outrageous bed. He was dressing. Around her neck was the gold necklace she had been worried about the day before on the settee. In the bedroom she had taken it off, along with her clothes, but now it was on again. No man could ever understand what went in a woman's mind or why she did what she did.

'I'm so happy you stayed with me,' she said.

Something in her voice made him wonder if she meant more than she way saying, but the idea left his head the instant she rose from the bed and stood close and put her hand down the front of his trousers. He was in the process of buckling his belt and he paused while her hand took possession of his limp part.

'I was exhausted when you woke me in the night,' she said with a tweak of his dangler, 'I begged you to let me sleep, but you were pitiless, you turned me on my back and got on top.'

In her hand his male part was losing its limpness and growing bigger. He laughed and put his hands on her slim bare shoulders and then slowly down to cup her spiky little breasts – each one exactly a handful.

'I hated you for molesting me like that when I was so utterly worn out,' she said, 'I bit your shoulder.'

'But not very hard,' said Pierre-Raymond with a smile, 'there is only the faintest red mark this morning.'

'Because while I was biting you I changed my mind,' she said, 'that great thick *thing* you were pushing into me suddenly

41

felt wonderful. So I opened my legs and let you do what you wanted – it was marvellous.'

Pierre-Raymond slid a palm down her narrow belly, between her thighs, to clasp her warm little *joujou* tenderly.

Not that he knew it, of course, but this was part of her plan to remind him how much he needed her.

'Do you remember what you used to do to me in the studio when time was short and a client was due?' she enquired, giving his upright and throbbing part a firm stroking that made him gasp.

'Standing against the wall, you mean?' he said.

'That too. But I was thinking of how you used to make me bend over the desk and lift my skirt from behind. I liked that.'

'You were enchanting,' he murmured, 'always enchanting.'

'For old time's sake, Pierre-Raymond – do it to me before you go – would that please you?'

'Ah yes, *chérie*.'

He loved doing it like that, nothing she could have suggested would have delighted him more. She knew that very well – it was a step in her programme to regain his interest in her on a more useful basis than consolation when he was distressed.

Her clasped hand moved up and down his stiff part and made it jump. His fingers were between her legs and then inside her to caress her slippery bud.

'Ah yes,' he repeated, 'for the sake of old times together.'

Liliane turned her back to him and bent over to put her hands flat on the rumpled bed. He contemplated the small round cheeks of her bottom and smiled in delight. He stood close behind her, undoing his belt buckle with hasty fingers so his trousers fell down around his ankles.

The sight of her bare pretty rump and her slender body at

his disposal was extremely arousing. Her little breasts hung pertly beneath her. And her gold chain, it swung loosely under her. He ran his hands up and down the insides of her thighs – she moved her feet wide apart. Seen from this angle her *joujou* was a soft fleshy mound with a long split, the dark brown hair very sparse here underneath.

Pierre-Raymond stroked her with slow sensitive fingertips, he opened the pretty lips, he made her so wet that forefinger and second finger together slipped easily inside. Liliane shuddered in little tremors of pleasure and gave long soft sighs until he presented the swollen head of his pride to the parted split and pushed slowly into her.

'Ah, how this brings back the old days . . .' she murmured.

'Lili, *je t'adore*,' Pierre-Raymond murmured, a stock response of his at sentimental moments such as this.

He was well mounted on her, his hands holding her narrow hips in a firm grip to keep her steady while he thrust in and out in a strong and deliberate rhythm that soon had her gasping. There was an overwhelming emotion of goodwill toward her in his heart at that moment.

'I'd forgotten how marvellous it is like this,' she murmured, 'no one but you has ever made love to me in this way. You are a master, Pierre-Raymond, I adore you for it.'

Her words made him smile with pleasure, the flattery made him even more aroused. He slid in and out of her wet warmth, on the brink of a crisis after twenty strokes. He lay forward over her bare back, his hands cupped her pointed little breasts while he rode her. Her gold necklace swung wildly to his thrusting.

'*Ah mon Dieu, oui*!' Liliane exclaimed shrilly.

All her body was responding to him – she was already as

43

close to orgasm as he was. His hands clenched over the soft flesh of her breasts. He moved faster and thrust deeper – she moaned and pushed her smooth-skinned bottom against him. Inside his belly he felt the golden moment arrive. He stabbed furiously into her and she convulsed under him and squealed faintly when he poured his ecstasy into her.

He'd been standing so long at the window, looking out across the Seine to Nôtre Dame and seeing nothing, an empty coffee cup in his hand, that Valerie spoke his name twice before he heard her. He came back to earth and turned to face her.

'What did you say?' he asked.

Her eyes flickered down to stare at the front of his trousers where a long bulge was plainly visible. She smiled to see that and he recognised the half-mocking smile that so disconcerted him.

'You were lost in thought,' she said in her cheerful way, 'is anything troubling you, that's what I asked.'

He shook his head and put his hands in his pockets. He was by the window still, his shoulder leaning on the wall.

'Then you were watching something outside,' she said, 'was it very interesting, whatever it was? Someone you know going by?'

'Come and see for yourself,' he suggested.

He had to get Liliane right out of his mind – the quicker the better. It was ridiculous to let himself become obsessed by any particular woman. Look at the emotional devastation when he let Claudia Deneuve insinuate herself into his deepest emotions and then leave him flat! Never again. The hours he had passed with Liliane were marvellous, but now it was time to forget her.

He knew precisely how to erase Liliane from his mind. Valerie had left her desk and crossed the room to stand at the window, looking down to see what had held his attention so long. There was nothing, only the old buildings and the river, pedestrians and traffic going past.

Before she had time to say so he put his arms round her waist and kissed her. He fondled her heavy round breasts through the thin black sleeveless pullover she was wearing. He pressed the tip of his tongue between her lips. Her wet tongue touched his, she sighed into his mouth.

After a moment or two she pulled back a little to smile that knowing smile of hers.

'Ah now I understand,' she said, 'there is nothing to see out there – you've been ill in bed for the past three days with no one to look after you. You are feeling neglected.'

If she was content to believe Pierre-Raymond had been without the comfort of a woman's charms for three days, he wasn't going to disillusion her. It would be unkind to do so.

'Ah yes,' he said, 'you understand. But there *is* something to see, Valerie.'

'What?'

He took her hand and pressed it to the bulge in his trousers.

'Oh that!' she said, her palm sliding slowly over the cloth, rubbing him through it in a provocative manner. 'That's on show every day of the week.'

When she first came to work for him, Valerie had refused outright to believe he could make it stand up stiff any time he wished. She'd had boyfriends, of course, and knew what they could do in this way. She'd never known a man – or even heard of one – able to achieve what Pierre-Raymond insisted he could.

When he proved by a daily demonstration that he was telling the truth, she became fascinated by his ever-staunch part. Many a time she persuaded him – never difficult – to perch on the edge of her desk so she could open his trousers and examine his aroused part – for at the first suggestion it went instantly hard.

She sat on her chair between his spread knees, both her hands circling round his uprightness, fingertips playing up and down, tantalising him till he was shuddering and gasping – frantic to attain release.

'So hard, so big,' she'd murmur, her face pink – Pierre-Raymond closed his eyes on these occasions and abandoned himself to her caresses.

Her face was close to her gliding hands, her tongue slid from between her lips and she licked lightly over the tip of his swollen part with each stroke.

After almost two years working for him Valerie had long since ceased to doubt his ability to produce instant hardness when it pleased him. 'That's on show every day of the week,' she said with her mocking little grin, standing close to the window with him, her hand stroking over the hard bulge in his trousers.

'So you have been ill and alone for three days?' she said in a doubtful tone. 'This *thing* you are so proud of has been small and soft all that time?'

'What do you mean, *chérie*?'

'I was worried about you, Pierre-Raymond – I phoned yesterday to ask how you were. And there was no reply.'

'In the morning was that?' he asked cautiously.

'About ten-thirty in the morning, yes. Where were you?'

'Sleeping – I didn't wake up till after midday.'

'I phoned again in the afternoon,' she said, 'and again there was no reply.'

There was an edge to her voice.

'I felt so much better when eventually I woke that I went out for a little stroll in the fresh air,' he said as convincingly as he could.

Before Valerie could pursue her inconvenient line of enquiry, he closed her mouth with a kiss and put his hand up her skirt. Under his fingertips the skin of her thighs was like satin and he intended to kiss it. But that came later. For now he slipped his hand into her knickers to touch her thick bush of curls.

'*Ah oui*!' she murmured, her mouth pressed hotly to his.

Pierre-Raymond turned her until her back was to the window – her feet apart to open her thighs for his caress on the fleshy split between them. He opened her neatly with a gentle finger.

'You are adorable,' he whispered, fingers busy down below.

'Have you told me the truth?' she breathed.

His fingers were between her warm and wet folds – flickering over the little bud that roused her passion. By now she had his trousers gaping wide open and her hand was pumping firmly.

'I missed you,' she murmured, 'three days without you here to do shameful things to me. I began to think it was an excuse you saying you were ill and you had a girlfriend in your apartment and were staying in bed with her day after day.'

'I assure you there was no one in my apartment with me,' said Pierre-Raymond. At least that was true – but then, he hadn't been there himself for the past day and night.

His cheek was close to hers but he didn't stare into her eyes while he was misleading her. He did notice how a corner of her mouth twitched in her mocking grin. Only for a second, then the little thrills his busy fingers were giving her wiped the grin from her face.

'*Ah non*!' she gasped, her parted legs trembling against him.

He pressed his mouth to hers in a hot kiss that held her head back against the glass of the window. Those passing outside, if they glanced up, would see a woman flattened against the window – her head of dark brunette hair, her shoulders in a thin black sleeveless pullover, her full round bottom in a grey skirt.

They would observe a man standing very close to her, her body shielding from the curiosity of passers-by what he was doing to her. Whatever he was doing, the result was to make her tremble against the window – that bountiful bottom was sliding a little down the glass.

Down in the road it was not possible to hear what the man and the woman might be saying to each other. And impossible to hear Valerie's sighs and moans. Or those of Pierre-Raymond for she had his trousers open and his stiffness in her hand and she was trying to push it up into herself, where his fingertips were dancing over her slippery bud.

He had forgotten Liliane, that went without saying – playing with Valerie had cleared his mind of entanglements. She wanted him inside her, they were both impossibly aroused, he and she. But there was no time left. While she was fumbling to steer his hardness past his caressing hand and up into herself, the phone rang insistently on the desk across the room.

An Unscheduled Visitor

Valerie's back was pressed against the widow, her back and her round bottom on the glass. Pierre-Raymond had his hand up under her grey skirt and inside her knickers, a fingertip teasing her slippery bud.

'Ah yes!' she was gasping, her legs shaking under her – when the phone rang on her desk across the other side of the room.

'Don't make me answer it,' she moaned, her hand holding tight to his upright part, 'not now!'

Pierre-Raymond pulled his hand from between her legs and took a step back.

'It may be important,' he said, breathing quickly but trying to calm himself, 'a client, perhaps.'

Where money was concerned he was very attentive, he never let an opportunity to earn a fee escape him. Valerie put her tongue out at him and went to the phone. She pulled her knickers up as she went, a comic process to observe. She had to hitch her skirt up to achieve it, displaying the backs of her plump thighs.

She sat down at the desk and answered the phone.

'It's Madame Marot,' she said to Pierre-Raymond, her hand over the mouthpiece. 'It's the second time this week she's phoned to speak to you. She says it's important. Shall I put her off till tomorrow? Or next week?'

Pierre-Raymond left the window to stand beside Valerie at her desk, thinking what he wanted to do. He could guess what it was that Madame Marot wanted. No mystery about that. She was a vain and wealthy woman of forty, past her best but trying hard by diet, make-up and self-delusion to present herself as desirable. Like many of Pierre-Raymond's clients.

He'd tucked *Grandjean* back into his trousers and done them up before crossing the room to Valerie's side. But his hand was in his pocket – he was too aroused to do otherwise – and his fingers were stroking along the quivering length of hard flesh and over the head.

He considered it natural that his female sitters expected him to make love to them. And it was his right to take his pleasure with them – when all was said, he was a man of fine appearance, broad of shoulder, tall, well-dressed. He had the reputation of being a fantastic lover. Women whose pictures he took chattered to each other on café terraces and in the expensive restaurants they preferred.

A regular subject for their gossip was Pierre-Raymond Becquet and his abilities. How this lady was shattered beyond belief by the repeated thrills he gave her, how that lady was devastated and speechless when he'd finished with her, how another fainted from the force of the orgasmic sensations he unleashed in her.

In consequence his photographic business thrived and he made love to a large number of women; elegant married women in their thirties, experiencing his talked-about abilities; elegant women of forty-something finding it hard to attract young men now; elegant women in their fifties, desperate for a man to strip them naked and give them the thrill of earlier years.

'Does she want to make an appointment for another sitting?' Pierre-Raymond asked Valerie.

'No it's about more prints of the last portrait you did. She wants to talk to you.'

In Pierre-Raymond's trousers his fifteen centimetres jerked to the slow rub of his fingers through the pocket. He placed a hand on Valerie's shoulder while he looked at the appointments diary on the desk, pretending he was thinking.

She wore a light floral perfume he found charming. Enticing, not intrusive. It hinted, not demanded, as some perfumes did. In his trousers there was a delicious throbbing that made him sigh and shiver a little.

He wasn't looking at the diary at all, he was staring down at the rounded swell of Valerie's heavy breasts in her thin black pullover. The most natural thing in the world was to reach down over her shoulder and feel her right breast. He would prefer to get his hand inside the pullover for a closer feel but it came up almost to her throat. At the waist it tucked down inside her skirt and she wore a broad black leather belt.

She had exciting breasts, Valerie, and he adored playing with them. Just now the pleasure was lessened by clothes between her warm flesh and his fingers, but it was still enjoyable to touch her. When they were bare, her breasts were imposing – round and heavy. Pierre-Raymond almost lost himself in a reverie, his two hands reaching down over her shoulders to lift and roll both of her big beauties through the pullover.

He bent lower to kiss the top of her head. She wore her dark hair parted in a fringe at the front and long at the sides and back – and she fastened it in a sort of horse tail with ribbons or tortoise-shell clips, according to mood.

'What shall I tell Madame Marot?' she asked.

'Ask her if tomorrow is convenient.'

While Valerie was talking into the phone and then listening, Pierre-Raymond reached down further over her shoulders to unbuckle her leather belt and pull her sweater out of her skirt – so he could get his hands up underneath it. He unclipped the capacious bra that supported her treasures – he was grinning as he leaned over her and dandled her big bare delights.

'Madame Marot says tomorrow is no good. It will only take ten minutes. She says she needs to talk to you about her daughter's pictures as well.'

'What daughter?' Pierre-Raymond asked dreamily, hands busy.

'She says she can be here inside twenty minutes if you have a moment free before lunch.'

'Very well then, if she insists.'

His fingertips were gliding over the prominent russet buds of Valerie's breasts and she was arching her back. Her voice was a little strained as she relayed the message and hung up smartly.

She clamped her hands on to her black pullover to hold Pierre-Raymond's hands still.

'You left me high and dry,' she said – a note of spite in her voice, 'now it's your turn – Madame Marot is on her way, so you can either wait for her or do it to yourself.'

She turned her head to glance up at him and he saw the corner of her mouth was turned up in a fierce little grin.

'Valerie, *chérie*,' he pleaded.

His tone of voice said he wanted to, but he removed his hands from her breasts and stood up straight.

'We must defer our pleasure,' he said, sounding regretful.

She said nothing. She eyed the long bulge in his trousers and looked pleased that he was frustrated.

'No need for you to wait for Madame Marot,' he told her, 'she may be delayed. Take your lunch-hour and I will stay here until she arrives.'

'As you wish,' she said, the corners of her mouth turned down in a disagreeable expression.

She stood up and lifted the front of her sleeveless pullover until her pale heavy breasts were exposed, then turned her back to Pierre-Raymond and calmly asked him to fasten her bra.

So openly provoked . . . how could any man resist handling those fleshy beauties? He moved closer, he put his arms round her to feel them. He pressed himself so close to her back she felt the hardness in his trousers against her bottom.

She heard his sighing and thought he was going to tell her to bend forward over the desk – he could have her skirt up and her knickers down in a second, then he would be inside her! But he was not going to have his own way so easily this time, she said to herself, not after he made her answer the phone when she was only two seconds from orgasm.

She intended to make him pay for that unkindness. By refusing to bend over for him. Or perhaps she *would* bend over – and when he tried to penetrate her she would clench her thighs together tight and pull away. And laugh at his discomfiture.

In the event Pierre-Raymond made no such demands – he stepped back and fastened her bra deftly. He smoothed her pullover down and tucked it neatly into her skirt, he held her belt in place while she buckled it. A kiss on the cheek, a pat on the bottom, that was all, before he left her standing by the desk and went from the office into the studio.

To say that Madame Marot was vain and wealthy, trying by diet and stylish clothes to remain desirable at forty was true – but it was by no means all of the truth. She had a natural elegance in her movements, she was intelligent and she could be charming if she wanted to be.

She had a long thin nose in a face dominated by the huge arch of her fine-plucked black eyebrows. Dark brown eyes that could stare without blinking at people she thought of as unimportant. And they were many.

She arrived at Pierre-Raymond's studio wearing a Chanel suit – a fine tweed in pink and white check, the jacket unbuttoned to show a black silk blouse. Her hair was a rich chestnut, parted in the middle and swept back in soft waves – by one of the most expensive hairdressers in Paris, naturally.

Pierre-Raymond kissed her hand – it seemed appropriate and it pleased her. Her fingernails were painted crimson and she had a large diamond ring on each hand. And diamond bracelets on each wrist – and diamond studs in her ears.

'At last!' she cried. 'I've been trying to get you all week, I must have phoned at least ten times! Where have you been?'

'A thousand apologies,' Pierre-Raymond murmured smoothly, his hand holding on to hers in an affectionate manner, 'I had to go out of Paris on a special commission for a day or two.'

'I wanted you to take me to see a film a friend told me about at one of those little cinemas no one admits to knowing. I don't mean the tourist places around the Place Pigalle where the touts stand outside – it is impossible to go to places like that. This is near the Boulevard St Germain. And very discreet. But you were nowhere to be found and I had to find someone else to take me. You would have enjoyed the movie.'

She implied that he would have enjoyed the performance after the film also.

'What a pity I missed it,' said Pierre-Raymond, 'another time perhaps – I adore pornographic movies if they are made with wit and panache. Was it French or foreign?'

They were standing just inside the door to the reception room that also served as office. While she was talking, Madame Marot moved closer to Pierre-Raymond, her luminous eyes gazing up into his face.

'That last portrait of me you did,' she said, 'the one in the black Dior evening frock. Everyone I know says it makes me look marvellous. I need another twenty copies.'

'Of course,' he agreed, knowing that was only a pretence.

Her hand, the one he had held and kissed, was busily opening the front of his trousers. Madame Marot was a superior person, not accustomed to being kept waiting.

'I'm meeting my husband and his mother for lunch at one-fifteen – at the Tour d'Argent,' she said.

Her hand was plunged into his trousers to hold his long stiff part – it had refused to subside after he had played with Valerie.

'I can only stay for a minute or two. Tell me why you are in this condition, Pierre-Raymond.'

'Dearest Joelle – as soon as I knew you were coming to see me I became aroused. It is the effect you have on me.'

'*Formidable*!' she murmured, her crimson-nailed hand gripping him voraciously.

Pierre-Raymond eased her backward, step by step, his hands on her hips, until the backs of her legs were against the desk. He put his hand up her elegant Chanel skirt – her expensively-shod feet had moved well apart.

Déjà vu, he thought, *second time this morning I've done this*!

His palm slid up the sheerness of her stocking – to the bare thigh above. He touched curls and moist flesh and she chuckled at his gasp of surprise.

'It seemed unnecessary to wear knickers when I was coming to see Monsieur Ten-times,' she informed him.

He smiled with a certain pride to hear her use his nickname. It had been bestowed upon him by a client as a comic tribute to his reputation. He didn't know who, but it was obviously one of the women who chattered to each other about their sexual adventures over drinks on café terraces.

Not that any of these women, chic and perfumed and dressed in the most elegant of clothes, could truthfully claim he had done it to her ten times without pausing for breath, so to speak. He had pleasured several of them three or four times in the course of an afternoon. And certainly during an evening, when they had that much free time from their more public social activities.

But ten times? That was for a weekend.

'My dear Joelle, there is a tiny touch of perversity in you,' he said, knowing how it flattered her to be thought outrageous. 'How can you consider sitting in a fashionable restaurant with no knickers under your frock – it is too provocative!'

His fingers were between the warm and very wet lips where her thighs met and he was caressing the firm little bud that triggered her passion. Inside his trousers her hand was pumping steadily.

'Oh yes!' she gasped, her parted legs trembling against him.

He bent his head to kiss her and she sighed into his mouth –

her wet tongue touched his. At another time he would be down on his knees to kiss the insides of her thighs – but time was short.

'*Ah mon Dieu*!' she murmured, her mouth pressed hotly against his. 'Don't keep me waiting.'

'You are adorable,' he whispered, his agile fingers busy.

'Pierre-Raymond!' Her grip was very tight. 'Put it in now!'

She guided his throbbing part into the wet lips of her *belle-chose*. He bent his knees a little and then straightened as he pushed up into her.

'How good that feels, Joelle!' he sighed.

His eyes shut and hands clenched on the cheeks of her bottom, he pressed his belly hard against hers and felt her press back. A disquieting thought was in his head. That mocking look on his receptionist's face before she left for lunch – was it possible that she regarded him as a gigolo?

Valerie understood that he did it to women clients who asked him to – but that didn't make him a gigolo. It was for his art and skill at portrait photography they paid him so highly, not for his willingness to pleasure them. Surely no one could be mistaken about so obvious a matter? Perhaps when the moment was right he ought to make sure Valerie understood.

'Yes . . .' Joelle Marot gasped, 'just like that . . . hard!'

Whatever Valerie's views were on Pierre-Raymond's approach to his clients, a simple truth was that handling her heavy breasts while she was on the phone had aroused him more than he realised.

It had been a miracle of self-control – an ability unfamiliar to him, very unfamiliar – that he had managed to take his hands off Valerie's bouncy flesh and step back from her. In four more seconds he would have been too far gone to stop.

He knew exactly what he would have done to her – made her get up on her feet and pushed her forward across the desk, flipping her skirt up over her plump-cheeked bottom.

Et voilà he would be inside her in an instant, his hands full of fleshy breasts – and she would receive his ardent desire.

Fortunately for his self-esteem he didn't know Valerie had had no intention of obliging him if he'd tried that. In his mind every woman over the age of sixteen wanted him to slide his hard part into her and reduce her to sobbing ecstasy. No mystery there, it was the natural order of things, it was how the world was arranged.

That Valerie would have managed affairs to discomfort him was not within his comprehension. She herself was somewhat confused about the precise way of turning his desire into farce. But she had a sort of plan. She would let him believe he was having his way with her, it was vital to the plan. She would bend over the desk and let him flip her skirt up and slide her knickers down.

Let him stroke the cheeks of her bottom and let him touch the brown-haired lips between them. By then he would be off-guard.

He adored his own *thing*, of course, he adored to see it stiff and pushing into a woman. She knew that before he put it in her, he would slide it up and down between the cheeks of her bottom, watching it grow harder and bigger at the stimulus.

He would be holding her by the hips, his knees bent. He would be staring down open-mouthed and fascinated by himself. And she would encourage him to continue this sliding of flesh on flesh until he was frantically aroused.

'Does that feel good, Pierre-Raymond?'

'*Je t'adore*, Valerie . . .'

She would be wriggling her bottom to increase the pressure on his throbbing part. His hand would fly to it, to steer it under her and between her legs and up into her *joujou* – he would babble her name as his crisis approached rapidly.

And then – at his desperate moment, she would flex her legs, sway her bottom, roll her hips – as if in the throes of orgasm – making it impossible for him to push up inside her. There would be moans and gasps of outrage from Pierre-Raymond when his desire splattered over the cheeks of her bottom.

For his self-esteem it was as well that this scene of revenge by Valerie did not take place. But that she could imagine it at all was significant – her attitude toward him was changing.

All that was for another time. At present, Valerie had gone to lunch and Joelle Marot was the recipient of Pierre-Raymond's desire. Joelle did not intend to frustrate him in any way, far from it. She moaned and shuddered against him – perfectly-manicured scarlet nails clawing the shoulders of his jacket.

He was deep in her belly – she pushed her tongue deep in his mouth. They were joined together twice, wet flesh embedded in wet flesh above and below. His hands were gripping the bare cheeks of her bottom to steady her for his thrusts and he sank his nails into her, making red marks on her perfect skin. He hadn't touched her elegant breasts silhouetted by her black silk blouse. She said she was in a hurry, there wasn't the time to uncover them and play with them.

'Ah, ah . . .' she was moaning deep in her throat.

Pierre-Raymond pounded at her and she went into ecstatic spasms, ramming her belly hard against him.

I am not a gigolo, he said to himself at the very moment

that he erupted in jolting delight. *I am Pierre-Raymond Becquet, the lover of many women – Monsieur Ten-times – women adore me . . .*

Long after it was over, Joelle still shuddered and pushed her belly rhythmically against him, reluctant to admit the pleasure was ended. She gave a last sigh and pulled away, his softening part slipping from the wet clasp of her flesh.

'That was beautifully brutal,' she told him, 'I'd love you to do it to me again. But I must go – I shall be late for lunch.'

She stroked his face lightly with the back of her hand and he felt the brilliant hardness of the diamonds in her ring against his skin. The contact was oddly arousing, he felt his softening male part give a little jump – he knew how exciting it would be to have Joelle's diamond-ringed hand fondling him to stiffness.

She could no doubt be persuaded to wear both diamond rings on the same hand for the experiment. And to bring on his climax in order to observe how the cold brilliance of the stones could be dulled by the smear of his sticky spurting. To make love to her massively expensive diamonds – what an entrancing thought!

Not that the concept was entirely new to him – something like it had happened to him the year before. With Madame Fabien – an exquisitely elegant lady who had amused herself in an unusual way. She noticed how fascinated he was by her necklace – a long string of black pearls. Worth a fortune – if they were natural.

Charming as she was, Madame Fabien was a cynic. Particularly about the motives of handsome men twenty or more years younger than herself who said they adored her. Even after she had been laid on her back on Pierre-Raymond's chaise longue, her knickers off and ridden to orgasm.

'Ah, my pearls arouse you more than I do,' she said with a wry smile, 'that is not very gallant.'

She swept aside his protestations and proved her point in the simplest possible way – she took the long strand of pearls from around her neck and wound it around his shrinking part. At once the process was reversed, *Grandjean* lived up to his nickname by growing long and thick again, less than five minutes after he'd done his duty in the traditional way.

'You are a charming man,' Madame Fabien told him, 'everyone I know is mad about you, Pierre-Raymond. They want this long hard *thing* of yours in them. But I think it prefers another lodging, a more expensive bed than it finds between women's legs.'

'Ah Marie-Rose . . .' he sighed, staring down in astonishment at what she was doing to him.

His length of stiff flesh strained upward, wrapped completely in rows of black pearls from its dark-curled root to its purple head. The appearance was artistically pleasing, though bizarre. The sensation was totally unfamiliar, that of smooth round hard pearls pressing into his flesh as he became more aroused and so thicker.

The psychological impact was tremendous – overpowering! Only seconds passed from the first delicate movement of Marie-Rose's hand on her pearls – five seconds, no more – and Pierre-Raymond cried out, his body bucking as his sticky desire flew wildly up into the air.

By the time he was tranquil again she had stopped laughing at his reaction. He unwound the pearls from his shrinking part and wiped them with his handkerchief, each pearl separately. He put the string around her neck and kissed her on both cheeks.

If pearls had so overwhelming an effect, what would diamonds do for him? Joelle Marot had a diamond ring on each hand. Just to look at them set Pierre-Raymond's fantasies racing. Did she also own a diamond necklace?

He thought it probable. Women with very rich husbands usually acquired diamond necklaces and fur coats as an ordinary part of their wardrobe. Well then, could she be persuaded to bring the necklace to the studio one day to play a little game . . . ?

Her hand was stroking his face and the touch of the brilliant hardness of the diamonds in her ring was arousing him.

'*Au revoir, chéri*,' she said, 'I must dash or I shall be late for lunch. I shall be wet between the legs because of what you have done to me. I shall be thinking about you.'

He took her hand in his and kissed it. He was hungry himself in spite of the big breakfast he had eaten in the brasserie at eleven that morning. He'd decided on lunch at his favourite restaurant – which was not the Tour d'Argent, even though he knew that was the supreme eating experience of the Left Bank. Duck cooked in fourteen different ways, a triumph of the culinary art, possible only in Paris!

'On second thoughts,' said Joelle, 'they can wait for me – it is idiotic to run away so soon – I want you again, I must have you, Pierre-Raymond. Let them wait, but you must be quick.'

He shrugged and smiled and held her by the waist to move her away from the desk and to the wall beside it.

'If you are sure . . .' he murmured, kissing her hand again. And then the bright hard diamonds of her ring.

The jacket of her elegant Chanel tweed suit in pink and white had been undone ever since she arrived. With expert fingers he opened the buttons of her chic black silk blouse and freed her breasts from the confines of a black lace bra. He had seen them many times, they were of middle size, still beautifully shaped.

Joelle took great care of her face and body. There was not a line on her long-nosed face. And as for her breasts, hardly the slightest droop was to be seen when the bra came off, though to the hands they had lost the firmness of a young woman. A little soft to the touch, but no worse for that. Pierre-Raymond rolled the balls of his thumbs lightly over the prominent tips.

'You are a never-failing delight, Pierre-Raymond,' she said.

He didn't bother to reply, he knew perfectly well that he was wonderful and women had no option but adore him and open their legs for him and beg him to pleasure them. He pressed his lips to hers in a passionate kiss that sent little shivers of purest delight through her body.

He reached down between her knees to slip his hand underneath her fine tweed skirt.

'I adore your perversity, Joelle,' he murmured, stroking her.

'No one has ever given me the pleasure you do,' she told him, 'it's too good to throw away in hurried ten-minute sessions – I want you for hours, for days, both of us naked, on my back upon a comfortable bed. You must make arrangements, Pierre-Raymond. A discreet hotel, perhaps. With your reputation you must surely know many convenient places.'

'Perhaps you'd prefer the Ritz hotel,' he said, attempting to be sarcastic – an almost impossible thing to achieve for a man whose fingers are between a woman's bare thighs.

'Not the Ritz,' Joelle murmured, 'too many people there know me. You must find somewhere else . . . I'll pay, of course.'

'Ah yes,' said Pierre-Raymond, uncertain of the implication

of her offer to pay for a hotel room. Did Joelle think of him as a gigolo after all?

While he was puzzling over it, she moaned at the touch of his clever fingers combing through the curls of her fleece. And she moaned again and her body shook when he caressed the soft lips of her *bijou*, and then again when his fingertip eased into her to find her bud.

'Flat on your back all through the day and night – you'd like that,' he said thickly. A fortunate thought of hers to wear no knickers when she came to see him – he steered his hard-rearing part between her open thighs and into her with a strong push.

'And I would live up to my nickname,' he gasped as he started to slide in her with nervous little jabs, 'Monsieur Ten-times – after you had screamed your head off in seven or eight orgasms, would you still be conscious when I spread your legs wide apart and lay on your belly to ravage you the tenth time, Joelle?'

At that she squealed faintly and bumped her loins against him fast – each time she jerked she felt his stiff flesh slither in her. Pierre-Raymond was experiencing the strong palpitations of pleasure in her belly – the regular contraction of the slippery velvet *joujou* containing him, the firm contraction that warned of the imminent onset of her climax of ecstasy.

He was panting, and his rhythm quickened until she shook like a leaf against him. Only his arms around her waist and the wall behind her kept her from sliding to the studio floor. A massive spasm took her at the instant his triumphant desire gushed into her in hasty flicks.

Joelle expressed her ecstasy in little screams, until Pierre-Raymond wondered if she'd ever stop. But finally she was quiet and she sank back against the wall, sighing her satisfaction.

'That was magnificent,' she said, staring at him with those unblinking eyes of hers, 'now I must go, I am late already.'

'You will have more appetite for your lunch now,' he said.

'I'll phone you as soon as I get a free hour and we can meet, Pierre-Raymond,' she said.

Madame Marot Goes Shopping

Pierre-Raymond's apartment was just off the rue de Sèvres, well away from his studio and within strolling distance of the great and celebrated brasseries of the Boulevard Montparnasse. At ten minutes past nine on Saturday morning, Madame Marot got out of a taxi outside the building in which he lived, looked around carefully, then found her way up the stairs and rang his doorbell.

After a pause the door opened and Pierre-Raymond in a crimson silk dressing gown looked out. His eyebrows rose in surprise to see who it was. He wasn't expecting her and he didn't know how she'd found his address. But she was a superior woman. And used to getting her own way.

And she was worth looking at. She was wearing a summer frock in narrow green and white stripes, tight at the waist and with a swirling skirt. Over it she wore a casual jacket of matt black satin – she stood posing on the landing, hands in pockets, as if on the catwalk at a couturier's show.

Her chin was tilted up as she looked at Pierre-Raymond in the doorway – large and luminous eyes stared unblinking at him. Her long thin nose was elegant – indeed, every part of her asserted her natural right to do whatever she wished.

'*Bonjour*,' she said, eyes never blinking, 'but I am impressed by your dressing gown. It is *très chic*. Are you going to invite me in?'

'Of course, forgive me. It surprised me to see you here.'

He took her to his sitting room, she glanced around and found nothing to displease her discriminating taste. She posed again, on the sofa this time, knees crossed to show off an elegant leg in silk. Her jacket was undone and her shoulders were well back – to show her breasts to good advantage under the thin frock.

'May I get you something, Joelle – coffee, perhaps?'

Pierre-Raymond had no illusions about why she was there – the purpose of her visit required little guessing. He was wondering why she had arrived so very early in the day. Ladies of her age didn't usually want to be pleasured before noon. The afternoon, that was their best time in his experience. And why was she at his apartment instead of his studio?

He hadn't taken her seriously when she told him he must make arrangements for a discreet hotel. He'd only shrugged and said whatever seemed appropriate at the time – he couldn't recall it now. It wasn't important.

Women often babbled suggestions about hotels and being taken away for weekends in the excitement of oncoming orgasm. Because they wanted him again and again. They wanted to be ravished and brutalised. They wanted to hang naked and screaming upside-down from the chandelier – that was the sort of thing they babbled.

It didn't mean anything. He forgot Joelle's command to find a hotel room and ravage her all day and night – forgot all about it as soon as she left him that morning to go to her lunch with husband and mother-in-law. But now here she was at his apartment!

'No thank you.' She dismissed his offer of coffee with a wave of her well-manicured hand. 'I'm having a morning's shopping. I thought I'd drop in for a moment.'

'I see,' he said.

'I phoned your studio and your secretary said you wouldn't be there until ten-thirty. I decided to drop in on you at home to discuss portraits of my daughter.'

Pierre-Raymond didn't believe a word of it. He knew perfectly well what she wanted. He sat down beside her, leaving a space between them so as not to appear eager to fall in with her wishes – as yet unspoken wishes but no mystery to him.

He was not pleased about being pursued into his apartment. He saw it as an important question of *not* permitting himself to be treated like a gigolo. He was Pierre-Raymond Becquet, a man of artistic talent. Women adored him and ripped their knickers off for his attentions. He was not there to be used casually by any woman who could afford his expensive photography.

Why had Valerie given Madame Marot his home address? he asked himself. She could be very assertive, this Joelle – but Valerie was trained to protect him, that was what a good secretary did. She would only reveal his address for a good reason. Or what to her seemed to be a good reason.

A dismaying thought flashed into his mind – not for the first time. Could Valerie think perhaps he was a gigolo? Selling his services to rich women? Could she have directed Joelle to him because of that? Had Joelle suggested she was a special client and had every right to his personal attentions?

If Valerie Charbonnet thinks that she is ridiculously wrong, he assured himself – while smiling his charming smile at Joelle Marot. *And if there is any such idiotic idea in Joelle's mind, she too is making an absurd mistake.*

But no, the reason she is here is not that. It is because she is enchanted by me and wants to die of delight in my arms.

If Pierre-Raymond's conclusion was true, there was no sign of respect or admiration on Joelle's face – nor evidence of it in her tone when she spoke. She reached over and flipped back his crimson dressing gown with a diamond-ringed hand.

'Ah, so it was a lie when we last met,' she said in modified outrage, 'I thought as much at the time.'

'What do you mean?' he asked. 'I don't understand you.'

'You know very well what I'm talking about,' she said coolly, 'I touched you at your studio and you were stiff and strong the moment I arrived.'

'Yes, of course,' he murmured, wondering what she was getting at. Her tone wasn't affectionate at all, as he would expect from a woman who came uninvited to his apartment to be pleasured.

'You claimed it was the effect I have on you,' she continued, a slight sneer in her voice, 'even then I didn't believe it – I thought you'd probably been handling your fat receptionist.'

'What are you saying!' He was indignant.

'I was right. You've proved it – I sit within arm's reach and you are as soft as cooked spaghetti.'

'She's not fat,' Pierre-Raymond said defensively, 'chubby, if you like, well-fleshed.'

'Pah!' Joelle exclaimed, her thin black eyebrows arching upwards. 'She's got a pair of breasts like water-melons. A backside like a barrel. Don't try to change the subject – I'm angry with you, very angry.'

Having flipped back his dressing gown, she'd put her hand in his pale-blue silk pyjama trousers to grope between his thighs. She brought out his limp part.

'No doubt I've come at an awkward time,' she said coldly, 'is there a woman in your bedroom, left over from last night? It's not the fat receptionist – she's at your studio because I spoke to her on the phone. But it's clear someone has exhausted you – *Monsieur Ten-times*?'

The sarcasm in her voice when she called him by his nickname was keen as a knife blade. He glanced down into his lap in time to see her fingers curling inward like claws – then her scarlet nails sank into the flesh of his cherished part.

'Nothing of the sort,' he said, wincing at the agony, 'I slept alone last night, if you really must know. Though I can't think why you should be interested.'

'Then I shall enlighten you,' she told him.

Before she attempted to do so, he thought it best to offer an explanation of sorts. For the sake of his pride and reputation.

'I was only half awake when you rang the bell,' he said, 'but as you can see, my sleepiness is disappearing very rapidly – in two more seconds I shall be fully awake. All of me.'

Indeed, in his lap where she had turned back the sides of his dressing gown and opened his pyjamas to expose him to her view, *Grandjean* had raised his head and grown strong.

'At last!' said Joelle – she sounded as if she had been kept waiting for hours. 'If you are sure there's nobody else in your bedroom, you may take me there.'

It would have been gallant – and doubtless Joelle would have enjoyed it enormously – to pick her up in his arms and carry her to the bed. But his pyjamas slipped to his ankles when he stood up and his fifteen centimetres stuck out of his open dressing gown in a comical way.

It was more prudent to kick off his crimson leather slippers, step out of the pyjama trousers and take Joelle's hand, leading her into the bedroom upright on her own two feet.

Her eyes glittered with greedy desire – as soon as she was in his bedroom her jacket and frock came off so smoothly it seemed as if they'd fallen off. She unhooked her lace bra and threw it aside – followed by her silk stockings. As he expected, she had no knickers on for a visit to Monsieur Ten-times!

Pierre-Raymond took off his dressing gown and pyjama jacket – he was staring thoughtfully at Joelle Marot stretched out naked on his unmade bed. He leaned over and kissed the russet tips of her breasts with his wet tongue. His fingertips flittered like butterfly wings on her belly and down between her parted thighs to touch the warm lips of her *belle-chose*.

This was routine for him, actions his hands performed without conscious direction from his brain. But women didn't know that, fortunately, and Joelle was stirred.

'I adore the touch of hands on my naked body,' she said with a lascivious smile, 'especially your hands, Pierre-Raymond, you are the best.'

It was not the sort of comment a man expected to hear when he was kissing a woman. Certainly not the sort of remark he *wanted* to hear. In these intimate moments a comparison with other men, if only implied, was distasteful. Even if the comparison was to your own advantage, it was still unnecessary.

His hand gripped her thigh hard, an iron grip near the groin. She gasped and her leg jerked. He stared down at her flat belly and the neat little triangle of dark brunette hair. At the thin long lips of her *abricot*.

Throughout this visual inspection he was asking himself if he was the last man who'd pushed into that pink split. All things considered, he doubted it. He suspected Joelle was like himself in one respect, she needed to feel the thrill of orgasm several times a day. Which meant she required several men to make love to her to attain satisfaction.

What of it? It made little difference where she went for her pleasure – perhaps even her husband had obliged her after their grand lunch at the Tour d'Argent. Perhaps he'd slithered on her belly and penetrated her insatiable *joujou*. Perhaps.

For Pierre-Raymond what went on elsewhere had no relevance or interest. Only the present had significance. Only here and now mattered, not yesterday, not last night – *now* when her body was his to enjoy. He got onto the bed with her and lay between her elegant legs to kiss the tender lips exposed between them.

'*Ah chéri*, you always know what I want,' she exclaimed with a wriggle of her bottom, 'you are the supreme lover, there can be no doubt of that.'

He kissed the insides of her thighs, the soft satin skin near her neat patch of brunette curls. He touched the tip of his wet tongue into her groin, flattered by what she said. *It is true*, he said to himself, *there is no one as expert as I am. She says no more than the simple truth.*

'Your tongue, Pierre-Raymond,' she said, 'only your tongue.'

She slid her legs wider apart to pull open the lips between – Pierre-Raymond pressed his tongue into her.

'I adore you – ah yes, do that – don't stop,' she sighed as little spasms of delight rippled through her belly.

Pierre-Raymond pulled her wider open with his thumbs while he rubbed the tip of his tongue over her exposed and slippery bud. She gasped and trembled, she shuddered and cried, she jerked to the furious rhythm of her sexual arousal. And he too was highly excited by what he was doing to her.

His stiff part was trapped between his belly and the bedsheet under him, it throbbed and twitched. He started to move up her belly to bring it level with her *jouet*, to plunge into her, in to the limit! She shrieked and gripped his hair and pushed his head back down between her shaking thighs.

Her bottom writhed on the bed while he pushed his tongue back into her. Her heels drummed against the mattress. 'Make me do it,' she was gasping, 'make me do it!'

She drew her knees up and squealed loudly when Pierre-Raymond slid a hand under her jerking bottom, his skilful finger probing delicately between the cheeks.

'*Ah Dieu*!' she moaned in delight, ravished front and rear at the same moment. 'I'm dying, Pierre-Raymond!'

In four more seconds her back arched off the bed in a massive orgasm. She screamed loudly enough to be heard a kilometre off. Her painful grip on his hair slackened at last – he wondered if she'd torn a couple of handfuls out completely.

As she lay gasping for breath, her long legs slid down to lie flat, still shaken by tremors while the experience faded away. Pierre-Raymond lay quietly, his cheek resting on her thigh, his male part jerking under him and demanding relief very soon – by any means available.

Joelle grinned and sat up. She smacked Pierre-Raymond on the bottom to get him to turn on his back, then sat over his loins. Her knees were up and her split peach a hand's breath above his rearing fifteen centimetres.

'That was superb,' she told him, 'unsurpassable! Now I shall return the favour.'

He thought she meant she was going to take his hugely swollen part in her mouth and use her tongue to assuage his desire. But Madame Marot was not one to trouble herself with

74

other people's gratification. She held herself wide open with two long fingers of one hand while she positioned his throbbing part at the pink wet entrance of her *joujou* with the other.

A large diamond glinted on the hand gripping him.

Mais c'est magnifique, he thought. If only she would reverse her hand and press the shiny many-faceted stone into *Grandjean* . . . press hard enough to leave a red indentation . . . a souvenir of love to remember her by for a few hours after she'd gone.

She did nothing of the sort – she impaled herself neatly upon his hard part by sinking down until she sat astride him.

'There – now you can have me,' she exclaimed.

It was untrue, of course. She was having him. It was entirely for her own pleasure she had let him penetrate her pampered and smooth body – for her own orgasm, not for his.

Nevertheless it was delicious, the soft sensation of her warm slippery flesh gliding up and down his proud hard part. To tell the truth Pierre-Raymond didn't mind who was on top and who was below. The result was the same.

The downward pressure of her body drove *Grandjean* right into her. She slid up and down, making Pierre-Raymond feel her full weight across his belly at each down-stroke. And threatening to rip his treasured part right off with each up-stroke, so strong was the grip of her *joujou*.

'Your favour returned, Pierre-Raymond!' she exclaimed as her soft breasts flipped up and down to her briskness.

There was no point in telling her he disagreed slightly – and anyway her bouncing up and down was having its effect. He shook and jerked with excitement, he twitched, squirmed, panted – and although it was hardly a minute since Joelle impaled herself on him, he felt his crisis arriving.

Then to his astonishment, she raised her arm to glance at

the little diamond-studded watch on her wrist. At once the already lively tempo of her up-and-down glide accelerated. She was bracing herself on stiff arms, her hands flat on his belly, bouncing as if riding a wild horse. Her elegant breasts joggled to the rhythm, leaping up and down her chest.

Pierre-Raymond lay on his back astounded, his eyes glaring up at her. To check the time at such a moment – it was incredible. An intolerable insult to him! Had she arranged to meet someone on her shopping trip? Was it more important to be there at the agreed time than to be here with him on the bed?

The unacceptable thought in his mind was that she really was acting toward him as if he were a gigolo. She was not treating him as a lover but as someone subservient to her desire and her convenience. This was atrocious – it was insupportable. Yet the sensations of sexual delight were no less for that.

He detested Joelle for the evidently low opinion she held of him – but in truth he was furiously excited by the sight of her naked body looming over him, her red-tipped breasts flopping up and down and her pale belly ramming at him in her frenzy.

The force of her assault carried him to the brink of ecstasy. And over it without pause, into the familiar yet always strange paroxysm. He gave a long ecstatic moan as she sat down hard on him and his sticky passion gushed up into her quaking belly.

Joelle cried out in triumph to feel his surge inside her. She jerked her body on him in rapid spasms, her head thrown back to show her long throat, her hair dishevelled.

But I hate you, Pierre-Raymond was saying in his mind even as his desire gushed into her hot belly. *I detest you and despise you, Joelle* . . . He didn't say it, of course, he only thought it. The sound he made was an incoherent wailing.

When Joelle dismounted from his body she gave him a sweet and knowing smile to indicate her approval of his abilities.

'Wasn't that marvellous!' she said. 'I wish I could stay for more, but I must dash – I'm meeting Giselle Picard at ten-thirty and we're going to do the shops together.'

It was not necessary to explain to Pierre-Raymond who Madame Picard was. He knew her very well – he had taken photographs of her for years. She was in her mid-forties now, a slender dark-haired woman of impossible elegance.

Pierre-Raymond had been accustomed all throughout their years of acquaintance to inviting Madame Picard to seat herself upon the green chaise longue in his office so that he could take off her expensive silk underwear. Then he would kneel beside her to kiss her soft little breasts that sagged hardly noticeably.

He didn't know it, but it was Giselle Picard who first gave him the nickname Monsieur Ten-times. That was a long time ago – she was talking about him to her women friends – boasting about his prowess, to make her friends jealous.

It amused them to exchange details of their intimate frolics, these middle-aged ladies of style and good breeding – adventures of a very discreet type, to be sure, never a breath of scandal. Monsieur Ten-times – the name made them giggle in surprise when they heard it and so Pierre-Raymond's reputation grew and grew.

The curiosity of women is legendary – they all wished to test the truth of Giselle Picard's claim – and it was easy enough to arrange an appointment to have a portrait taken. And afterwards to have an enthralling tale to tell over a drink on the terrace of a good café.

Marguerite said she was shattered by the experience and would return to Pierre-Raymond for more. And then more. Lucienne said she was so completely devastated by what he did to her that she was speechless for twenty minutes. Her friends thought that was doubtful, she was never silent for more than a few seconds at a time.

She too believed it necessary to return to the studio to find out what it was about Pierre-Raymond that had so devastating an effect. Not to be outdone, Thérèse claimed she had fainted from the incredible strength of sensation Pierre-Raymond released in her . . . she too thought it important to repeat the experience to understand it better. On a regular basis.

It went without saying none of these ladies really wished to be ravaged ten times, that was excessive. Twice in an otherwise uninteresting morning, and then a slimmer's lunch at one of the chic little restaurants where these privileged ladies met for a long spicy gossip.

It must not be thought that Pierre-Raymond's experiences were limited to wealthy women in their forties, bored with husbands, unoccupied and anxious to find romance in their lives before it was too late. There were actresses too, they needed photographs all the time for publicity – no one else in Paris had the skill of Pierre-Raymond to transform a moderately gifted and plainish actress of thirty-something into a woman of instant allure by means of lighting and retouching in the darkroom.

Actresses had, it went without saying, spectacular and public love affairs with actors. How else could picture magazines make a profit and stay in business? But such liaisons were normally the clash of grossly inflated egos, they gave rise to

78

publicity on a vast scale, but to hardly any emotional satisfaction.

As all the world knows, good-looking actors are usually left-handed and take far more interest in young men than the sexiest actress. And those who do appreciate the pleasures of women are too concerned with themselves to be satisfactory as lovers over any length of time.

In these vexing circumstances, Pierre-Raymond could be relied upon to provide that instant adoration without which ladies of the stage cannot live for more than twenty-four hours. He also provided ecstatic episodes without tantrum or argument or discussion as often as required. Many an actress had displayed more dramatic talent on her back for Pierre-Raymond than on the stage.

There was Denise Lafontaine, to take one name of the many who came often to him to be photographed. Denise was not exactly a star but she appeared regularly in comedies and light dramas. A long-legged woman with yellow-dyed hair and a lot of dark eye make-up. Her mouth was very broad and she laughed a lot.

On the first appointment she sat on his lap after he finished taking photographs of her – and she chuckled to feel him slip a hand up her skirt and between her legs.

'I've heard all about you,' she said, her thighs moving apart to let him have an unimpeded feel.

'What have you heard?' he murmured.

His hand was in her knickers, his fingers stroking the curls between her legs.

'You're famous, Pierre-Raymond – women call you Monsieur Ten-times.' She was opening his trousers with eager fingers to see what he had in there to become so celebrated.

It was long and stiff, of course, when she pulled it out into the light of day.

'It's impressive, I'll say that much for you,' she conceded – and though she laughed she sounded slightly disappointed. 'I've been told so much about you and what you can do that I expected to find something thick as your arm, rearing up to your chin.'

He chuckled at that. He played with her deftly, middle finger gliding round her hidden bud till she started to sigh and arch her back like a cat that is stroked.

Before very long he had her on her back on the studio floor – her frock turned up to her waist, her white satin knickers off, her surprisingly sturdy thighs wide apart. He balanced upon his arms above her, his stiffness poised at the moist lips in their nest of dark curls.

'You will feel me slide into you,' he murmured, 'and you will adore the sensation. This is me, Pierre-Raymond Becquet, not an unnatural monster with a thing half a metre long.'

'All this talk!' Denise gasped. 'Give it to me.'

He lowered his belly to touch hers and penetrated her slowly, centimetre by centimetre, drawing from Denise an exclamation of delight as she felt *her* jouet opened and stretched and filled.

'There!' he said. 'You have all of me now – is it enough for you, Denise?'

'*Ah mon Dieu*!' she gasped and he began to jerk his bottom up and down smartly. What he had offered seemed to be enough – her eyes were closed and her mouth was open in continuous sighs.

Her legs shuddered and her sturdy thighs strained outward to open herself to the full. Spasms shook her belly and she opened her pale brown eyes to stare up at him curiously.

'It's all true, what they say about you,' she gasped.

He maintained his strong and steady stroke, it seemed to him that he was growing bigger and harder all the time. Denise made little gurgling sounds as she jerked beneath him.

Pierre-Raymond never knew, but it was this little episode on the studio floor that made Liliane decide to resign her job and leave his employ. She opened the studio door quietly and looked in – at the moment Pierre-Raymond felt the first quick surge of his sexual climax.

'Now, Denise, now, now!' Liliane heard him cry out as he stabbed hard into the belly of the actress under him.

Liliane saw the woman's long legs kick in the air and Pierre-Raymond's bare bottom driving between her spread thighs. It was too much – Liliane turned away and closed the door and decided it was time to look for a job elsewhere. Charming, fascinating, exciting he might be, this Pierre-Raymond – but to be number thirty-six in his harem was no longer amusing.

That was long ago, almost two years – since then he had taken many more photographs of Denise Lafontaine, and demonstrated to her the excellent reasons why he had so high a reputation among adventurous women. One of whom was Joelle Marot, who had arrived at his apartment unexpected at nine on Saturday morning and proceeded to almost rape him on his back before rushing away to meet Madame Picard and go shopping.

He was still lying on his rumpled bed while Joelle dressed to leave. She cupped her breasts into her lace bra, she smoothed her stockings up her slim legs, standing by the bed facing him with her feet apart. He stared at the join of her slim thighs and at her brown-haired *bijou*.

He thought of his fifteen centimetres of hard flesh inside it, the hot clasp of her soft and slippery flesh – and Joelle bouncing up and down on him, her head thrown back, her hair dishevelled. The rush of his desire up into her belly – he detested her!

She was a selfish, demanding woman, this Joelle. It had been pleasurable to have her straddling his belly, but the truth was she had used him as if he were a machine, not a human being.

She raised her slim arms and slipped her green-striped summer frock over her head, revealing her smooth little armpits. Would it be amusing to use them for lovemaking? Pierre-Raymond asked himself. How could it be done? Lie facing while she pressed an arm against her side? Kneel behind her and push into that soft little hollow? The mechanics were not obvious – it required experimentation to get it right.

Joelle tightened the belt of the frock around her waist, then cocked up each leg in turn behind her to put on her shoes. She sat before the mirror and, without troubling to ask, made use of Pierre-Raymond's ivory-backed brushes to attend to her hair.

Finally, she got up and put on her little black satin jacket.

'I'm ready,' she announced, 'I'll let you know when I've time to drop in again. *Au revoir, chéri.*'

Pierre-Raymond got off the bed and stretched, shoulders back, belly pulled in – his male part dangling limply from his thatch of dark curls. Joelle gave it the most indifferent of glances, her luminous eyes unblinking. Her desire was satisfied for now.

He put on his silk dressing gown to take her to the door.

'My handbag,' Joelle said, 'it's in the sitting room.'

It was lying on the sofa, an expensive creation in soft cream leather with a shoulder strap and her initials in small letters of

82

gold. She leaned over the sofa arm to pick it up – instantly Pierre-Raymond stepped close behind her and placed his hands on her hips. She was startled – she could feel his stiffening part pressing on the back of her thigh through her thin silk frock.

'I've no time for that now,' she said, trying to stand up and shake him off.

He gripped her hips hard, flipped her upward off her feet and forward over the sofa arm. With a hand flat on the small of her back, he was easily able to hold her down now her feet were off the floor. He kept her face down while he turned up her frock – he moved in close between her legs, forcing them apart.

'Let me up,' she said crossly, 'I've no time for games now.'

Pierre-Raymond was determined to use her as she had used him. It was to his advantage that she had no knickers – although she might not now agree about that. His free hand stroked the bare cheeks of her bottom, smooth and perfectly rounded despite her years. Then between her thighs to probe the soft lips there.

'Stop this now,' said Joelle, 'I shall get very angry!'

She tried to push herself up with her hands flat on the sofa. Pierre-Raymond pushed down hard on her back to keep her pinned. Helpless and bare-bottomed, the situation excited him.

Joelle glared at him over her shoulder and commanded him to let her up at once.

'I cannot let you go without a final proof of my adoration,' he said mockingly, 'it will take only a minute, *chérie*.'

A Lurking Threat Appears

There she was, the elegant Madame Marot, face down over the arm of the sofa in Pierre-Raymond's sitting room. She was angry and wriggling – her green-and-white summer frock turned up over her bare bottom. Pierre-Raymond's hand pressed down on her back held her helpless.

He was standing between her thighs, forcing them apart, while his fingers caressed the warm soft flesh of her *belle-chose*. He had unfastened his scarlet dressing gown and it hung open – his stiff part was sticking out, nodding up and down in approval of what he was doing. Joelle gave a shriek to feel it touching her bottom.

'I cannot let you go without the final proof of my adoration, Joelle,' Pierre-Raymond announced with mocking courtesy.

'No, no, no – not like this!' she exclaimed. 'Let me up!'

His agile fingers opened her for easy penetration. He pushed slow and steady and she squealed to feel his stiff length entering her. He slid in all the way, the whole fifteen centimetres – she was loose and slippery from their games in the bedroom, when he had been virtually raped by her, flat on his back.

The position was reversed – he had the upper hand now. Joelle squirmed and made moaning noises as he slid up into her *joujou* until his bare belly was hard against the cheeks of her bottom.

'*Et voilà, chérie!*' he exclaimed. 'Now you feel the strength of my devotion to you!' He started to thrust in and out to a quick smooth rhythm.

Joelle's outrage knew no bounds. She squirmed and complained, she kicked back in the hope of scoring a hit on any vulnerable part of his anatomy. Nothing did any good, he held her while he slid in and out, not hurrying, not dawdling – he was doing this for the simple pleasure of getting his own back on her.

'Ah, that feels good,' he gasped, 'what a pity you have to go so soon, Joelle. I would like to take you back to bed and amuse you for the rest of the day . . .'

Joelle's limp body shook across the sofa arm to his now rapid stabbing.

'*Ah bon Dieu!*' she moaned.

She had clenched her fists and was beating at the cushions of the sofa. The scintillating diamond rings on her fingers caught his attention – big hard stones, marvellously expensive. If only she had a necklace of these glittering diamonds to wind around *Grandjean* in his pride! Or suppose somewhere in the world was a diamond ring big enough to slip over his big purple-red head, to glitter around him like a jewelled collar . . .

A diamond collar for his cherished part – it would be a well-deserved acknowledgement of his imperial worth, an outward sign of his unsurpassable abilities. This image of *Grandjean* crowned was so astounding and appropriate that Pierre-Raymond sank his nails into the flesh of Joelle's hips while he slammed into her fast and furious.

'*Ah Dieu!*' she moaned again, loudly now. '*Dieu!*'

To Pierre-Raymond's amazement a tide of ecstasy swept through her body, from her loins up to her breasts. The sudden heave of her back showed him what was happening – she was in orgasm. She sobbed and squirmed and pushed her bare bottom hard against him to drive him in deeper.

But this wasn't supposed to be for her pleasure, that was the half-coherent thought in his mind. Yet she had again scored a victory over him, he realised to his consternation.

He was annoyed with himself, but that didn't stop him ramming hard into her, smacking his belly against her bottom, till with a cry of success he shot his revenge into her convulsing body.

'Ah yes!' she moaned. 'Ah yes, Pierre-Raymond!'

His knees were shaking under him. He lay forward, trembling on her back while his breathing slowed to normal. When he stood up and eased his slackening wet part out of her, he wondered if she would turn and attack him with her fingernails. He took a step backwards as a precaution.

She got up briskly, smoothing her frock down as she turned to look at him. His dressing gown hung limply open, all he had was exposed to her unblinking gaze.

'Pierre-Raymond, that was tremendous,' she said, 'even though you've made me late for lunch. Is my hair all right or does it need combing again?'

She was so casual that he was taken aback.

'Your hair is perfectly all right,' he assured her.

'Then I must dash,' and she kissed him on the cheek, gave his softening part a quick little tap with her fingertips and made for the door.

'*Au revoir*,' she said, 'I shall phone you.'

It was impossible to understand women, he thought as he

stood under the shower two minutes later. *I tried to show Joelle who is the man and who the woman – and instead of being humbled she turned it into a demonstration of her superiority. Damn her.*

He was under the shower, washing away the lingering traces of her expensive perfume that clung to his body. It was Givenchy, he thought, and she used it on herself generously. He had found it under her breasts and in her armpits and between her thighs. Wherever her body had rubbed against him there was her perfume. It was very exciting, but he couldn't go to the studio smelling of Joelle.

He washed his hair under the warm water cascading down on him and soaped his arms and body. He remembered with annoyance what Joelle said about Valerie, that she was fat. *But Valerie is not fat*, he said to himself, *she is comfortably round*. It was only jealousy speaking, nothing more, particularly that remark about Valerie having breasts like melons.

To an unbiased eye, such as his own, Valerie's breasts could be said to be formidably beautiful. Statuesque, admirable. Each was, at an estimate, three times the size and weight of each of Joelle's. Which perhaps accounted for the jealousy he detected in Joelle's criticism. And, it could be said, full as Valerie's breasts were, they sagged no more than Joelle's smaller ones.

Ah, they were very beautiful, Valerie's, he thought dreamily, the warm water pouring down over his body. When he had them out at the studio, her bra undone and pushed aside – when he kissed them bare and delightful, their red-brown buds stood up boldly. The times he'd put his head down and sucked her prominent nipples, until she sighed in slow ecstasy.

His mind was so completely occupied with Valerie's breasts

he was unaware that his soapy hand was circling his most treasured part – which was standing up stiffly again. Long and hard and swollen, twitching to the splash of warm water on its uncovered head.

Large or small, elegant or plump, massive or girlish, women's breasts were a delight and a comfort that Pierre-Raymond fully and enthusiastically appreciated. To stroke them and cup them in one's palms – there was no aesthetic experience known to man to match it. Music, paintings, statues – inspirational to every civilised man, but they faded out of serious consideration when compared with the pleasures of baring and feeling and kissing a pair of pretty breasts.

Pierre-Raymond's feet had slid apart and his back now rested on the wet tiles. He was iron-hard and he was sighing as his fingers fluttered on his jerking part, the warm water running down his chest and belly, soothing and arousing at the same time.

'*Ah non, non,*' he gasped, suddenly aware of what he was doing, 'she never fails to leave me upset and distraught, that Joelle. She uses me like a gigolo for her pleasure. It must stop before she reduces me to a nervous wreck . . .'

Pierre-Raymond's day had started strangely with Joelle Marot at his door. It continued in the same way when he arrived late at his studio by the Quai St Michel. Valerie smiled at him and said Madame Marot had phoned at nine that morning and had been told he was not expected till ten-thirty.

'She didn't tell me what she wanted,' Valerie added, her tone uncomfortably close to sarcasm, 'perhaps she will come in later and tell you herself.'

'Perhaps,' Pierre-Raymond muttered.

He had no intention of telling her that Madame Marot had conveyed her wishes to him already. She hadn't actually said what it was she wanted, she simply took it. That was the type of person she was, impatient and demanding.

There was no necessity for Valerie to know that Madame Marot had exploited him on his own bed, straddling him naked upon his back. The information would certainly bring that slyly mocking look to Valerie's face.

'A man came in,' she continued, 'he said his name was Leduc – he insisted that he must talk to you but he refused to say what he wanted.'

'Leduc?' said Pierre-Raymond. 'Do I know a Monsieur Leduc?'

Valerie shrugged.

'There was a certain air of menace about him,' she said, 'and he is a big man. I thought perhaps you owe him money and he had come to collect it. So I told him you weren't coming in today.'

'Leduc, the name means nothing to me,' said Pierre-Raymond, a puzzled frown wrinkling his brow, 'what did he look like?'

'As I said, big. He's about thirty, with a thick moustache like an old-time bandit in movies. Roland Leduc.'

His heart sinking, Pierre-Raymond realised the caller had to be Liliane Bonchamp's boyfriend. The man she lived with. He had seen a framed photo of Liliane and a moustached man with an arm around her waist, the two of them posed on a beach. And when he phoned before he went to see her, she said Roland was away.

Oh la la! Pierre-Raymond said to himself. *He's found out I was in that absurd bed with Liliane and now he's going to make trouble. But there was no harm in it – all I wanted was someone to talk to about my problems. I wasn't there to get Liliane on her back, it was just by chance that happened – it didn't mean anything to either of us.*

'I remember him now,' he told Valerie, 'you did right to send him away. He thinks I owe him something, but he is mistaken.'

His ten-thirty appointment was with a lady he had known for a long time, Madame Fabien. It was she who had amused herself one day by taking the strand of fine pearls from her neck to wind about his exposed part. That had been one of the most memorable days of Pierre-Raymond's life – the experience had made an indelible impression on him.

'Ah Marie-Rose,' he had sighed in amazement as he stared down at what she was doing. His stiff part strained upward, wrapped in rows of black pearls from root to tip, throbbing and leaping in her hand.

But today the reason she was at his studio was not to play exciting little games. She had brought her grandson to be photographed, a little boy of six. She wanted a portrait to put in a silver frame and stand on the piano in her salon.

Pierre-Raymond kissed her hand. She wasn't wearing her pearls today – she had a double strand of crimson coral beads about her slender neck. She saw him looking at it and knew what was going through his mind – she hooked a finger in the necklace to shake it a little and wink at him.

Nothing could take place while the little boy was present, of course. Pierre-Raymond became as charming as only he knew how – he took many pictures before he was certain he'd achieved what Marie-Rose wanted for her family album. Now and then he glanced at her necklace and smiled a little.

There had been an occasion – it made him breathe more quickly even to recall it – when Marie-Rose Fabien had arrived at the studio with a handbag filled with jewellery. After a little episode with her pearls, she considered it amusing to discover just how susceptible Pierre-Raymond was.

He took her portrait, not hurrying though he was keen to get her clothes off. Professionalism came first – it must never be said that a photograph by Pierre-Raymond Becquet could fall short of being a masterpiece!

But eventually they were alone in the reception room that was also the office – the famous chaise longue stood ready, a piece of furniture on which many married women had been shown ecstasy far beyond anything they had experienced in the marriage bed or ever dreamed of in their wildest flights of imagination.

The receptionist – it was Liliane in those days – had the day off when Marie-Rose turned the tables by showing Pierre-Raymond an ecstasy even he never believed possible. And to a man of his vast experience of women almost nothing was impossible. But she had understood him better than he knew. The little episode with her pearls had revealed something of interest to her.

She said nothing in advance but let him think it was a usual encounter until the right moment. He unbuckled the shiny black patent leather belt around her waist and tugged her cream silk blouse out. Her skirt slipped down her slim legs and she sat upon the green chaise longue in an almost transparent slip.

Through it he observed she was wearing no bra that day – just to provoke him. Her small breasts still rode high on her chest, though she was fifty. She took her own knickers off, then swung her legs up on the chaise longue. Pierre-Raymond perched beside her and stroked her full-handed, from her knees to the joint of her thighs.

His open palm glided on her sheer silk stockings, lingered on the bare skin above them, his fingertips creeping into her groin. He prised her thighs apart and smiled in anticipation.

The curls between Marie-Rose's legs were a rich chestnut. But they were sparse. They lay against her pale skin and nothing at all was covered. This he knew well from his previous experience with her. He intended to kiss her open groin and her belly and inside her thighs, but she had other plans in mind and told him to take her stockings off.

'Ah yes,' he sighed, 'how charming, *chérie*.'

His fingers roamed over her groin and thighs, fluttering and caressing and pressing between the cheeks of her bottom, over the thin lips of her *joujou*, down inside her thighs – all this and more to undo her suspenders and roll her stockings down her long legs! Was it any wonder that Marie-Rose became aroused to an exemplary degree just by having her silk stockings removed?

When she was completely naked he resumed his original intent, he licked her groin. He moved by exquisitely lingering stages to her peach, parting the thin curls with delicate fingertips.

Marie-Rose's face was flushed a charming pink as she lay back and gave herself up to the sensations of the moment. She sighed when Pierre-Raymond opened her deftly to caress her little bud. But she was not so carried away that she lost sight of what she had planned to do.

Her black crocodile-skin handbag lay on the floor beside the chaise longue. While Pierre-Raymond was licking the buds of her breasts she reached down to the bag, rummaged about inside it – and brought out a handful of necklaces of different types.

Her famous black pearls were there – the string she had once wound around his upright part. There were other pearls – two or three strings, cream coloured. She had square-cut amethysts set in a heavy gold chain. And gemstones – red and green in precious settings. There was a necklace of pink coral beads, long enough to go round her neck twice and still reach her waist.

The psychological moment had arrived – Pierre-Raymond watched in fascination and raging passion while she arranged her jewels. She was smiling at him all the time, as if enjoying a joke he didn't understand. Which was, of course, perfectly true.

She put strings of pearls between her open thighs, she draped them up her groin to frame her *belle-chose*. She put the string of black pearls in a straight line on her belly, from her split peach to between her small breasts.

She laid strands of gemstones across her belly, from side to side, over her bellybutton. She draped the string of amethysts and the other jewellery over her belly and thighs until at last the dark pink lips of her *joujou* were all that remained visible in this mélange of precious stones.

'*Ah mon Dieu*!' Pierre-Raymond gasped hoarsely, his eyes were almost bulging from his head.

'I know how much you like jewellery,' she said, eyes shining, 'I thought you might enjoy making love to mine.'

He was unable to restrain himself – he ripped off his clothes and hurled himself on top of her. He slid deep into her without a pause, so far gone that he didn't feel her legs embracing him and her heels thumping on his bottom. He thrust fast and hard, moaning incoherently, his mind wiped out by the hardness of gemstones and pearls pressing into his flesh.

Marie-Rose was completely overwhelmed by his unaccustomed and exciting savagery – his brutal onslaught on her naked body. Or on her jewels, who could say which he was ravaging? She writhed under him and cried out shrilly to his thrusting. Her body was hot and sweating and she felt his skin slide on hers. She too felt the hard round pearls pressed into her groin, into her belly.

She clawed at his bare back and rammed her loins hard against him to take all he had to give her, then she heard his sudden cry of exaltation as he spurted into her belly.

When he came to himself again, Marie-Rose was staring at him in stupefaction. She took a deep breath or two and smiled as if unable to believe what had just happened to her.

'Pierre-Raymond, you are amazing,' she whispered, 'I've never felt anything like that in my life.'

All that was a long time ago. She'd been to the studio plenty of times since, but had never again brought her jewels. Perhaps the force of her own response that day had been too much for her to accept. These days when she came to be photographed she wanted him to make love to her more delicately.

She let him arrange the pink coral beads in an oval round her chestnut-haired *joujou* before he slid into her, but that was as much as she permitted. And the effect on him was never the same as that first incredible psychological devastation.

Today it was her grandchild whose picture was being taken and there was no question of lovemaking, not of any kind. Even so, being a woman she was unable to resist teasing

Pierre-Raymond a little by fingering her necklace of pink coral.

While he was chatting to the little boy and making him laugh, Pierre-Raymond couldn't stop worrying about Roland Leduc – that big man with the bandit moustache. He'd been to the studio once – he would come back, that was certain, to pursue his grievance! What else could it be but a grievance if he knew a stranger had taken liberties with his girlfriend? For half a day and all of a night.

On that ridiculous imitation leopardskin settee. Then on the more absurd bed with the brocade-type curtains and gold tassels – what appalling taste the man had!

If a full confession was needed, Pierre-Raymond had also made use of Liliane's beautiful body standing beside the monstrous bed. It was Liliane's idea, not his own, while he was dressing to leave. 'For old time's sake,' she'd said, bending over to put her hands on the bed and present her small round bottom to him.

No man alive could resist so provocative a sight – certainly not Pierre-Raymond. He slipped his hands between her thighs and opened the pretty lips of her joujou. He positioned the purple-red head of his stiff part to her moist pinkness – and slid up slowly into her.

The old days – yes, doing that to her most certainly reminded him of when Liliane worked for him and he had her in the studio or in the office whenever there was time. Mounted on her back, hands holding her narrow hips in a firm grip to keep her steady while he thrust in and out, strong and deliberate. Ah, the good old days, those happy times before he met Claudia!

Which was all very well – but if Leduc had in some way found out what Pierre-Raymond had done to Liliane, there was going to be trouble. Leduc would be very angry if he knew his girlfriend had used his bed to bend over and present her bottom to another man. Violently angry, no doubt. Dangerous, perhaps.

Pierre-Raymond knew he must get in touch with Liliane to ask what was going on – how much had she told Leduc and what did he mean to do in retaliation. And had he vented his anger on her? Had he beaten her – the man sounded like a barbarian. Perhaps he had already thrown her out of the apartment.

But was it safe to phone? Suppose Leduc answered, what then? Say nothing and put the phone down? But Leduc might guess who was calling and become infuriated . . . and rush out to find him.

Good god, what an imbroglio, he said to himself, *and so very unjust – I never intended Leduc any harm – can't he understand that? It was just two old friends meeting and perhaps becoming a little carried away.*

By eleven-thirty Madame Fabien and the boy were gone.

'You look worried,' said Valerie, 'why – is it because Madame Marot might turn up? Did she say anything about her daughter's picture to you when she was here?'

She had a less than respectful gleam in her eyes and the half-grin on her face. This was in the darkroom – they were standing side by side at the workbench in the dim red glow.

'Her daughter's picture, ah yes,' he said vaguely.

His hand moved casually down Valerie's back until his fingers were in the cleft of her plump bottom. She had come to work that day in a pink shirt tucked into the waist of a grey skirt. To touch her was a reflex action for Pierre-Raymond, there was not a conscious decision involved in the gesture. But that said, it helped to sooth his anxieties about Roland Leduc.

He was much too concerned with his problem to give a thought to Valerie's reactions to what he was doing – the gentle rub of his fingers through her skirt was arousing her.

'When Madame Marot phoned the other day before she came in to see you, she mentioned a photo of her daughter,' Valerie said a little breathlessly, 'it wasn't clear what she wanted. When she talked to you while I was at lunch, didn't she explain?'

'She said something of the sort to me,' Pierre-Raymond said.

But Joelle had mentioned it only in passing. In effect, she spoke of nothing much at all, being exclusively concerned with sexual gratification at the time. Her own, naturally.

Pierre-Raymond put his hands on Valerie's hips and turned her with her back to the filing cabinet. She stared at him with the expression he interpreted as mockery, but he was never entirely certain. He shrugged and put an arm about her waist and a hand up her skirt.

Perhaps he was wrong about her expression. In the subdued red light of the darkroom it could be a smile of pleasure – after all, he was caressing her thighs above her stocking tops, warm flesh bare between stockings and knickers. His touch must give her sensations of pleasure, that went without saying. But just to reassure himself that it was so, he asked her.

'Oh yes,' she murmured, 'I love the feel of your hand between my legs, Pierre-Raymond.'

So that was all right. And certainly it felt good to him, his fingers sliding over her bare warm flesh, edging upward to that beautiful mound where her thighs met. His worries receded until they were forgotten.

'So why haven't you put the appointment in the book,' Valerie asked.

For a moment he was baffled, then he realised she was talking about Joelle's daughter.

'Madame Marot was in a hurry,' he murmured, 'we were not able to decide on a convenient time.'

Valerie's legs were as far apart as her skirt allowed and she was squirming in delight as he slid her knickers down till he could stroke her *bijou*.

'Yes, I understand,' she gasped, her knees trembling.

This talk of Joelle Marot had served to remind Pierre-Raymond of how his day had started. How she had used him for her pleasure. Flat on his back on his bed – his pride sticking straight up in the air – Joelle straddling his hips and jolting up and down on it with a smirk on her red-painted mouth.

True, it had felt good, but that was not the right way of things. After all, he was obliging her, not she him. He had no need for the attentions of women of a certain age. He was Pierre-Raymond Becquet, he could have all the pretty young women he wanted.

He sighed to feel Valerie's round belly pushing at his hand – *she* appreciated him. He had two fingers inside her now and with his other hand he opened his trousers all the way down, took her by the wrist and pushed her hand inside.

'*Enorme*,' she whispered when her fingers closed on *Grandjean* and she felt the strength and hardness, 'much too much!'

A contented smile crossed Pierre-Raymond's face and he raised her thin skirt to her waist. This was how things ought to be.

'But what if Madame Marot arrives and finds us doing this? I told you she rang to ask when you would be here,' she said.

That look was in her eye again, a corner of her mouth turned wryly up.

'She won't come here today,' Pierre-Raymond insisted.

He was fumbling under her clothes – her knickers were halfway down her thighs. She was open and ready for him and he pressed straight in, his strong hard flesh pierced her like a blade.

'But you can't be sure . . .' she gasped.

He slithered in and out – and Valerie no longer cared whether Madame Marot came looking for him or not. His hands were behind her, up her skirt to grasp the soft plump cheeks of her bottom. She pushed her loins rhythmically against him, meeting his long thrusts – and could hear the creak of the wooden filing cabinet she was leaning against.

'Oh Pierre-Raymond, oh yes,' she was sighing.

Her eyes were closed, her face was almost cherubic in the dim diffused red light of the darkroom. Outside in the office the phone rang. Pierre-Raymond was thrusting busily. Valerie moaned and turned her head to stare at the door as if she thought that she ought to go and pick up the phone.

'Leave it!' he gasped hoarsely.

'And if it is Madame Marot?' she sighed.

Her legs were shaking – she was only two seconds from orgasm. She bounced her belly and thighs against Pierre-Raymond, breath rasping in her throat. And in his mind was the thought that the inconvenient caller was Leduc, checking to ascertain if the man he believed had wronged him was there.

'It is no one of importance,' he gasped, 'leave it!'

'But . . .' she managed to say at the instant his passion gushed up into her wet *joujou*.

Darkroom Longings

Pierre-Raymond assumed that Joelle Marot's suggestion of having her daughter photographed was only an excuse, not a reality. It was a reason to phone – an excuse to visit the studio in search of sexual gratification. He had been happy to accommodate her, with her bottom on the desk and her feet on the floor, well apart.

It was brief and vigorous, almost like doing exercises. Well-known exercises that are good for toning up the system. And she had enjoyed it so much she didn't rush away to meet her mother-in-law and husband for lunch at the Tour d'Argent. She demanded he do it again, and Pierre-Raymond saw no reason not to.

Against the wall this time, not the desk – with the jacket of her elegant Chanel suit undone and her blouse unbuttoned – and her black lace bra unhooked and pulled up to let him stroke her well-shaped breasts.

This time when he pushed up inside her he made it last longer, taking her deeper into ecstatic sensation. She'd squealed and bumped her loins against him and she was shaking so furiously that only his arms around her waist prevented her from sliding down the wall to the floor.

Then she dashed off belatedly to her lunch party. Then she

turned up outside his apartment door early on Saturday morning – for more of the same. She'd said something about her daughter and a photo, either at the studio or at his apartment – he couldn't remember when she said it. He'd paid no attention.

Such excuses were familiar to him – many of his clients made up little reasons to arrive at the studio. When Joelle took him by surprise at his apartment he knew what she wanted and it had nothing to do with photography and portraits. The true focus of her interest was between his legs.

But he was mistaken. Though not about what Joelle wanted from him – he never misunderstood that. Events proved she really did want him to take photographs of her daughter. And there the two of them were in his studio.

Joelle's daughter, Monique, was seventeen. In many ways she resembled her mother – she had the same long thin nose, large dark brown eyes, determined chin. Her hair was the same dark brunette, but it was worn shorter and had been brushed back in a style that flattered her youthful appearance.

In one important respect mother and daughter differed vastly. In spite of her slenderness of body and limb, Monique had large breasts! Her mother's were average-sized and elegant, set high on her chest. But Monique! That was another story altogether. Somewhere back in the family, conveniently forgotten, there was an ancestress with the heavy breasts of a peasant woman.

At the sight of Monique's over-developed bosom a brief smile flickered over Pierre-Raymond's face. He was careful not to let Joelle see his amusement – he hadn't forgotten how scornful she had been about Valerie, for no good reason, merely to be offensive.

Breasts like water-melons – that's what she said. And her

own daughter had a pair just as big, evidently a source of maternal embarrassment for Joelle!

But there was another reason why Pierre-Raymond was affected so strongly by Monique – her youth. In the usual way of things, the women he made love to were mostly in their forties, like Joelle. And Giselle Picard. Marie-Rose Fabien and the others.

They were immensely elegant, of course, chic beyond words and hard-dieted down to a stylish thinness, perfumed to perfection, with face, neck, breasts, thighs pampered and smoothed by every expensive cosmetic on sale in Paris.

Valerie was younger, only twenty-five – but she was an employee and it didn't count in the same way. Liliane was a year or two younger still – she was the youngest woman Pierre-Raymond had made love to since Claudia left him.

It wasn't that he was attracted to older women, it was merely part of his profession as a society portrait photographer, that was how he saw things. Middle-aged women could afford the price he charged for his services. And if they wanted another type of service as well, on their back with their legs apart, why not?

But a girl of seventeen, slender and beautiful, with those beautiful breasts – *ah, Dieu*! It was with a tremendous effort of will he forced himself not to stare at the tempting mounds in Monique's white silk blouse.

He listened with only half an ear to Joelle chattering away in her usual manner. His fervid imagination was occupied with a vision of her daughter naked to the waist for him to admire. Ah if only!

They were bigger than Valerie's, he thought, although Monique was almost 10 years younger. A delicate young girl –

very lithe and slender of body – endowed with those round heavy delights! She was a virgin, he was certain – a raging temptation to every man who laid eyes on her!

Were hers bigger than Valerie's? To judge accurately by eye alone was very difficult. It was mere guesswork when comparative sizes were close. As they seemed to be. Valerie, Monique, which had the bigger pair? Impossible to be precise by weighing them in the mind's eye, so to speak.

To reach a reliable decision it would be necessary to handle both pairs, one after the other. To run one's hands over them. And under them. To gauge the weight and solidity.

Yesterday, in the darkroom before leaving for the day, he'd gauged Valerie's beauties thoroughly and professionally. He had stripped her to the waist and handled her until she was frantic with desire and pleading with him.

He prolonged her ordeal by sliding his hands down her body to her waist. He undid her skirt so that it fell down her legs and lay around her ankles till she kicked it away. His hand slid inside the top of her knickers and down her belly until the tip of his middle finger touched curls and then soft lips.

In another second he was on his knees. He pulled her knickers down and off and laid his flushed face against her thighs above her stockings. She moaned and beat her fists on his shoulders – his tongue probed into her *joujou* to find her bud. He flickered his tongue over it until he felt a throb begin in her body.

'Ah!' Valerie moaned, her belly bucking against him.

He licked faster at her and felt her body shaking in orgasm – her little cries echoing in the closed and confined darkroom. His determined tongue flung her from climax to climax.

'Stop . . .' she gasped, 'let me breathe – stop for a moment, a moment, Pierre-Raymond . . . only for a moment . . .'

By his reckoning she had experienced orgasm four or five times by then – although it was not easy to tell where one ended and the next started. In the process of doing this to her he had become desperately aroused. He stood up and steered his palpitating hardness up between her legs, her back to the wall.

Her loose-lipped and very wet *jouet* was waiting and he pushed up into her easily and fully, till their bellies were touching and his curls entwined in hers. It seemed to him that she was more completely his in those moments than any woman that he had ever been with – it was a strange impression and it aroused him more highly yet.

She couldn't respond again – whatever he did to her now. He'd finished her off with his tongue to a point where she as only just conscious. But she was his. She leaned heavily against the wall with her legs spread and surrendered herself completely to his desire. He plunged into her slippery depths – he could feel the trembling of her belly in response to his strong thrusts.

His hands were on her big soft breasts – he rolled them under his palms, he bounced them on his open hands, he sank his agile fingers into their tender warmth, he handled them savagely – he was making love to her breasts as much as to her *joujou*.

No doubt of it, he had a very clear impression of the weight and size of Valerie's breasts. And today, standing there in the studio behind his camera and assessing the size of Monique's in her thin silk blouse, he tried to make up his mind.

In his trousers there was an awkward stiffness, a weightiness that caused him to move carefully. He was hiding his arousal as best he could from Monique's mother, not from embarrassment, of course – he knew Joelle too closely to be embarrassed.

But she would give him that unblinking and most disconcerting stare of hers if she became aware of his condition – a superior and silent sarcasm was the least he could expect.

However aroused he was, nothing could possibly happen. Joelle had made herself comfortable on a wicker fan-backed settee that was a studio prop. She'd had Pierre-Raymond move it from the wall to nearer the camera so she could observe him at work.

She talked incessantly – she instructed him at short intervals to take the photograph this way or that way, she suggested that the lighting could be improved, she instructed Monique how she should sit and which way to turn her head . . . and so on, advising Pierre-Raymond how to do the job he was famous for.

Nevertheless, he was able to touch Monique while he posed her for various shots. Delicately, of course – a finger beneath her chin to lift her head, a light touch of his hand on her spine. He wanted her shoulders well back to make her glories stand out to their very impressive best.

Ah, if only he dare put his hands under those breasts to lift them a little . . . if he dare suggest her bra needed the tiniest rearrangement . . . unbutton her blouse and put his hand inside to cup those fleshy delights while he was pretending to adjust her bra strap . . . His fingers curled in anticipation. But no.

If Monique were alone with him here in the studio, perhaps he might risk touching her. He told himself that he would – but it was only a dream. Joelle was sitting watching, her head on one side and her legs crossed suavely.

He knew very well why she had chosen to sit on the

Indonesian wicker settee. It was to taunt him, to remind him without words that this bamboo settee was the scene of their first encounter. He couldn't recall exactly how long ago it was when he made her acquaintance but it had been when Liliane was still working for him, before Valerie.

The unknown Madame Marot had had a late afternoon appointment, he remembered that clearly. By the time he completed his portraits of her, Liliane had gone – she'd left early to deliver a set of proofs to a client. Although Madame Marot was a stranger to him he knew she was a vain and wealthy woman – and elegant. So much was evident. What he had still to discover was how selfish she was, and that would be no surprise with a woman of her type.

For her final portrait that afternoon long ago, he sat Madame Marot on the Eastern fan-backed settee, her chin up and her eyebrows arched in a haughty stare, her long thin nose raised. The camera shutter clicked. Pierre-Raymond informed her he was finished.

She smiled curiously and said he was by no means finished. A friend of hers had told her he had the stamina of ten men. She eased her skirt up her thighs, almost to her stocking-tops, and she moved her knees apart. The pose was inelegant – but it was provocative. Pierre-Raymond smiled and asked who was the friend who had recommended him.

'Giselle Picard,' she said.

'Ah,' he said, 'of course.'

There was no doubt remaining in his mind about the direction of Joelle Marot's interest. Her skirt had moved up higher yet – he now had a perfect view of bare skin above silk stockings. To say nothing of the view of a fascinating strip of shiny black satin between her legs, covering her *lapin*.

'As it happens, several of my friends spoke well of you,' she said casually.

'May I ask who, besides Madame Picard?'

'Marguerite Lagarde was one, Fleur Duval another. And others, if you are interested, Nicole Gentilly, Lucienne Aragon. Need I go on? Come here, Pierre-Raymond – and show me this marvellous *thing* they rave about.'

And that was how it happened with her. In no time he was down on his knees before the high-backed wicker settee, his trousers open and his stiff part exposed for her admiration. She held it in her hand to feel its size and strength.

'You had my friends on this settee, I suppose,' she said very casually, her fingertips sliding up the smooth skin of his long hard pride, 'who was the best with her legs apart?'

'Ah no,' he breathed, 'comparisons are impossible! Women are all adorable.'

'Your discretion is admirable,' she said, 'but tell me how it is possible to do anything interesting on this little settee – it is only long enough for two persons to sit side by side. You can't ask a woman to lie on it – her legs would be over the end and her neck twisted up against the arm.'

'There are thirty-six ways to pleasure a woman,' said Pierre-Raymond, his stiff part jumping in her hand.

And certainly, when her little black knickers were off, Joelle showed herself to be very adaptable. She understood well enough that it was not a question of lying on her back. She raised one foot and placed it on the settee, her knee level with her chin.

The other expensively-shod foot stayed on the floor while her thighs moved apart as far as they would go – stretching herself open for Pierre-Raymond's grand entrance. He kissed

110

inside her warm thighs, he kissed her open groin, he kissed her belly. He gripped her legs with eager hands and she set the bare head of his twitching part to the wet lips between her thighs.

'Slowly,' she said, 'I want to watch myself being violated.'

He pushed into her very slowly. He and she stared down at his centimetre by centimetre penetration of her belly – and when at last he was fully in her, they remained still to enjoy the view of his preliminary achievement.

'The best sight in the world,' she murmured, 'and by far the best sensation, a man's long hard *thing* inside one.'

Pierre-Raymond agreed completely with that. This sensation of being engulfed by Joelle's warm and wet *joujou* was so enjoyable and the sight of those long lips forced open by his penetration was so exciting – he knew this first time with her would be of brief duration.

He stared at her face and saw her dark brown eyes gleaming in the intensity of her emotions. He wanted to stroke her breasts, but her frock had no opening he could discover. He cupped them in his hands and sank his fingers into their soft flesh through the silk of her frock and her unseen bra.

Then he was thrusting rapidly into her belly, only a heartbeat or two from ecstatic release. Joelle took his flushed face between her palms and held it firmly – her unblinking eyes watching for the change in his expression when his moment arrived.

Since that first day a great deal had taken place between him and her. Mostly to her advantage – although he would never deny the pleasure he had from her elegant body. He detested her now because she behaved as if she owned him body and soul. But that was no reason to refuse her when she opened her legs for him.

Now she had brought her pretty young daughter to his studio – a portrait, yes – but he understood enough about Joelle and her ways to realise she was also taunting him. Arranging it so that he became aroused in an impossible and absurd situation.

Tricks of that type amused Joelle, she had a cruel nature. He was certain she would return to take advantage of his condition the moment she could get rid of her daughter.

While he was working he could stare at Monique all he liked – it would be a strange photographer who didn't study his sitter with great care. He could stare at every part of her he wished, at her pretty face and her long slender legs. At her thighs and hips and graceful neck.

All very true, all quite professional perhaps – but mainly he was looking at Monique's bountiful breasts, those beauties that swayed under her thin silk blouse when she moved.

The hardness in Pierre-Raymond's trousers was almost painful, so insistent had it become. He busied himself with viewfinder, lens settings and camera. He was obsessed by the idea of taking Monique into the darkroom, away from her mother. To do what he had done to Valerie in there the evening before.

In Pierre-Raymond's feverish imagination Monique *wanted* to go into the darkroom as much as he did. But she was so young – so young and so virginal! For that reason it would be considerate to do it to her in complete darkness, to spare her blushes.

Naturally, in the dark she would press herself close to him – he would feel her marvellous breasts squashed against him! He would stroke her back from shoulder blades to waist through her silk blouse and feel the delicious warmth of her body. Then the cheeks of her bottom, soft and springy through her skirt.

Standing, sitting, how? In the drama playing out in his mind he swayed this way and that, wanting it all at once – then made up his mind. He switched on the dim red light of the darkroom, he wanted to see Monique while he was playing with her.

He lifted her and sat her upon the workbench facing him. His male part throbbed in his trousers, demanding and impetuous as he opened her blouse and her bra to bare her fleshy delights. A long sigh escaped him while he stared as if mesmerised by their sumptuous shape. His hands were trembling when he touched her.

'But Monsieur Becquet,' she murmured, her mouth close to his face and her sweet breath on his cheek, 'you know we mustn't do this, not you and I.'

'You are very beautiful, Monique,' he answered.

His palms circled gently over her bare breasts. He could feel their gentle bounce under his touch and he heard her sighs.

'No, it's impossible!' she said and grabbed at his wrists.

'Do not blame me, *chérie*,' he sighed, 'you are so beautiful that to be near you robs me of all sense of responsibility.'

It went without saying that she enjoyed having Pierre-Raymond play with her breasts. In his mind he resumed his caresses till her body was trembling. Only then did he open his trousers and guide her hand inside.

She gasped when she touched his hardness. He was leaning half over her, using his tongue on her breasts. She had a tight hold on his upright part but she did nothing to it – so young a girl couldn't be expected to know how to give pleasure to a man. Not that any stimulation by her was necessary – his hard flesh was leaping in her nervous grasp.

113

'Monsieur Becquet!' she gasped. 'Stop this now before we do something we shall regret later.'

'Monique, *je t'adore*,' he murmured as he rolled the firm buds of her breasts expertly between his fingers.

Her body was shaking, she pressed her legs tightly together, she jerked her hand out of his trousers. In doing so she pulled *Grandjean* unintentionally out. Pierre-Raymond gasped as he felt the uncovered plum-purple head touch her skirt – in a moment he had his quivering length under the hem.

His desire came surging out instantly as he slid his hardness along her stocking, vigorous little jets that reached right up to the bare skin. He gripped her heavy breasts tightly while he spurted, hearing her whimper of *Non non non* . . .

In his racing imagination he spurted again and again, higher, up past Monique's bare thigh to her little knickers. Ah, he was soaking the narrow strip of satin between her legs, wetting the thin material over her little *joujou*. She would feel his sticky desire soak through to the soft virginal lips . . .

'I think that half-profile will make an interesting picture,' he said, reloading the camera, 'it will show that delicate jawline to perfection. What do you think, Madame Marot?'

Joelle pretended to think about his suggestion, sitting there on the Indonesian wicker settee with the fan-back, elegant legs lightly together, back straight – a picture of propriety on the very piece of furniture she had been ravaged on countless times by the photographer.

'Very well,' she agreed eventually, 'her face in half-profile but the torso full-on to the camera.'

Pierre-Raymond nodded. He knew precisely what was in her mind – she disliked her daughter's oversized breasts and would have no pictures of her sideways to the camera. Monique mustn't show her bounties protruding to their superb fullness. And evidently Monique understood her mother's unspoken criticism – her cheeks turned a pretty rose-pink for a moment.

But Joelle is a monster, Pierre-Raymond said to himself while he set to work – she makes her daughter ashamed of the beauties Nature has bestowed upon her. Oh for an opportunity to take all the dear girl's clothes off and explain to her how she has been superbly endowed!

He touched her cheek with respectful fingers to turn her head to the side for the proposed portrait. He put his hands lightly on her shoulders to straighten her body and keep her square-on to the camera. He couldn't help looking down the slope of those sumptuous breasts under the white silk blouse. Monique knew why he was looking down and blushed again.

In his mind he took her into the darkroom again and stripped her naked – in pitch darkness, by touch alone, not even the red working light on. Ah, the feel of her full breasts, soft and so vulnerable to his eager hands.

This time she didn't say anything to discourage him. That was only the first time around, before he spurted his sticky desire up her thigh. She was bolder now, ready to go further with him. She stood in the total blackness, naked and warm and delightful while his hand glided on the smooth flesh of her girlish belly. He touched soft curls and warm lips.

Monique, *je t'adore*, he thought. He was playing out the ardent little drama in his head. Monique sank to her knees at his feet and he jerked his trousers open – out sprang his fifteen centimetres of hard flesh. He sighed to feel Monique put her arms about his waist and smother *Grandjean* between her magnificent breasts . . .

She murmured his name adoringly. Then she got to her feet

to press her naked young body against him. Her feet were apart – she had his hardness in her hand to guide it into her.

But she is too young and inexperienced to succeed in this. He takes charge, his hands on her hips to lift her bodily till her legs curl around his waist and she can grip him tight. They are both naked now – in the imagination everything is possible – he revels in the feel of her warm young flesh against his body.

His hands are under her bare bottom, he touches the curls and pries open the soft wet lips. He positions the swollen head of his proud part where he wants it to be. *Ah Monique*, he sighs as he pushes strongly up into her. She winds her arms tight around his neck and she makes little mewling sounds of excitement. His throbbing flesh is inside her *joujou* . . .

'But that's enough now,' Madame Marot's voice interrupted his frantic imagining, 'you've taken enough pictures of her.'

It was true. Pierre-Raymond nodded, hardly able to speak.

'Monique darling,' her mother said, 'your portraits are going to be absolutely beautiful. There is no one half as talented as Monsieur Becquet in a photographic studio.'

Monique stared at her mother and then at Pierre-Raymond – she said nothing, but it was obvious to him what she was thinking – and if it wasn't obvious to Joelle, then it ought to be. Monique knew her mother visited his studio to be ravaged on a regular basis.

'Go and ask Mademoiselle Charbonnet to let you use the phone, darling,' said Joelle briskly, 'ring your Aunt Felicie and tell her we haven't left the studio yet – we'll see her a little later than we thought.'

Pierre-Raymond watched the beautiful girl's lean round bottom as she walked across the studio to the door. With her hand upon the handle Monique turned to smile at him and thank him for all the trouble he'd taken. He said he wished all his sitters were as patient as she had been. And as beautiful.

The door closed behind her. He turned and there was Joelle at his side. Without a word she flicked his trousers open and slid her hand inside. He drew in his breath sharply to feel her long cool fingers close around his throbbing flesh.

'We have only a minute,' she said, 'why were you staring like that up my skirt while my young daughter was sitting there – I don't know how I stopped myself from blushing. I know how hotly you desire me and I feel the same about you – but I must insist that you control yourself when other people are present. I have a certain reputation to preserve, do you understand?'

Her fingers stroked up and down in a nervous little movement. Pierre-Raymond was unable to speak a word for the overwhelming sensations surging through his body.

'As for *this*,' Joelle went on, 'I could hardly prevent myself from laughing out loud when I saw your enormous bulge. It stuck out as if you had a bunch of bananas in your trousers! Suppose my daughter noticed it and asks me the reason for your shameful condition? How could I explain it to her? Children talk – and if my husband ever suspected me, what then?'

It was in Pierre-Raymond's mind that Monique was not a child. At seventeen she must know what men and women did together and she had probably guessed the reason for the bulge in his trousers – her own big beautiful breasts.

He was totally unable to answer Joelle's question. He gasped and shook at the knees to the sudden spurt of his desire up his belly under his shirt – wetting Joelle's fingers.

'This is intolerable!' she shrieked, her fingernails biting

into his flesh as she tried to cut off his flow.

But no explosion can ever be stopped once it has started – he teetered on his rubbery legs, his sticky passion shooting into her hand. And realising there was nothing she could do now, she snatched her hand away.

'So! You insult me!' she said with an unpleasant smile. 'We shall see who will have the last laugh, Monsieur Ten-times.'

She put so much derision into his nickname he almost quailed.

'Ah, Joelle *chérie*,' he murmured in an attempt to retrieve an irrecoverable situation, 'but you have this overwhelming effect on me – what can I do?'

She swept out of the studio without a word – leaving the door open behind her. Valerie sat at her desk, Monique stood beside her talking into the phone. Whether they saw Pierre-Raymond as he turned his back quickly and did up his trousers, he couldn't be sure. Joelle was deliberately trying to shame him.

Her anger sprang from disappointment, of course. She had sent Monique out of the studio to give herself a moment of privacy to take advantage of Pierre-Raymond's capabilities. Two minutes with her back to the wall and her feet apart, knickers down – if she had any on – and his hands grasping the cheeks of her bottom.

So simple, so very exciting – now he had ruined everything by his failure to restrain himself until the proper moment. He had cheated her of her due. It was infuriating. But he was going to regret his lack of consideration, she would see to that.

Liliane Brings Awkward News

It was past four in the afternoon when Madame Marot and Monique left Pierre-Raymond – he decided to go home. He needed the use of his bathroom after the debacle with Joelle and a clean shirt to replace the one sticking clammily to his belly.

He kissed Valerie lightly on the cheek and told her to lock up at the usual time. She gave him a doubtful look, perhaps she believed he'd arranged to meet Madame Marot for the usual. Not the friendliest of looks on her part – it worried him slightly.

He tried to improve the situation by the way he knew best. He put his hands on Valerie's big soft breasts for an affectionate squeeze – doing so reminded him of Monique's untouched beauties and something of his dismay must have showed in his expression. The look on Valerie's face became even more mocking.

'*Au revoir*,' he said quickly.

All in all, it had been a vexingly difficult time for Pierre-Raymond, this past hour or so.

The day was not over by a long way. Fate had more vexation in store for him. As he was leaving the building, who was just about to enter but Liliane Bonchamp?

119

'Pierre-Raymond, are you leaving so soon?' she exclaimed. 'I must talk to you – it is absolutely vital. I couldn't phone you because of Roland. We have to talk.'

Roland Leduc, the boyfriend with the moustache who burst into the studio to assassinate the man who had made love to Liliane. At least, Pierre-Raymond assumed he burst in, though he wasn't present himself and Valerie hadn't described the event in terms suggesting actual violence.

It was Pierre-Raymond's uneasiness and vague emotion of guilt that caused him to assume Leduc intended to harm him.

'Yes, we must talk urgently,' he agreed with Liliane, 'do you have an hour, or is Leduc waiting somewhere for you?'

'He'll be back about seven. I must be home before him.'

Pierre-Raymond took her arm and walked her to the taxi stand on the corner of the Boulevard St Michel. Once they were inside a taxi and rolling toward the rue de Sèvres he put an arm about her trim waist and stared at her mournfully.

His other hand was up her skirt, of course, between her legs. He did that without even thinking about it. Liliane had become accustomed to his mannerisms when she worked for him. She moved her knees just a little to allow him to continue without making runs in her stockings. They were a new pair.

The only surprise was that he had commenced by putting a hand up her skirt rather than undoing a button or two of her blouse to fondle her breasts. That's what he had nearly always done before. It meant nothing, this touching her body, she understood that. In some countries men carried a string of worry-beads to finger while they talked. Pierre-Raymond made use of women's bodies in the same casual way.

Naturally, it was impossible for Liliane to know how an image of Monique Marot's oversized breasts was dominating his mind to the exclusion of other women's advantages. Nothing smaller than Monique's could capture his attention just then.

Liliane had little spiky breasts. Normally he would feel them and kiss them till she almost achieved the peak of delight. But today he paid them no attention. He put a hand up her skirt and stroked her thighs where the flesh was smooth as fine satin. He felt higher, under the lace edge of her little knickers.

He was worried about Roland Leduc and any unpleasantness to come, but that didn't stop him remembering with pleasure when he last touched Liliane. It was beside that absurd bed of Leduc's, that tasteless affair of ironwork and brocade curtains like a tent – Liliane was standing with her back to him, bent over, her hands flat on the bed. While he was behind her, half dressed, feeling the pretty *lapin* between her thighs.

Liliane's bottom was very pretty. She had small round cheeks, marvellously smooth and firm to the fingers. And her *joujou* was a soft fleshy mound below, split like a peach. He'd stroked her with delicacy, just as he was stroking her now in the taxi, and he opened the pretty lips to feel how wet she was inside. She'd shivered in little spasms of pleasure as she waited to feel his hard flesh slide into her.

Standing by that absurd bed, she'd said it brought back the old days – he recalled her words. For him too it had stirred up the memory of those distant days when she worked for him, days when he bent her over the desk or over the chaise longue or over the wicker settee whenever he had a mind to. Which was often.

Naturally, he couldn't do more than caress her *joujou* sitting here in a taxi with the driver less than a metre away. Although she was sighing and trying to force her legs apart to the limit of her skirt. Pierre-Raymond was sighing in unison with her, remembering that day standing by Leduc's monstrous bed, mounting her from behind, holding her hips while he was thrusting in and out of her warm softness.

He recalled how he'd cupped her pointed little breasts in his hands while he rode her. And the gold chain round her long neck swinging to the jolt of his thrusts into her body.

'*Ah mon Dieu, oui*!' she'd shrieked. He adored it when women cried out in ecstasy at the moment of crisis, specially if they cried his name. That never failed to bring his maleness gushing out of him.

But that was last week. Now here they were in a taxi and much had changed since then. But not for the better.

'Is your heart still broken, Pierre-Raymond?' Liliane asked, a note of irony in her voice.

Her thighs closed, trapping his hand between them and holding it still. He said nothing but looked at her doubtfully. She was not so far gone in delight at his touch as he expected – not if she could trap his hand and ask idiotic questions.

'Or has the Claudia you were weeping for had a change of mind and returned to you?' she added.

Pierre-Raymond ignored her words. If she wanted conversation instead of sensation, he had urgent matters to raise – starting with what had taken place at his studio in his absence.

'Roland Leduc stormed in,' he said, with a dramatic intensity sufficient to describe an armed police raid. 'By good fortune I wasn't there, God knows what would have happened otherwise. I'm sure he came to do me harm. What have you told him?'

'I've told him nothing!' Liliane protested. 'Nothing!'

She emphasised her words by striking him several times on the thigh with her little hand clenched into a fist. High up on

122

his thigh, nowhere near his knee. Almost in his groin. Almost.

'You think I'm such a fool as to tell him I let you stay with me all night?' she demanded, her fist landing on the same spot again and again to impress her words on him.

'Then why did he come looking for me?' Pierre-Raymond gasped wildly, flinching under her blows to so sensitive an area.

The truth was that he had been limp since the little accident in Joelle Marot's hand. Even when he'd stroked Valerie's chubby breasts by way of bidding her *au revoir* – and it was unheard of for *Grandjean* to be remain *petit Jean* while Pierre-Raymond had his hands on a pair of breasts.

A psychological depression was affecting his natural response – even in the taxi while he was feeling between Liliane's legs he remained soft and small and pathetic. Until this moment. Her clenched fist thumped him and he grew thick and hard.

'Roland suspects,' said Liliane.

She knew from the old days that Pierre-Raymond was in a state of arousal more often than not. She wasn't aware of his target of being stiff for two-thirds of his waking hours. That was his own secret ambition and he never mentioned it to anyone.

But she knew he loved to feel himself stiff and strong in his trousers all day while he was working. She saw it as an idiotic male conceit but harmless, and she'd helped him to remain hard for hours on end. Sometimes by raising her skirt to let him see her bare thighs, sometimes by bending over to show him how taut her skirt was over her round little bottom.

There were times when she aroused him by slipping a hand into his trouser pocket, down into the warmth of his groin, to find and stroke his dangling part with her fingertips until it stood up. And with this knowledge of his nature, she was surprised in the taxi that he was soft and limp – even while his hand was up her skirt.

The only explanation she could think of for this most unusual state was that he must have pleasured his present receptionist-secretary just before leaving the studio. Or perhaps he'd done it to his last client of the day, some over-made-up middle-aged lady with thin thighs who'd taken her knickers down and lain on her back for his attentions. He did a lot of that.

Whatever the reason might be, it was an annoyance to Liliane, this lack of response – because she was trying to make progress on her plan to regain his favour and leave Roland.

She took encouragement from the knowledge that Pierre-Raymond recovered his strength and appetite very quickly. At least when she worked for him he had. If all else failed, when she got him to his apartment she'd sit him in an armchair and kneel down to take his limpness into her mouth – that never failed.

But now suddenly he was stiff. She hit him once more with her clenched fist, a few centimetres higher. He moaned softly while the hard part in his trousers bounded. Liliane had a programme, a plan of what she hoped to achieve at this meeting and Pierre-Raymond's response indicated all was going well at last.

'How can Roland suspect us?' he asked in a quavering voice. 'If you have admitted nothing, there can be no suspicion.'

'He is very friendly with the man in the next apartment,' she explained, 'they go to football matches together. And drinking. His name is Lemall. Roger Lemall. He was on the stairs when you arrived. I saw him when I opened the door to let you in.'

'Oh,' Pierre-Raymond said mournfully.

'He must have kept watch,' she continued, and her fist struck once more, hardly more than a light tap now he was in the state she required for her scheme. 'He knows you stayed a long time – but not how long. If he'd seen you leave the next morning, that would have been catastrophic.'

'You believe he informed Roland of my visit?'

'I know he did, because Roland asked me why you were there.'

'*Bon Dieu*,' Pierre-Raymond sighed, 'it gets worse and worse.'

The taxi ride was not a long one – they arrived at the rue de Sèvres before anything of further interest could happen or even be thought of or discussed.

Pierre-Raymond withdrew his hand from under her skirt, kissed her cheek briefly – and arranged matters in his trousers before paying the driver and helping Liliane out of the taxi.

In his apartment he sat her on the grey suede sofa – upon the very spot graced by Joelle Marot's elegant backside the morning she arrived out of the blue and found him in his dressing gown.

He had urgent questions to ask Liliane, but there was another matter that needed his attention before that. He poured a glass of white wine for her from a bottle in the kitchen refrigerator and begged to be excused for two minutes.

He dashed into his bedroom to take off his suit and the shirt stuck to his skin as a result of Joelle's badly timed advances. In the bathroom he washed with warm water and scented soap, and in the mirror the reflection of his long hard part seemed to be mocking him.

What had happened to him in the studio was absurd and disgraceful, he told himself. Joelle Marot behaved toward him

125

as if he were a gigolo she was paying! She'd snatched his trousers open and grabbed what she wanted the very second her daughter was out of sight. He was no hired gigolo – he was Pierre-Raymond Becquet, the greatest lover of women in Paris.

He knew what he ought to have done to humble Joelle's absurd disdain and make her understand her position in relation to the man they nicknamed Monsieur Ten-times. When she ripped open his trousers he ought to have pushed her down on her knees in front of him and taken advantage of her, not let her choose the tune.

Joelle's opinion of herself was so ludicrously inflated that she thought he'd been trying to look up her skirt while she sat on the fan-backed settee. He was photographing Monique – that was the reason he was so stiff and strong when she grabbed him. She valued herself too highly, Joelle. It was the sight of Monique's big bouncing breasts that aroused him – and of course his fantasies on what he would do to them if ever he had an opportunity! Ah, if only!

That was the moment he ought to have taught Joelle a lesson – he saw it now in his mind's eye. Monique sent out of the studio by her mother and the sight of the charming up-and-down jilt of her lean round bottom as she walked across the studio.

Pierre-Raymond knew that if ever the possibility came his way to watch Monique strolling naked across a room – to observe the bare cheeks of her bottom sway to her steps – that would be one of the high points of his life. It had been in his mind at the time, but Joelle flicked his trousers open and her fingers were inside groping for his stiff part.

He ought to have forced Joelle down to her knees at that very moment, his hands locked behind her head to hold her face close to him. *Grandjean* sticking out of his trousers and jerking, the pink-purple head touching Joelle's scarlet-painted mouth.

'Open your mouth for me,' he'd have said. If only he dared.

'*Ah non, jamais*!' she'd gasp.

Instantly he'd have slipped *Grandjean* between her parted lips and over her wet tongue. With her mouth full of hot hard flesh she wouldn't be able to resist him, not Joelle. Her anger would vanish at once and he'd feel the lick of her tongue on the warm and sensitive plum in her mouth.

It would have been very quick, because he was so aroused from staring at Monique's heavy young breasts. In seconds he'd spurt into Joelle's sucking mouth, staring down wide-eyed to see his thick outpouring trickle from the corners of her mouth and down her chin.

Except that it wasn't Joelle he'd really wanted then – it was her seventeen-year-old daughter. And standing naked in his bathroom at the washbasin, staring goggle-eyed in the mirror at his stiff and jerking part as he washed it, he could very easily envisage that scene too.

Beautiful young Monique on the green chaise longue that stood in his reception room for the easier entertainment of women. It had seen much service since he installed it, and would see much more – unless it went creaky with constant use and needed to be replaced.

Monique had taken off her white silk blouse to let him admire her full round breasts – in his vivid imagination. She took her bra off too when he asked her. He was Pierre-Raymond Becquet, famous over all of Paris for his tender skills with women – and naturally she'd been willing to please him, darling Monique. In his imagination.

Her hands were cupped under those magnificent fleshy mounds – she was looking at him with a half-smile on her face, as if she was asking for his approval.

'They are superb,' he sighed, 'superb, Monique *chérie*.'

She was offering him her breasts. He had his trousers open at once to permit his hard-swollen flesh to leap out like a sabre unsheathed. His knees were on the chaise longue to straddle her lap. He held her sumptuous breasts with hands that trembled and pressed his stiffness to the warm skin between her bounties.

'Oh but that's marvellous,' she'd have exclaimed for certain, her dark brown eyes shining and her girlish surprise swept away by natural admiration for his impressive male part.

He pressed her breasts together around his stiffness – and he thrust strongly between them. Monique stared up open-mouthed at his handsome face, then she smiled and pushed his hands away so that she could squeeze her breasts together herself to receive his long sliding movements.

To have achieved this was so arousing that Pierre-Raymond was instantly at the point of release. His hard naked part sliding between the beautiful big breasts of this delicious seventeen-year-old young lady! A dream of delight come true! He thrust into the soft fleshy pocket she was creating for him. He stared down at the shiny purple head emerging and disappearing between her big receptive breasts – then his passion spurted up the satin skin of her chest, all the way up to her throat.

That's how it should have been that afternoon in the studio – that's what he should have done to Joelle and her daughter. Not let Joelle determine events as she had, and then go away angry because he'd disappointed her expectations by doing in her hand by mishap. He should have used *her* instead – abused her for his own pleasure by making her take him in her mouth.

He had very nearly humiliated her when she came to his apartment. He had her face down over the arm of the sofa and turned up her frock over her bottom. Bare, naturally, she wore no knickers to visit Monsieur Ten-times. His hand flat on her back to keep her helpless while he stood between her legs and forced them apart.

How she'd struggled and kicked – such a delight to observe her. He'd really humiliated her, feeling between her thighs while he held her down against her will. She squealed when he parted the lips of her *belle-chose* to slide into her. Then he was in her – having her against her will and she couldn't stop him.

She wriggled and tried to kick his legs while he was sliding in and out to a nice smooth rhythm – he was gloating to himself at Joelle's discomfiture and anger. And then two seconds before his victory the damned woman spoiled it for him by flying into an orgasm!

He'd been too vigorous, he realised that later. If he got her into the same situation again, he'd know how to ensure she felt fully shamed. He'd slide in and out slowly and deliberately and then stop. And after a little while he'd start again. Never let her become really aroused, torment her and frustrate her – make her suffer and beg. But never let her reach a climax.

When he was ready, he'd suddenly slam hard into her, smacking his belly against her bare bottom till he shot his triumph into her. She wouldn't moan *ah yes* then, she'd be shrieking *no* as he laughed out loud and spurted hotly into her squirming body. And there'd be no question of treating him like a gigolo after he'd ravaged her brutally and left her frustrated and twitching with shame and rage.

He should have done that at the studio – fling her face down and humiliate her. And then, elated by success and ready for anything, he'd leave her flopped over the chair with her bottom bare, sobbing and broken in spirit while he dragged Monique into the darkroom!

He'd rip Monique's blouse open to make use of her magnificent breasts to relieve his bursting desire . . . have her gasping down on her knees with blouse and bra torn open and the evidence of his fulfilled desire trickling wetly down her bare skin to her bellybutton . . . her brown velvet eyes gazing up at him troubled and uncomprehending at what had been done to her.

Used and abused like her mother to satisfy his injured pride at being treated like a gigolo. Yes, that's what he should have done and didn't. The regret everyone felt afterwards for things left undone and for chances missed . . . but that was life.

With an effort Pierre-Raymond turned away from the mirror and went back into his bedroom, stiff part nodding in front of him. A clean shirt and underwear and casual trousers and he returned to the sitting room where Liliane was waiting. It had taken longer than the two minutes he promised.

He sat down beside her and sipped from his own glass of wine.

'So Roland suspects that you and I . . .?'

He let the words trail away and completed his meaning with a casual flick of the wrist.

'But you have denied everything, of course, *chérie*?'

'I had to think of a reason why you came to see me and stayed for two hours,' she said.

At least she had managed to reduce eighteen hours to two, he thought. That was resourceful – he had always acknowledged and respected her intelligence when she worked for him.

'What reason did you give him?' he asked.

'There was only one thing I could think of on the spur of the moment – I said you came to ask me to work for you again.'

'Ah,' Pierre-Raymond was suddenly very thoughtful, 'I see. To come back to work for me. What did he say to that? And why did he come to my studio?'

'He wants to see for himself if it is a suitable place for me to work in. And to see if you are a proper person for me to be with for several hours each day. Roland is a man of determined views – he is very old-fashioned about some matters. He can be extremely difficult.'

'Aggressive, you mean?'

'At times, yes,' she said, with a wry little smile. 'What are we going to do, Pierre-Raymond?'

Her hand lay palm-down on his thigh, he could feel its warmth through the material of the blue trousers he had put on. If she asked him why he'd changed his clothes as soon as he arrived at his apartment, he'd hardly know what to say. Not the truth – it was too ridiculous, and impossibly humiliating.

She didn't ask. Her fingers danced lightly over the big bulge and her other hand was on the nape of his neck to hold his face against hers.

'What are you going to do?' she asked. 'I rely on you to get me out of the impossible situation you've put me in. I took pity on you because your heart was broken by a faithless woman – and look at the difficulties that has created for me.'

'Liliane,' he sighed, 'trust me – I will find a way.'

But not at the moment, it went without saying. His trembling fingers opened her silk blouse. He opened the waistband of her skirt – in five seconds he stripped her to her bra and knickers there on his grey suede sofa. But he left her new stockings on.

'No,' she murmured, as if resisting him, 'this is exactly how the problem started in the first place, Pierre-Raymond, you and me sitting together on a sofa. We must be practical now.'

She leaned back and Pierre-Raymond sighed as he looked at her long slender body in bra and little white knickers – her dimple of a round bellybutton peeping over the waistband.

'Yes, we must be practical, *chérie*,' he said as he bent down to kiss her belly and then lick it.

'What are you doing to me?' she moaned, her hands behind her back to unclasp her brassiere.

'*Je t'adore*,' he said, as if that explained everything.

From her belly he looked up to her bare little breasts, then to her face, and he saw a smile on her lips.

'You were licking me,' she said, 'you put your tongue into my bellybutton – is that what you mean by being practical?'

'Perhaps not,' he admitted with a tiny shrug, 'but you are so delicious, Liliane – I want to kiss you all over, starting with the tips of your elegant breasts.'

'Swear to me you will find some way out the mess we are in and you may kiss me anywhere you choose,' she said graciously.

'But of course,' he promised.

He showered little kisses on her bare breasts, his mouth and tongue moving lightly and quickly to cover her smooth flesh and her upstanding buds. Her brown eyes closed and her mouth opened a little. Her hands rested on his shoulders.

'I truly adore you, Liliane,' he murmured between kisses, 'you understand me – no one else does, no one in the entire world.'

'Yes, you adore me,' she said, eyes still closed and a little smile on her face. 'I know that, *chéri*. And I adore you – it is why I allow you do anything you desire to me.'

He sat up on the sofa and slid her knickers down her legs and threw them across the sitting room. He clasped his warm hand on the brunette curls between her long thighs. She moved her knees apart to let him touch her just as he wished – the prospect of pleasure to come aroused her but she did not lose sight of her plans for her own future, not for a second.

She sighed when Pierre-Raymond slid two fingers into her. In another moment she was straddling him as he sat – her nakedness pressed against his clothed body. Her eager fingers ripped open his trousers and seized his stiff flesh, tugging it toward her. He cradled her pretty little breasts in his hands, rubbing his thumbs gently over their firm tips.

'Do I have your solemn promise?' she gasped. 'I want to know for certain you will settle those difficulties with Roland – or there's no telling what he'll do to me!'

'I swear to you!' Pierre-Raymond babbled.

He was in so advanced a condition of sexual frenzy he'd agree to anything she asked, promise anything she wanted, anything in the world, to get his bounding part into her. Liliane knew that and she was relying on it, impatient though she was to feel him pushing up inside her.

She held *Grandjean* tightly while she impaled herself. She was on her knees across his lap. He stared with shining eyes at the upright strip of hair between her legs, at the soft fleshy lips forced open by the insertion of his hard length.

'Ah Liliane, you are exquisite,' he murmured.

At the instant his hard part slid up into her, she started to sigh loudly and jerk her belly backward and forward in a rhythm that was insistent – demanding. Her *joujou* was deliciously warm and slippery, so much so that it seemed to him she must already be in the throes of orgasm.

He dragged her closer to him with hands gripping the cheeks of her bottom. She was bouncing on him like a jockey on a horse – he stabbed upwards into her to respond to her excitement. His tongue was in her mouth. He felt her sucking at it strongly and the sensation aroused him even more furiously.

His fingers were sinking into the soft flesh of her bottom – she'd have red marks when she went home to Roland and if he saw marks on her body he'd know for certain she'd been with another man. But neither Pierre-Raymond nor Liliane were worrying about such considerations just then, they were dizzy with sensation.

'Ah yes!' he cried out – his belly straining upward to force his hardness deeper into her.

'Yes!' she echoed back, rising and falling on him faster and faster.

'*Je t'aime*, Lili!' he wailed when his desire spurted up into her belly.

'Ah yes, yes!' she shrieked as she squirmed on him in sudden racking ecstasy. Her plan was working out very well.

Claudia Returns

After dinner Pierre-Raymond took a stroll down the Boulevard du Montparnasse and found a vacant table outside the brasserie Le Dôme. There he sat with a small cup of black coffee and a small glass of cognac, watching people go past. It was a fine evening, but not very warm – he sat outside because the chatter of people in the restaurant made it difficult to think.

What was occupying his thoughts and giving him cause for deep despondency was Liliane and what to do about her. Her boyfriend Roland Leduc was suspicious, he'd proved that beyond doubt when he had turned up at the studio and threatened Valerie. She hadn't said so but Pierre-Raymond assumed he had threatened her. It was too terrifying to contemplate what the madman would have done if Pierre-Raymond had been there.

Could Liliane's version of events be believed? As devoted to her as he was, Pierre-Raymond knew better than to trust women's assurances when matters of the heart were concerned. According to her she had told Leduc that she'd been offered her old job back. And according to her, Leduc wanted to investigate if the studio was a suitable place for her.

Perhaps, perhaps not, who could possibly say? But one thing was certain – Pierre-Raymond had given Liliane his word that he would get her out of the impossible situation she was in. Which again according to her was entirely his doing. As if she hadn't opened her legs willingly for him on that terrible leopardskin settee!

Nevertheless, he'd undeniably promised to resolve the problem for her. And one second later she had demonstrated her gratitude by allowing him to strip her naked on his sofa and lick her belly and her pointed little breasts.

He adored Liliane, of course. He'd adored her from the first day she started to work for him. Which didn't mean he wanted her to be with him twenty-four hours a day and seven days a week. It would be convenient if he could give her the job back. She could find a small apartment . . . in the daytime he'd love her whenever time and business allowed . . . his evenings would be his own.

But he didn't want to sack Valerie, there was the problem. He adored her too. Feeling her big soft breasts and putting a hand up her skirt, perching her on the desk edge to feel between her thighs – his working days were satisfactorily organised. And if it became necessary to choose between her and Liliane, it would be an impossible decision.

If women were rational, of course, he could have both of them working at the studio and play with them by turns. But optimist though he was, he recognised that was out of the question. What a great pity, he said to himself – he had a great affection for both women.

A girl on her own was walking along the Boulevard, toward the corner where the café stood – she glanced at the people sitting at each table as she passed it. Pierre-Raymond was staring into his empty glass, sunk too deep in thought, until she stopped at his table and spoke to him.

He looked up, recognising the voice – it was Claudia Deneuve, the woman who had broken his heart by leaving him when he was desperately in love with her. He smiled bitterly and stood up and said that he was pleased to see her. Any man would be – Claudia was very attractive. She had blonde hair, large dark blue eyes, a nicely shaped body on long legs, pretty breasts, a pouting mouth – the list could continue. In short, she was a catalogue of desirable attributes.

And she was eighteen years old. To be exact, eighteen years and two months.

Pierre-Raymond loved all women, that was understood. He would kiss their breasts and part their legs with the same enthusiasm whether they were twenty or forty. He wasn't attracted to older women particularly but his profession made it necessary for him to put his hand up their skirts.

But Claudia – this was a different tale and had nothing to do with his profession. She was unspoiled and beautiful – her face was angelic, her body was a delight. Pierre-Raymond's heart was bounding in his chest as he looked at her across the table – he remembered how madly he had loved her and decided he still did.

He guessed she'd been looking for him – though she didn't say so. But why else was she checking the Boulevard du Montparnasse cafés where she knew he often went in the evenings? Not for a reconciliation it seemed, she hadn't thrown her arms about his neck and kissed him.

He waved to attract the waiter's attention and ordered cognac for Claudia and more for himself. They talked like old friends, but warily, the conversation never approached anything of true emotional importance. During the chatter Pierre-Raymond watched her closely, the exquisite smile she had, the way her long fair hair floated when she tossed her head. He adored her, he wanted to tell her so but thought it better to wait until he found out what she was after.

The elegant way she crossed her legs – the delicious swell of her breasts under her saffron-yellow frock – a million memories went through Pierre-Raymond's mind as he looked at her fondly. *Grandjean* was long and hard – dare he allow himself to hope?

By ten o'clock it was too chilly to sit outdoors, even though Claudia had a charming little jacket over her dress. And to his great surprise she suggested they should go to his apartment – it was a pity to part so soon, she said.

Pierre-Raymond could hardly believe his luck. He flung money on the table to pay for the drinks, leaving far too much in his eagerness to get Claudia into his apartment before she changed her mind. And within ten minutes there they were, sitting side by side on his big sofa, each with a glass of excellent cognac.

She took off her little jacket. They chattered away and Pierre-Raymond eyed her pretty breasts under the yellow silk – they were high-set and round, he knew very well, with dark red buds. He looked down the curve of her belly to where her thighs joined inside the dress and in his mind's eye he saw her fleece of blondish curls. And the tender peach they covered.

Claudia was smiling as she saw the recognisable emotions flit across his face.

'I know what's in your mind,' she said amiably, 'but you know very well that my answer is no.'

'Why?' he asked. 'And how do I know that?'

He was encouraged that she had raised the subject. If a woman says *no* she often means *perhaps*. This is a well-known aspect of the mystery of feminine logic. And everyone understands that a *perhaps* may become *yes* with a little persuasion.

Since arriving at the apartment Pierre-Raymond had controlled his normal instincts to touch – to caress Claudia's breasts as an adjunct to conversation. That was his way, and she must have been surprised he hadn't tried to touch her. Until now – he put his hand lightly on her silk-stockinged knee.

'Pierre-Raymond, let us be sincere with each other,' was her response, while she pressed her knees decisively together.

'Of course,' he agreed, wondering what she meant.

'For reasons I am not going to explain,' she said with a grin that made his heart lurch, 'I have nowhere to sleep tonight and not enough money for a hotel room.'

'Ah!' he said thoughtfully, feeling the stir in his trousers in anticipation of her next request.

'I'd appreciate it very much if you would let me stay here tonight. I'd be forever grateful,' she said, 'and perhaps tomorrow night as well, though probably not. As a dear friend I'm sure you'll let me stay. On the understanding that we're friends, only that – not in the same bed.'

'I understand all too well,' he said sadly, 'there's another man – you've quarrelled and you want to teach him a lesson. You storm out and leave him for a night – and he suffers because he thinks you're with someone else. And you have come here because you believe I am the idiot who will make this possible.'

'You are my dear friend,' said Claudia, dazzling him with her smile, 'that's why I am here, Pierre-Raymond. Friends help each other. I won't be in the way – I'll sleep here on the sofa with a blanket.'

'Who is this man you left me for?' he demanded.

'There is no other man.'

He didn't believe her. But he followed up his advantage.

'If there is no one else, then why not share my bed, *chérie*? You know I adore you, I have been desolate since you left me.'

'No,' she said firmly, 'if I stay, then you sleep in the bed, I sleep on the sofa. Is it agreed?'

'You might as well have the bed,' he said morosely, 'I shan't be able to sleep a wink all night for thinking of you – so near and so unattainable. This is torment, Claudia, it is cruelty to someone who adores you, it is not the act of a friend.'

'What a fuss you make,' she said, 'all the women who call you Monsieur Ten-times would be astounded to see you agitated like this – your reputation would be ruined.'

'Don't laugh at me, Claudia – I truly adore you. Come back to me, I implore you.'

'You think you adore me,' she said with a pout, 'all it means is you want to take my clothes off and get on top of me. But we have decided that's not going to happen.

'Have we decided?' he asked in surprise.

'We agreed,' she said, 'because we are such good friends.'

'You said that friends help each other,' he reminded her.

She looked at him thoughtfully. At eighteen Claudia was wise in the ways of men. Particularly the ways of Pierre-Raymond. So without another word she opened his trousers and hitched up his shirt to bare his belly.

He was not in his usual state of hardness. He had been while they sat talking at the Dôme and all the way to his apartment – and massively so when they chatted casually on the big sofa and he had stared at her with hot eyes and recalled the beauties of her body. But the conversation since then had depressed him and disheartened *Grandjean* – who had lapsed into sulky limpness.

'Well!' Claudia exclaimed, eyebrows arching up her forehead. 'I've never seen you so small and soft before, Pierre-Raymond.'

'Come into the bedroom,' he murmured ardently, 'I want to see you naked and lying on your back, *chérie*.'

'Don't be absurd,' she said calmly.

In her clasping hand his cherished part grew stiff and thick. With a graceful little move of her wrist she aroused him fully, her face close to his, her dark blue eyes gazing into his. Her lips brushed across his mouth lightly and he tried to slide his hand up her skirt. She pushed it away.

'Sit still, Pierre-Raymond,' she breathed, 'because I am your dear friend I want to make sure you'll sleep quietly tonight.'

The thought that entered his mind was that she was paying the rent. He sighed and gave himself up completely to the rhythm of her manipulating hand. A night's rent would turn out to be more than Claudia imagined.

The truth was he'd never yet known a woman who'd handled that tireless part of his and refused afterward to part her legs for him. He was certain in his mind that he'd have Claudia stripped naked and on her back before the night was out.

'Claudia, Claudia,' he sighed, '*je t'adore, chérie*!'

He had been forbidden to touch her, but in his mind's eye he was able to see and enjoy the little blondish curls between her legs. And those delicious full soft lips he had kissed so often – into whose warm wet embrace he had slid *Grandjean* hundreds of times. And gushed his hot desire into her girlish belly . . .

'You are throbbing in my hand,' she said with a giggle.

'Claudia!' he gasped. '*Chérie*!' and he felt his belly quake in the final moments before sensation swamped his mind.

'Yes, Pierre-Raymond,' she said calmly, 'yes, *chéri*.'

His eyes widened to the familiar throb in his groin. Claudia stared curiously into his very soul as he spurted on his belly to the beat of her hand.

'There,' she said when he was done, 'that will quieten you.'

Later on, toward midnight, after another glass of cognac, she decided she was tired and wished to go to bed. There followed a lengthy discussion as to who should have the bed and who the sofa, since she refused to share with him. Eventually she let herself be persuaded to take the bed – though she'd most likely decided on that before the discussion began.

That settled – the broad comfortable bed for her and a blanket on the lonely sofa for him – they went into the bedroom, both of them – Pierre-Raymond explaining he had to collect his pyjamas. Then she agreed there could be no harm if he undressed and put his pyjamas on in the bedroom, as was his usual way. She sat on the side of the bed with her legs pressed together and watched him without comment as he stripped.

'Claudia,' he said, knowing how good he looked standing there in his plum-red silk pyjamas, 'we are such close friends I can speak with total confidence when I give you my word that if you will permit me to watch you undress I will sit quietly here on this chair and make no attempt to touch you.'

'No,' she said, 'go to your sofa, Pierre-Raymond.'

'Do not be cruel,' he pleaded, 'it can't hurt you in any way, but it will make me happy.'

'You're being stupid,' she said, knees still firmly together.

'Love makes all of us stupid,' he said, 'humour me.'

'If I must,' she sighed, 'but give me your solemn word

you'll stay where you are and not come any nearer.'

'I swear it,' he said fervently.

Claudia stood up from the bed to unfasten her yellow dress at the back. Pierre-Raymond watched breathless as she pulled it up over her head and emerged in her pretty white bra and knickers. His best-loved part was standing stiff and thick in his pyjamas and he crossed his legs to disguise it – it would be too tragic if darling Claudia took fright at this stage.

She sat down on the side of the bed again to remove her high-heeled black shoes and her stockings. And then to his desperate disappointment she threw back the covers and swung her legs up onto the bed.

'But . . .' Pierre-Raymond said in amazement, 'surely you do not intend to sleep in your underwear!'

'I have only the clothes you see,' she said, her grin showing she knew he felt cheated, 'there is no choice.'

There was a faintly teasing note in her voice – his extensive experience of women made him recognise such nuances instantly. Claudia's *no* had softened into a *perhaps* – if he was clever now he could turn her *perhaps* into a *yes*.

She was lying on her side grinning at him. She had not pulled the covers over herself – it was almost as if she wanted him to see the delights he had lost forever. He glanced with affection at her long shapely naked legs – and told himself he'd be lying between them soon.

'You must remember that time when we were even closer friends than we are now,' he said, with his charming smile. 'You always slept naked with me – why not sleep naked tonight? There is no reason for shyness between you and me.'

'You'll be offering to take my knickers off in a minute,' she said. 'Remember your promise and keep your distance.'

'Of course,' he said smoothly, 'would you like me to help you off with your pretty underwear, Claudia?'

'You don't seem to understand,' she said, flicking the covers over herself, 'I let you look because we are close friends, but you are forbidden to touch.'

She put her arms into the bed and from her wriggling about he guessed she was removing her little white bra. Her hand emerged from under the sheet with it. Pierre-Raymond realised that her delicious breasts were bare – he sighed and squeezed his thighs tight together to control his bounding part. Claudia's hand was back inside the bed, she reached down – Pierre-Raymond's heart missed a beat at the realisation that she was about to take her knickers off!

'Wait,' he said quickly, 'I have an idea, Claudia, may I tell you what it is before you undress any further?'

'I don't really care what it is,' she said, 'but I'll listen, as long as you don't suggest getting into bed with me.'

'The difficulty we have is this,' he said, keeping his voice tranquil, 'because you are so very beautiful and I adore you so much, what I want most is to see you naked. Then I shall always have that memory of you when you leave. But because you are in love with someone else, you do not wish me to touch you. That I understand completely, just as I hope you understand why I want to have one last glimpse of your beautiful body.'

'It seems to me that the difficulty, as you call it, is yours and not mine,' said Claudia, her dark blue eyes mocking him, 'I will not let you touch me and that's the end of it.'

'I accept that without reservation,' he answered, 'that's why I have this simple little suggestion to make to you.'

'What then?'

'I will clasp my hands together behind my back,' he

explained to her, 'I swear I won't touch you. My hands will remain behind me, locked together, while I take off your knickers and look at your beautiful body for two minutes – no longer than that.'

'With your hands behind your back?' she asked, dark eyebrows rising. 'How do you propose to get my knickers down – with your toes?'

'With my teeth,' he said serenely.

She burst out laughing.

'If I agree,' she said at last, 'will you then leave me alone to sleep?'

'Yes,' he said, sounding very sincere.

'You promise?'

'You have my word of honour.'

She was laughing again as he left his chair and stood at the bedside, his hands clasped behind his back. His male part stuck out of his red pyjama trousers, nodding up and down – he could think of no way to conceal it. Claudia seemed not to see it, at least she ignored it. She threw back the sheet and turned on to her back to wait for his bizarre attentions.

Pierre-Raymond stared down at her, his face flushed pink with emotion to see that beautiful young body again. Her yellow hair was loose about her head on the pillow, her pear-shaped breasts stood bare and firm. And her thighs were definitely together.

'Teeth!' she exclaimed, she was laughing again as if it were the funniest thing she'd ever heard.

Pierre-Raymond, hands behind his back, got down on his knees beside the bed and leaned across to grip the waist of her white little knickers with his teeth. Claudia was still laughing when he pulled the front down a few centimetres.

Her belly was a girlish delight, the skin smooth as satin. He tugged the knickers lower, until he saw the top of the blondish curls. For one brief instant he let the tip of his tongue touch the skin between her belly button and her curls.

'Oh,' she said, and she wasn't laughing now, 'keep your hands behind your back, Pierre-Raymond – you promised.'

'I never break a promise,' he assured her, 'you may rely upon that. Raise yourself a little, if you will be so kind.'

He gripped the waistband between his teeth again and she lifted her bottom off the bed. He pulled her knickers over her hips to her closed thighs. From a distance of ten centimetres he stared adoringly at her little patch of soft blondish curls and at the pretty peach they adorned.

In the time when they were lovers, it always pleased him that the pale pink inner lips of Claudia's *joujou* protruded between her permanently parted outer lips. It was as if she was pouting between her thighs, just as she pouted with her pretty mouth.

He got on the bed and knelt beside her to ease the knickers down her long legs with his teeth. She raised her heels off the bed to help him get them off – and when her legs stretched out flat again, her feet were a little apart. Only a little, but it was enough. Pierre-Raymond dropped the knickers and pressed a kiss on her soft pouting *joujou*.

'Ah no!' said Claudia. 'No touching. Look but don't touch.' Her hand lay on his head, ready to push him away if it became necessary. He licked the soft skin of her belly with the tip of his tongue, doing it delicately.

'I should have known better than to trust you,' she murmured.

Her hand reached down to grasp the throbbing monster sticking out of his pyjamas. Her fingers played up and down it

146

swiftly. He gasped and caressed the pouting lips between her thighs with his tongue. But he did not try to press inside – if he went too far too fast she might easily take fright and make him stop.

'I knew it would come to this,' she said as her hand moved up and down unconcerned, 'you can forget about Monsieur Ten-times, tonight you're only Monsieur Two-times. And that by hand.'

It didn't take long at all – he was too aroused from removing her little white knickers with his teeth and the close sight of her delightful body and the sweet scent of her warm flesh . . .

'Oh Claudia!' he gasped as her fingers worked and his desire gushed out briefly over her left thigh.

When it was over he lay down beside her on the bed. His hands were no longer clasped together behind his back – it had become uncomfortable – but his arms were by his sides and he took care not to touch her.

'Before I leave you to sleep,' he said conversationally, 'let me ask you just one question – you needn't answer if you don't want to. Between close friends there is no reason for secrecy – only between lovers.'

'What is the question, Pierre-Raymond?'

'A little while ago you assured me there was no one else. But I am forbidden to kiss you or touch you – though until ten days ago we were lovers, you and I.'

There was no need to state his question, Claudia knew what he wanted to ask. She sat up in bed, arms clasped round her drawn-up knees, her long slender naked body a sight to make any man's heart race.

'I didn't say there was no one else,' she said, 'I said there is no other man. And that is the truth.'

'No other man – another woman?' he exclaimed. 'Unthinkable – unbelievable! But who?'

Claudia shrugged her pretty shoulders and said nothing.

'This is impossible,' he said, 'only ten days ago you were as eager to make love with me as I with you – I refuse to believe you've changed so completely.'

'I understand more now than I did then,' she told him calmly, 'being so young I didn't realise how men exploit women in their so-called love making.'

'Ah, I see it all,' Pierre-Raymond muttered, 'you have fallen into the hands of an older woman – someone who is discontented and unfulfilled and who envies your young body. Surely you must see that *she* is exploiting you?'

'She is about the same age as you,' Claudia said.

'That's different,' he said, 'I'm a man.'

'You're the one who exploited my body for your pleasure,' she countered. 'It is you who wishes to brutalise me with your long thick *thing* and crush me under your weight while you ravage me. Be truthful – you never truly loved me as a person. Not love as I have come to understand it. Your interest is in reaching your little spasm as often as possible.'

'This is not true,' he said, thumping the bed with a clenched fist, 'your heart has been poisoned against me by whoever it is you allow to possess your mind and body.'

'Believe what you will,' she said unconcerned, 'now I know the pleasures of being loved by a charming woman I refuse to permit my body to be brutalised by you or any other man.'

'We will not quarrel, not close friends like us,' he declared at once, changing his line of approach to the problem. 'I adore you and I wish you well, Claudia, whatever you choose to do. As a gesture of trust, to put my mind at rest, why not tell me who your new lover is? Is it someone I know?'

'I am in love with Janine Bonnard,' she said boldly, 'and she is in love with me.'

'Ah,' Pierre-Raymond murmured, as if he understood everything now, 'you met her with me when I took you to the theatre where she was playing.'

Mademoiselle Bonnard was one of the actresses who came to him for publicity pictures. She was a tall dark-haired woman in her early thirties, attractive and vivacious. She was not perhaps in the first rank of the acting profession, but nevertheless she was always on the stage in some part of Paris.

The first time she was at Pierre-Raymond's studio she flirted with him during the photographing and took a glass of champagne with him afterward. She sat on his Indonesian wicker settee and he gave her his charming smile and put a hand on her knee – his casual overture to new female clients.

Mademoiselle Bonnard smiled back at him – but with total lack of interest. She took his wrist and moved his hand off her knee and shook her head. He concluded she had not come for the usual reason, to be solaced – her interests were elsewhere. From then on he discontinued all advances, though she came to him twice a year for new photographs.

'You see how impossible it is for you to even think of making love to me,' said Claudia.

'Oh, I understand completely,' he assured her, and he propped himself up on an elbow to gaze at her face as they talked, 'you need have no anxiety now you have confided in me – I shall make no attempt to persuade you to anything against your will.'

'I am pleased I can trust you,' she said, 'it is a proof that we truly are friends.'

149

It was maddeningly difficult for Pierre-Raymond to refrain from touching Claudia's beautiful naked body lying so close to him. He gazed sadly at her upstanding breasts and at her smooth belly and at her long shapely thighs. They were spread a little apart now – was that a promising sign? he asked himself. And at the patch of blondish curls between those slender young thighs. His fingers curled with the effort of stopping himself reaching out to touch her.

'We are true friends,' he agreed, his male part standing hard and ready again inside his plum-red pyjamas.

Fortunately Claudia couldn't see the condition he was in. She was lying on her back with her head turned on the pillow so she could look into his eyes.

'How did it happen between you and Janine Bonnard?' he asked lightly. 'I mean, how did she convey that she wanted to be your lover? Did she say so outright, did she simply kiss you?'

'I knew she was interested in me,' Claudia told him, 'and she phoned me after you introduced us. She asked me to meet her – I liked her and so I agreed.'

'You said nothing of this to me at the time.'

'There was no reason to,' she said. 'We met at the Café de la Paix one afternoon and talked for an hour. Janine is a charming and fascinating woman. We walked up to the Boulevard Haussmann to the Printemps department store to look at the summer styles. Janine saw a dress she liked – very chic, stripes in black and white – and decided to try it on.'

Pierre-Raymond was listening intently, his stiff part jumping to a slow rhythm against the silk of his pyjama trousers.

'She asked me to go into the changing room with her,' Claudia went on, 'to give my opinion on the dress. She took off the one she was wearing and had only her knickers and bra and stockings – she took her bra off and looked at herself in the long mirror on the wall. I'm not a fool, Pierre-Raymond, I guessed what she felt about me. She asked if I thought her breasts were starting to droop.'

'And are they?' Pierre-Raymond asked.

'Hardly at all. She put her arms round me and kissed me – and pressed me back against the wall with her body. I knew what she would do before she did it – she put her hand up my skirt while she was kissing me full on the mouth. It troubled me – I didn't want her to touch me because I still adored you, Pierre-Raymond, and nobody else. I tried to explain, but I couldn't speak while her mouth was crushing mine.'

'And in another instant her hand was in your knickers and you forgot that you adored me?' Pierre-Raymond suggested.

'It is impossible to explain, I shouldn't have tried – you'll never understand – but while Janine was kissing me and stroking me I realised slowly that I didn't want her to stop after all – I knew in a second that I was in love with her.'

'I am honoured that you have confided in me,' Pierre-Raymond said, 'it is another proof of our sincere friendship.'

'You aren't angry with me or jealous?' she asked.

'Not at all,' he assured her, 'I am fascinated by what you've told me about your new lover. It seems to me that in your first encounter she behaved exactly as I would myself – the long kiss and a hand stroking your thighs.'

'No, it was totally different!' Claudia insisted. While she was caressing me I knew there was no question of brutalising my body by pushing a long thick *thing* into me.'

'Brutalising your body,' Pierre-Raymond repeated thoughtfully as he stared into her dark blue eyes, 'you have used the phrase several times. It is her phrase, I think, and she has impressed it on your mind.'

'It is true, nonetheless,' she said.

'And since Janine acted exactly as I would that first time, I think it only reasonable for me to act now as she would.'

He leaned over Claudia and kissed the buds of her pear-shaped breasts lightly, his tongue lingering for only a second.

'What are you doing?' she demanded. 'You gave me your word.'

'And I shall keep it,' he said, sliding down the bed till his head was poised over her smooth girlish belly. For no more than a heartbeat she felt the tip of his tongue in her bellybutton and then he was kissing the protruding pink lips of her *joujou*.

'No, no,' she said, 'out of the question.'

He heard her protest and paid her no attention. For a man who had been her lover not long ago – and who had done a million exciting things to her – it was not difficult to arouse her. His tongue slipped over the plump lips between her legs, and slowly those long legs parted, until he could lick her exposed bud.

'No,' she said again, 'I don't love you, Pierre-Raymond – you mustn't do this to me!'

His hands were flat on her thighs, pressing them gently apart to let him change his position and lie between them. He aroused her slowly and deliberately with his agile tongue, no haste and no dominance – the opposite, in fact. He was her slave and his only desire was to serve her and please her . . .

After a while her legs spread apart as wide as they would go, he felt them trembling and the little spasms in her belly. Soon she would be in orgasm – she would moan and writhe and arch her back off the bed as his tongue drove her wild.

He raised his head from between her splayed thighs to look up the length of her beautiful body.

'Is this how she makes love to you?' he asked softly.

'Don't,' she gasped, 'I love her – you must stop this.'

'*Je t'adore*, Claudia,' he answered, and applied his tongue to her slippery bud again, hearing her little moans begin.

His cherished part was hard and frantic between his belly and the bed. He wondered if a man could reach a climax and gush his desire into his pyjamas without being touched. *Be patient, your turn will come soon*, he assured his throbbing length of flesh. *Before the night is over you shall plunge as deep as you please into Claudia's darling little slit, I swear it!*

A Disillusionment For
Pierre-Raymond

Claudia lay on her back with her legs spread wide, eyes closed and her whole body shaking. Pierre-Raymond's tongue lapped over her secret little bud, his hands pressing her thighs apart, his cheek against the inside of her satin-smooth thigh.

He could feel the little spasms in her belly – soon she would be moaning in orgasm, writhing and arching her back off the bed as his agile tongue drove her frantic.

He raised his head from between her legs to look up along the length of her beautiful young body, over her palpitating belly, between her firm pear-shaped breasts – to her face, angelic of expression even on the brink of orgasm.

'Is this how Janine makes love to you?' he asked softly.

'Don't,' she gasped, 'I love her – you must stop this.'

'*Je t'adore*, Claudia,' he said, and he heard her soft moaning as he applied his tongue to her slippery bud again.

He slipped his hands under her bottom, grasping and squeezing the bare cheeks, the tip of his tongue vibrating urgently.

'*Mais non*!' she panted as her loins lifted upward toward him. 'I do not love you, Pierre-Raymond, I love someone else.'

The rise and fall of her loins was rhythmical and urgent. She was almost at the climax of her pleasure. And this was the very moment when Pierre-Raymond's tongue left her and he raised his head from between her legs.

'*Je t'adore, chérie,*' he said, 'and I cannot believe that you have fallen out of love with me.'

Claudia made a gurgling sound and her bare belly jerked up in little spasms to lift her *joujou* eagerly towards him.

Her hands were flat on the bed for support as she raised her knees and forced them out to the limit. Pierre-Raymond observed in delight how the sinews showed in her groin and how the muscles were stretched taut along the insides of her thighs.

She was so young and so lithe and so desirable . . . and unless he managed to get into her soon he would do it spontaneously in his beautiful silk pyjamas!

'*Je t'aime*, Claudia,' he murmured, fascinated by her body.

He stared into the wet pinkness of her joujou pulled open by the strain of her legs. But she wasn't offering herself to him as she used to, she was demanding release into ecstasy from the overwhelming sensations he had aroused in her. *But my turn will come*, he vowed silently to himself. He bowed his head again and pressed his tongue between the open velvet petals before him.

'Ah, yes, Pierre-Raymond, ah yes!' she wailed deliciously.

He tantalised her until her body was shaking violently in the spasms that announce the onset of orgasm – his tongue flickered like a striking cobra and she shrieked in convulsive release.

When she collapsed at last he lay full-length beside her, his hands well away from her so she couldn't claim he'd broken his promise. True, he had put his hands on her thighs and under her charming little bottom, but she had been too far gone in pleasure at the time to notice. Or to remember now.

He looked with longing at her pink-flushed face. He stared

AMOUR INTIME

at the rise and fall of her breasts to the irregular rhythm of her
breathing. He saw the little after-tremors of her belly and he
was tempted to throw himself on top of her and push up into
her wet openness whether she denied him or not. Five seconds,
maybe six – that's all it would take before he gushed into her.

He controlled his urgent need. He wanted her to want him
and to ask him to make love to her – not to force himself on
her.

She opened her eyes and smiled at him and she told him he
was mistaken if he believed he could imitate Janine. He was a
man – he hadn't the least idea of the delicacy with which
women made love to each other, she told him. But she was
smiling while she said these things – he saw a chance to pursue
the conversation along a line useful to his aim.

'Very well,' he said, 'I am a man and therefore I cannot
hope to be the equal of a woman in these matters. Can you
explain to me why? For example, I assume Janine took you to
her apartment after declaring her passion in the department
store.'

'Yes, we went to her apartment,' said Claudia with a smile
of tender reminiscence, 'she did more than declare her passion
for me in the changing room. She whirled me into instant
ecstasy so incredible I wanted to go down on my knees and
kiss her feet. I knew I adored her and she said she adored me.
After that we had to find out if we were truly in love with each
other.'

'Of course,' said Pierre-Raymond, very understanding, 'so
how did matters continue – my guess is she made love to you
exactly as I have just done.'

'You're wrong,' Claudia said firmly, 'you don't understand.'

'Because I am your dear and reliable friend, I want to try to

157

understand. Help me – tell me how it was.'

'When we reached Janine's apartment we went straight into the bedroom – we both knew that was what we wanted. We had our arms around each other's waist – she walked me to the bed so quickly it was almost like being ravished. We kissed and she pressed me down on the bed . . .'

'Ah,' Pierre-Raymond sighed, his hand on the stiffness in his pyjama trousers to stop its jerking, 'on your back on the bed.'

'Janine knelt down and took my skirt off. And my knickers, to kiss me.'

'As I have just done,' said Pierre-Raymond, satisfied that he had made his point.

'No, it was the kiss of love. It lasted only a moment or two, then we stood up and undressed completely and lay on the bed in each other's arms. We kissed and stroked each other. We laughed and cried a little in delight. No man can ever understand this. Janine's hand was between my legs, my hand was between hers, we were open and wet, both of us, though I hadn't touched her till this moment.'

'She caressed you in the changing room, but not you her?' he asked, holding his stiff part tightly to comfort it.

Claudia nodded and propped herself up on an elbow to face him – her beautiful bare breasts were so close to his chest that he was sure he would fountain his urgent desire into his pyjamas. She'd see a dark wet stain on the silk in ten more seconds.

'In the store she did it to me while she had me pinned to the wall,' Claudia explained. 'I couldn't believe how quick it was. I cried out when it happened, I couldn't stop myself – we were both afraid in case anyone heard me and came to investigate.'

'Fascinating!' Pierre-Raymond muttered. 'What you tell me is that she took you by force the first time. Then later in bed it was a slow and indolent caress of tongues and fingers?'

'The first time in bed, yes,' said Claudia, 'to show our love and devotion to each other. But later on Janine pushed me on my back and forced my legs wide apart. Her hands were all over me, so strong and demanding, and her tongue too. In three hours she took me to the peak of love more times than I thought possible. She conquered me utterly.'

'More than with me?' Pierre-Raymond asked, feeling outraged.

'Oh yes, more than with you, Monsieur Ten-times.'

He couldn't decide if she was telling the truth or if she was mocking him. And he was far from certain now whether he had the upper hand or not. The earlier belief that he would succeed in getting his throbbing hardness into her now looked doubtful.

Claudia was aware of his continuing state of arousal – and of his urgent desire to lie on her belly and penetrate her. But it was right out of the question. She reached into his pyjamas and took his stiffness from his hand into her own.

'Ah no,' he said, 'not that way again.'

'Why not?' she replied. 'It's all you'll get from me.'

With each stroke of her hand *Grandjean* grew stronger and more insistent – he protruded from the silk pyjama front and touched the smooth skin of Claudia's belly, his head rubbing there with the movement of her fingers. Pierre-Raymond was sighing in pleasure in spite of his protest against being aroused in that way once more.

His hand insinuated itself between Claudia's thighs. She was on her side facing him, propped on an elbow, and she raised her knee so he could feel her. She smiled at him while she played with him – her pear-shaped breasts touched his chest. She was so close. She was teasing him, asserting herself over his male brutality.

Or so she believed. In five seconds it would be over – he was shaking against her, on the extreme edge of sensation. And then in some way she couldn't understand, the velvet head of the hot flesh in her hand was touching the open wet lips of her *joujou*, where his fingers had been only an instant before.

'No you don't!' she said quickly.

Her hand tightened its grip to stop him pushing into her. She grinned into his face from two or three centimetres, seeing his eyes roll upward as the orgasm started. She felt the warm rush of his release on the soft lips between her legs. She gasped in horror at this male desecration of a shrine dedicated to female love alone.

Then she remembered that until she met Janine that particular shrine had been thoroughly desecrated by Pierre-Raymond day and night – and she had adored it. And had used her mouth and hands to stiffen his resolve if he went limp. But that was before she understood about love and the rapacity of men. Nevertheless, he was her close and trusted friend still.

'That's as far as you're going to get,' she said with a grin. She pulled the sheet over herself to the waist – and used the edge to wipe herself dry.

'Go to your sofa now,' she said, 'you have tired me out and I want to sleep.'

'Of course,' said Pierre-Raymond, very sympathetic – as if in complete agreement with her wishes.

Secretly he was more determined than ever to get between her legs and into her and enjoy the delights of her beautiful young body. He owed it to himself, he was Pierre-Raymond

Becquet, the most capable lover and the most desired man in Paris.

Naturally any beautiful naked girl in his bed must spread her legs for him. But with Claudia in so unusual a state of mind it was necessary to proceed slowly and with great care.

'Just one question before I leave you,' he said, 'why are you here tonight, Claudia? Is it because of a quarrel?'

She yawned and turned away from him.

'Why do you want to know?' she asked sleepily. 'It's none of your concern.'

'I am concerned for your happiness,' he said, 'a quarrel with someone you love means you are unhappy. You're here tonight for more than somewhere to sleep, you came looking for a friend to comfort you.'

'There *was* a quarrel,' she said sadly.

Her naked back was toward him, her shoulders uncovered by the sheet. Pierre-Raymond was tempted to slide forward and kiss her back, but he refrained. For the moment.

'A serious quarrel?' he asked.

'We went out to dinner. Afterwards we sat outside a café with a drink, on the Boulevard St Germain. A woman came to the table and greeted Janine and hugged her and kissed her on both cheeks and sat down with us.'

'Ah,' said he thoughtfully.

'I guessed she was an old love of Janine's – I am not a fool. It didn't upset me because I know I am the love of her life and she of mine. I expected Janine to introduce us and we'd talk a little and then this stranger from the past would go away.'

'She didn't?'

'Janine introduced us – her name is Lucienne. She didn't send her away, she ordered a drink for her. They talked – and it

161

was clear they knew each other very well. They talked of friends I didn't know I felt completely left out and humiliated.'

'Is she pretty, this Lucienne?' Pierre-Raymond asked.

'No,' Claudia said very definitely, 'she's tall and thin with dark hair cut very short and flat to the head. She smiles a lot and talks non-stop.'

'My poor Claudia,' said Pierre-Raymond, 'what a hateful scene for you – my heart goes out to you. The quarrel began after she left, I suppose.'

'This beanpole had the effrontery to suggest the three of us should go to a *café-dansant*! I'm not a complete idiot, I could see what that was leading to. Janine told her it was impossible – but she said it with regret in her voice. Even then the beanpole didn't go away. She stayed and talked till Janine paid the bill and we left her.'

'And then you quarrelled.'

'Not right away, though I was very angry. We went to Janine's apartment and she had her hand up my skirt and her tongue in my mouth as soon as the door closed. I wasn't ready for that.'

This Janine acts much like a man, Pierre-Raymond thought, *she does almost exactly what I would do myself.* He kept the thought to himself in case it annoyed Claudia.

'You walked out?' he asked.

Claudia yawned again.

'She begged me to stay,' said she with some satisfaction. 'I slammed the door hard and ran down the stairs and found a taxi. She doesn't know where I am and she'll be in a dreadful state.'

'Tomorrow you'll return and forgive her and there'll be tears and kisses,' Pierre-Raymond said casually. 'It is an old

162

drama, one that lovers continually play out.'

Claudia said nothing. She was breathing regularly and gently, her shoulder uncovered – she'd fallen asleep, forgetting he was still there on the bed beside her, not on the distant sofa. And he lay quietly behind her, thinking and wishing and hoping. The light was still on – he stared at Claudia's uncovered shoulder, at the back of her blonde head on the pillow and he thought his thoughts.

Why Claudia had formed this deep attachment to Janine Bonnard was beyond him. She was very young, perhaps that was part of the reason. Young and impressionable. And in justice it had to be confessed that she'd formed a similar deep attachment to Pierre-Raymond himself when they first met.

They were in bed less than two hours after being introduced – she was insisting that she loved him truly and eternally before he parted her legs the second time. And inside a week he was in love with her – he, Pierre-Raymond Becquet, lover of thousands, in love with a little eighteen-year-old blonde!

Claudia's deep and eternal love for him had lasted two months and eight days. Perhaps her attachment to Janine would be about the same duration – though one did not wish to sound cynical or scoffing about the emotions of so very beautiful a young woman. The question was, would she return to him when she left Janine, or would she form a similar deep attachment to someone else?

Could he take comfort from the way Liliane so obviously regretted leaving him two years ago and now wanted to come back? She hadn't said so outright, but he knew. She was hiding behind her boyfriend with this story of telling him she'd been offered her job back at the studio.

According to her that was her excuse to the boyfriend when

he demanded to know why Pierre-Raymond had been to see her. It was plausible up to a point, but it left many unanswered questions. Evidently Liliane had become tired of Roland Leduc and his ugly curtained bed – she had been willing to let Pierre-Raymond take her clothes off and play with her all evening and all night.

But this Roland was surely not stupid, he guessed the truth – that Liliane had been on her back for Pierre-Raymond. Which was why he visited the studio – to punch Pierre-Raymond's head, not for the idiotic reason Liliane invented. The unavoidable facts were that Roland was enraged and there would be trouble with him.

But it was worth it, those hours with Liliane on the leopard-skin settee and on the pompously designed bed. What a pity that she wasn't here in Pierre-Raymond's own bed tonight, then there would no necessity to play this comedy with darling Claudia. By now he would have made love to her two or three times properly, lying between her legs. They would fall asleep in each other's arms – when they woke in the morning they would do it again.

Liliane had been very passionate at his apartment after she'd come to the studio to find him. She started by saying she must be home before the boyfriend returned at seven, then she forgot about that when they were naked and in bed and she stayed until after nine.

She was devastatingly pretty, dark-brunette Liliane, with her slender and narrow-hipped body and her pointed little breasts. When she was naked Pierre-Raymond could play with her for hours and hours, kissing and stroking her, then parting her thighs to slide into her warm and slippery *joujou*. Back in the days when she worked for him, he would often long for a slack day so that he could devote himself to enjoying her for a whole afternoon.

In his apartment only yesterday, she had sat with him on the grey suede sofa and let him pull her knickers down her legs and clasp his palm between her thighs. She moved her knees apart to let him touch her and sighed when he slid two fingers into her.

Looking back now he saw that was the moment when Liliane took charge of events. She straddled his legs as he sat on the sofa, she ripped his trousers open. While he was cradling her pretty breasts she was busily impaling herself on his upstanding part. He thought he was having her, but the truth he now saw was that Liliane was having him, sliding up and down and sighing loudly.

To give him his due, he had gripped the cheeks of her bare bottom and dragged her towards him – he stabbed upwards into her belly and thrust his tongue into her mouth. He felt her sucking at it strongly and the sensation aroused him even more furiously.

'Ah yes!' he cried out, his belly straining upward to force his hardness deeper yet into her.

But he was deceiving himself. Liliane was in control, she was the one who bounced up and down on him till she made his desire gush into her. Only then did she shriek and squirm in ecstasy.

'You've given me your promise,' she said when she could talk sensibly again, 'you'll get me out of the mess you've put me in with Roland.'

When they moved into his bedroom she retained the initiative, he saw that clearly now, though it hadn't seemed so at the time. On the bed together, stark naked, his fifteen centimetres standing up hard and ready – while he was kissing her belly she sat up fast and rolled him on his back and straddled his loins again.

It was in his mind to laugh and say it was his turn to be on top. But he was enchanted by that upright little strip of dark brunette curls between her parted thighs and in another moment she slid her slippery *joujou* down his jerking shaft. Then it was too late to say he wanted to do it otherwise. Lazily he had accepted her right to call the tune – the pleasure was all that mattered.

She rode him with zeal and energy, her hands cupping her spiky little breasts 'Lili, Lili,' he sighed as a marvellous sensation in his belly informed him that his moment of crisis was soon to arrive. He jerked upwards into her slippery clinging warmth and fountained his virility into her. He heard her moaning and knew her ecstasy had begun three seconds after his own.

With the benefit of hindsight he understood that she had come looking for him that day with the intention of manipulating his emotions and sensations to make him fall in with her plans. And she'd gone a long way towards success. He had promised to extricate her from Roland's tent-shaped bed, but he wasn't sure how.

And now another woman he adored had come to wheedle him round to her wishes. Claudia. She wanted his shoulder to cry on and a bed for the night. In a way she was exploiting him too, he saw that now. As Joelle Marot also exploited him – although for different reasons. Joelle wanted him to make love to her, Claudia didn't.

This is absurd, Pierre-Raymond said to himself, *I will not be a victim! From now on I shall be less obliging to the whims of women and assert myself. I am Pierre-Raymond*

Becquet, the lover of innumerable women – their greatest pleasure is to part their legs and invite me to do what I wish.

Beside him Claudia was so still that he assumed she was fast asleep. Thinking about Liliane and how she had straddled him on this very bed had made him stiff again – his male pride pointed up at Claudia's back to indicate its wishes. Carefully he eased the sheet off her until she was completely uncovered except for her feet. He sighed and pressed his palms lightly on the round and beautiful cheeks of her bottom.

He wanted to slide down the bed and kiss those beautiful warm cheeks. And nip them gently with his teeth. Out of the question at the moment, it would wake her up and she'd tell him to go to his sofa. He must be contented with the touch of his palms and fingertips on those delicious rounded curves.

Even that caused her to stir a little and murmur incoherently. He paused and waited for her to settle back into sleep. It took a little time, her long bare legs twitched and changed position on the bed.

When she was quiet again he slid forward on his side, until the red-purple head of his hard-swollen pride touched her bottom. But lightly, in the deep crease between the cheeks. Any firmer pressure of his stiff part against Claudia's smooth warm flesh would hurl him into involuntary release, he believed, and he'd see his creamy desire jetting into that pretty crease.

Even the light touch against her body made her restless – she moved a little. He waited, not retreating and not advancing.

I am no woman's victim – I am Pierre-Raymond Becquet, he told himself as he burrowed his throbbing part slowly in between her thighs. She was lying with her knees bent a little and her left leg forward. After some gentle probing, *Grandjean*'s hot head touched the lips between Claudia's thighs. They were loose and moist after the orgasms he'd had given her with his fingers and tongue before she fell asleep.

He pushed steadily – and felt himself slip in a centimetre or two. He paused, there was no reaction from Claudia. He pushed a little further – and soon he was halfway inside her, her bottom against his bare belly.

When he was all the way in Claudia shuddered from head to toe as if waking with a start.

'No, no – that's not what I want!' she exclaimed.

'*Je t'aime,*' he murmured, his face against her hair, his hand on her waist to hold her gently as he began long slow strokes.

He was half intoxicated by the scent of her hair – it was the insanely expensive perfume he'd given her for her birthday only two months ago. He had recognised it early, in her groin, when he'd kissed her *joujou*. For a moment or two he thought bitterly of Janine Bonnard enjoying that perfume on Claudia's body.

But he was too eager now he was inside Claudia to bother with such considerations of rivalry. His solid flesh was sliding in and out of her in an easy rhythm. This was the moment he'd been waiting for since she appeared at his table outside the Dôme.

'We love each other,' he said softly, 'you know it.'

'Perhaps I love you,' she sighed, 'it is hard to say. But not as I did once. It is wrong of you to force me to be unfaithful to Janine. You know that without being told by me.'

'It cannot be wrong when I love you to distraction,' he said, 'and at heart you want me to do this, admit it!'

'This is not love,' she gasped, 'whatever you say, you cannot persuade me this is true love.'

'Your own feelings will persuade you,' he answered, 'not me.'

At that she stopped complaining, as if examining her feelings to judge if he was stating the truth. Whatever the progress of her emotions, her body was trembling against Pierre-Raymond in little spasms of delight very familiar to him.

'Open your legs wider!' he commanded her, determined to make her understand she was his again, 'give yourself to me.'

'Ah!' she gasped, 'ah, *yes* Pierre-Raymond . . .'

To his delight she drew her knees up till they almost touched her breasts, letting him push in deeper yet. He reached over to feel her breasts and hold them – he was certain now that she accepted him. Her head turned on the pillow and she tried to reach his mouth with her tongue.

Her little spasms were becoming more and more insistent. Very soon they would devastate her, he realised, his own excitement mounting out of control. Claudia was his again – he was sure of it in his heart. Another part of him was equally sure of it and slid in and out of her beautiful body with zestful enjoyment.

'Claudia,' Pierre-Raymond murmured, holding her tight to him, his face pressed into her soft blonde scented hair.

She moaned and shook, he felt the jerking of her body against him as the moment of her orgasm arrived. He thrust passionately into her slipperiness, her head jerked up and she screamed. In a blaze of ecstatic sensation he jetted his desire into her and felt her body convulsing against him.

'*Je t'aime*, Claudia,' he sighed,' I cannot live without you.'

At The Movies

Madame Marot told Pierre-Raymond that the cinema she wanted him to take her to was near the Boulevard St Germain. That meant it couldn't be far away from where he lived – although he couldn't recall ever noticing a secret cinema in that part of Paris.

It was in one of the narrow little streets that ran down from the boulevard to the Seine. A doorway between two shops – there were no posters, no name, no electric sign. Nothing to draw the attention of passers-by. Just a private rendezvous for those in the know.

The price of two tickets made Pierre-Raymond blink. But since Joelle had given him the money in advance it didn't matter. He handed over the banknotes to a woman in black with a shady look about her, and followed Joelle into the interior.

It was small and dimly lit. There were seats for sixty people at most and the screen was half the size one expected in proper cinemas. But the seats were very special, deep and comfortable, thickly padded, almost armchairs. They were coupled in twos and had no armrest between, only at the outside, to mark out one's territory so to speak.

Even with the lights on there was very little chance of being

171

recognised. It was so dark that patrons entering stumbled about and risked tripping over in the search for seats. Joelle showed herself to be well acquainted with the Cinema Drapp, that being the name she gave it. Pierre-Raymond assumed it was the name of the proprietor.

He didn't want to be there with her, he had many other things on his mind. But Joelle had phoned and said she wished to go to the cinema that evening to see a new movie that was showing. It was no use Pierre-Raymond saying he had other arrangements, she had simply insisted. And she was accustomed to getting her own way.

Joelle Marot was important to Pierre-Raymond. In his business at least. If she lost her temper with him and never came to his studio again, that in itself wouldn't be a disaster. But if she persuaded her friends to stay away, the loss of so many regular clients would have an unpleasant effect on his finances. And on his reputation.

So here he was, humouring her. Sitting in the dark with forty or so other people, the situation doubtless illegal, watching a movie he had no particular wish to see. His own tender episodes with women were so numerous and frequent and so intense that it was out of the question to think actors could acquaint him with aspects of lovemaking he hadn't experienced.

The dim lights went out completely and the performance began. According to the credits that appeared on the screen, the movie was called *The Widow*. The stars were not named and nor were the producer or director. Or the company responsible.

The action opened in a street with traffic and pedestrians – a man in a blue suit and a hat with a wide brim, sitting alone at an outside café table. The style of his hat suggested that the location might be foreign. When the man got up and walked away, Pierre-Raymond studied the surroundings carefully in an attempt to place the scene.

For anything he saw to the contrary it could be Paris, though as no street signs were shown it was impossible to be reach any certain decision. The soundtrack music was undistinguished to the point of being unrecognisable – no clues there.

The man halted outside a door and looked over his shoulder as if suspicious he was being followed. He went into the building – it was an old building with a circular staircase going up five or six stories, from the entrance hall to the top floor.

On the second floor a woman was leaning over the wrought-iron railings. Her arms were folded on it and her breasts lay on her arms. She was about twenty, dark hair cut short in a fringe and wide cheekbones, more Slav than true French.

She was wearing a long-sleeve black dress that reached to her knees and was cut square and low over her heavy breasts. Expert in these matters, Pierre-Raymond regarded with interest the way they swelled out over her folded arms – evidently they were big and loose, unconfined by a bra. About the same size as Valerie's, he judged, good fleshy double-handfuls to get hold of.

He assumed she was the widow of the movie title. She had been waiting for the man in the broad-rimmed hat, it seemed. She waved and smiled at him in welcome and leaned over the railing – her breasts very prominent under the black frock.

The scene was banal, but it had possibilities. It became more promising when she stood upright and hoisted her black dress up to her hips.

A faint sigh passed through the darkened cinema, perhaps from the men in the audience acknowledging the raising of the skirt on the screen. The Widow wore no knickers, she displayed strong bare thighs and a curly black bush where her thighs joined.

The man in the entrance hall below was standing in the centre of the floor, staring upward. As well he might. He took off his black hat and waved it at her. She moved her feet apart and put one hand over her exposed bush and caressed herself.

'Only if you dare,' she said, 'there are no illusions here.'

Pierre-Raymond's heart sank instantly. From the solemnity of tone he guessed that the movie was going to be heavily symbolic of god knew what. The eroticism would have a deep philosophical message, an existential undercurrent, an intellectual content.

That was something he regarded as totally superfluous. In his own life he found not the least necessity to look for a meaning when he played with a woman. To do it was reason enough, and no complicated explanation was required.

In the dark Joelle reached for his hand and squeezed it hard. Perhaps she found some interesting significance in the movie so far. Pierre-Raymond remembered what he was there for – he placed his hand on Joelle's thigh. For her outing to the cinema she was wearing a chic cream linen costume with a pink silk blouse under the little jacket.

On the screen the woman smiled again as the man below set his foot on the first step of the circular staircase. He must have taken the Widow's word for it that there were no illusions here and wanted a closer look at the black bush she was stroking.

'Each step that you take,' she called down, 'is a step nearer to realisation and a step nearer to nothingness. Do you dare?'

Mon Dieu, what nonsense, Pierre-Raymond thought, *drop all the farcical philosophising and climb those stairs, you idiot – do something interesting to her!*

Joelle's knees were apart. Pierre-Raymond slid his hand under her linen skirt and up the expanse of silk stocking to the bare flesh above. Like the Widow on the screen Joelle wasn't wearing knickers. She never wore knickers when she came to meet him – it amused her to believe that Monsieur Ten-times was too impatient for her body to delay himself by taking her knickers down.

But unlike the woman up on the screen, here was no thick bush of curls. Joelle sighed faintly in the dark as Pierre-Raymond's questing fingers found her neat triangle of dark brunette hair, and the thin long lips of her *joujou*.

The truth was there was a certain perversity in her character that excited Pierre-Raymond, although he disliked her. She took her pleasure where she chose – these warm soft lips his fingers were playing over had been used and abused for her delight more times than anyone could guess. And by more shafts of hard flesh than could be envisaged.

Or so Pierre-Raymond liked to believe. Whether it was true or not didn't matter – only to believe it was exciting enough. The strange and inexplicable truth was that Joelle Marot had a hold over Pierre-Raymond that was not entirely financial. After all, he was no gigolo. To be perfectly honest, it surprised him that a disdainful and upper-crust lady like Joelle would ever permit herself to be played with in public – even in the darkness of a private cinema.

Evidently she must find it exciting, the flirting with danger and running the risk of exposure and shame. And worse than that if she was recognised. Madame Marot was no widow to display her charms on a staircase, she had a rich and important husband who would take action against a woman who disgraced him and brought him into derision.

Nostalgie de la boue it was called, the wish to taste dubious pleasures – pleasures which had their existence far more in the mind than in reality. But the lure was strong – and Joelle felt it, that was never in doubt.

Up on the screen the man had reached the landing on which the Widow waited. She dropped her skirt at his approach and reached out to clutch at the fork of his thighs. He took her shoulders, turned her about and bent her forward over the bannister again. Instantly he had her black dress up to her waist to expose her bare bottom – on which the camera lingered.

'Have you ever done it on a staircase?' Joelle whispered.

'Never,' Pierre-Raymond confessed, 'once in a lift, but never on the stairs.'

'Nor I,' Joelle whispered, 'but I mean to try.'

The Widow had good strong thighs, Pierre-Raymond noticed with approval, and a solid round-cheeked bottom. The man behind her had a hand between her legs to stroke the lips hidden under the black curls. With his left hand he dropped his trousers and out sprang a commendably long and thick male part.

'Ah yes,' Joelle murmured in Pierre-Raymond's ear, 'he's well cast for the role, don't you think?'

Pierre-Raymond said nothing. He did not feel that he was out-classed by what he saw. Joelle was close to him and the perfume she was wearing was arousing him enormously. He opened the soft petals between her legs – his fingertip pressed inside.

The Widow's arms were flat along the bannister and she braced herself on spread legs. Her visitor held her hips and the blunt head of his stiff part was between her thighs, poised. He stopped at this vital moment to make an utterly meaningless remark.

'There is no uncertainty,' he said, an inane sort of thing to announce at so crucial a time. And having delivered himself of the unwanted ethical gem, he pushed quickly into her until his belly touched her bare bottom.

'You are at the brink of nothingness,' said the Widow.

Whether he believed her or not, even if he understood her, he wound his arms about her waist and held her tight while he rode fast and hard.

'*Ah Dieu!*' Joelle gasped, her hand on Pierre-Raymond's thigh, gripping so tight her fingernails were cutting into him through his trouser-leg. 'Look at that – they're really doing it – it's not just simulated!'

The Widow's head jerked up and down to the fast rhythm of the man's stabbing. Joelle was staring fixedly at the screen, mouth open and her breathing rapid. Pierre-Raymond's fingers moved inside her gracefully, not trying to keep pace with the thrusting into the mythical Widow.

'Oh yes,' Joelle sighed, 'you always understand what I want.'

Pierre-Raymond remembered the last time she'd said those very words to him. It was on the Saturday morning she had arrived at his apartment unexpected. She was lying naked on his bed and he lay between her legs, so long and so elegant, to kiss her *joujou* as a preliminary to plunging his fifteen centimetres into it.

'You always know what I want,' she'd said.

She wriggled her bottom on the bed when he kissed the insides of her open thighs.

'Your tongue, Pierre-Raymond,' she said, 'only your tongue!'

To gratify her wish he'd pulled her wide open with his thumbs and flickered the tip of his tongue over her little bud. She'd gasped and shook as he forced her up to unbelievable heights of arousal. She shrieked and gripped him by the hair, she held his head between her thighs.

He'd done it to her not because he wanted to, but because she was who she was and he was who he was. Not a gigolo, of course, but a man who relied upon her for his living and wanted to stay in her favour. And he did it to her until her back lifted right off the bed in a massive orgasm and she screeched.

This time, in the darkened cinema, it was his fingers playing inside that long pink split of hers, not his tongue. And it was in his mind to do it to her again and again and again with his clever fingers, until she cried for mercy. Then he'd put her in a taxi, wrung-out and limp, and send her home alone.

Up on the screen the man bucked and writhed as he reached the culmination of his rough ride. The Widow shook underneath him – she said something or other so pretentious that Pierre-Raymond didn't trouble himself to listen properly. Her friend slid out of her and stood back, leaving her round bottom exposed for a camera close-up. Her sturdy thighs were well parted and there was a creamy trickle down the inside of one of them.

It was more than Joelle could tolerate in her highly aroused condition. Pierre-Raymond heard her low moan and he could feel the muscles of her belly tighten and clench. Her nails sank deep in his thigh, making him wince, and she was jerking out of control in her plush seat in a long orgasm.

'Pierre-Raymond, you know so well what to do to me,' she said when she was able to speak rationally again. 'I really do adore you – but you know that.'

He didn't believe her, of course, he knew her too intimately. But it was convenient for him to pretend, as it was for her, that they were drawn together by more than sexual rapacity. '*Ah chérie*,' he murmured to please her while he started to take his hand away. She put her own hand over his to keep it in place.

'Again,' she murmured, 'I want you to do it again.'

The action of the film had moved on and the scene had changed to a deserted bar. Perhaps it was to do with the removal of the illusions, or the state of nothingness. It seemed to be late at night, chairs were turned upside down on the tables and all the lights were off except one.

The man who had ravaged the Widow over the landing balustrade was now flat on his back on the zinc-topped bar. His black felt hat had vanished, his trousers were down about his ankles, his shirt was up to his armpits, revealing how dark haired were his belly and chest.

The Widow was with him – she was naked. As Pierre-Raymond had deduced earlier, her breasts were heavy and superb, their flesh pale as milk, their buds dark red and erect. She was on the bar too, on her knees – she was sitting over her friend's face with her wet-lipped *jouet* pressed to his mouth.

'It is time to lose your final illusion,' she informed him.

'Look at that,' Joelle said breathily to Pierre-Raymond, 'I'm going to do that to you tonight.'

Pierre-Raymond pressed his middle finger up into her slippery warmth and let it flutter, as light as a butterfly wing, on her little bud. This was a trick he had perfected in years of games with women. He could hurl them into shrieking orgasm in seconds if he chose. And he could stretch out the sensation until their nerves were twisted tight and their bodies were shaking so hard that they could hardly breathe.

While he attended to Joelle in this way, he thought with some determination that the question of which of them would do what to the other later that evening was by no means settled. Joelle might think so, but she was mistaken. Tonight he refused to let her dominate him.

She had done that all too often in the past. But only because he permitted it out of good nature and friendship. Tonight he intended to reverse the situation – he hadn't wanted to be with her in the first place. He intended using Joelle's body for his own pleasure. She could like it or not, as she chose.

The simple truth was he wanted to be with Claudia, not Joelle Marot. He was in love with beautiful Claudia, he knew it and he had told her so in his bed the night she stayed with him after her quarrel with her actress lover.

Darling Claudia had agreed finally that he loved her, but she insisted she didn't love him, not since meeting Janine. Nothing he could say convinced her. He babbled and implored and argued, he held her little bare feet and kissed them. She was not moved in the least.

Worst of all was that while he was declaring eternal love to Claudia, he couldn't rid his mind of the image of Janine and Claudia together in the department store changing room. Janine kissing Claudia and putting a hand up her skirt.

He hadn't seen Claudia since that night she came to stay with him. It was a night that would live in his memory always, every word, every touch, every moment. Claudia asleep on his bed with her back to him – his throbbing part sliding between her thighs until it found what he wanted desperately to penetrate.

She didn't wake until he was all the way inside her and ready to spurt his passion at the least provocation. She asked him to stop and pull out at once. But old customs count for something. Her naked body was trembling in his arms, her bare back was hot against his chest.

Whether Claudia loved him or not, at that moment she had desired him as strongly as he desired her. She wanted to feel that hard part sliding into her, opening her soft flesh, penetrating her, bringing her to ecstasy.

She had forgotten about Janine's fingers inside her, Janine's tongue in her. What she wanted most in the world right then was what she had, Pierre-Raymond's stiff flesh in her, sliding smoothly in and out. Piercing her until his passion jetted into her and hurled her into orgasm, deep and long and overwhelming. Like the happy times when she and he were lovers.

The next morning she was out of bed while he was asleep. She was bathed and dressed and drinking black coffee in the kitchen when he got up and went looking for her, afraid she had already gone. She looked so beautiful sitting at the kitchen table with a breakfast cup in her hand that his heart thumped in his chest and he was breathless for a moment.

Her blonde hair was combed back and tied with a velvet ribbon at the nape of her neck. Her dark blue eyes stared up at him in a thoughtful way and she pouted deliciously as he bent down to kiss her cheek lightly and say *bonjour*.

Only eighteen years old, so young and desirable, he loved her to distraction. When she was ready to leave he went with her to the apartment door, reluctant to let her go. She was going back to Janine Bonnard, he knew that. He put his arms around her and kissed her, hoping it was *au revoir* and not *adieu*.

Then she was gone and two images remained in his memory – two contrasting pictures he could not lose, either of them. Claudia naked in his arms in the night, her back to him, his stiff part inside her warm wet *joujou* and his entire being – body and mind and soul – at the very instant of ecstatic release.

And the other image, the one he didn't want but couldn't lose – Claudia in the changing room with Janine Bonnard. The actress kissing Claudia's mouth, Janine's hand up her skirt and between her legs, above her stocking tops, touching the warm bare skin. Janine's hand in Claudia's little knickers. Janine's fingertips stroking Claudia's blonde-haired delight.

He was so jealously preoccupied with this disturbing image he had forgotten Joelle beside him in the dark cinema. His fingers had worked their magic without conscious direction – Joelle was rigid in her plush seat, her thighs strained apart in her linen skirt. She was sighing open-mouthed in the throes of orgasm. He finished her off and saw how she slumped against the seat back, limp and perspiring.

On the screen, the naked woman sitting over her friend's face jerked backwards and forwards to rub her *joujou* over his mouth. Evidently she was in the throes of tremendous ecstasy. Her head was thrown back and her eyes were rolled up in her head to show only the whites. She began to wail mindlessly, her breasts were shaking and jiggling to her spasms.

The Widow's orgasm seemed to last forever. The man underneath her beat his hands and drummed his heels on the zinc-topped bar and his thick length of flesh strained stiffly up in search of release that never came. His role was to suffer, that seemed to be the existential meaning of this otherwise puzzling scene. Or so Pierre-Raymond concluded.

When the woman was at last tranquil, her beautiful naked

body shiny with perspiration, her companion's ordeal still wasn't finished. She made him get up on his hands and knees on the bar, then she held an empty wine glass under his belly and milked him into it as if he were a beast. As perhaps he was – perhaps that was the point being made. Pierre-Raymond didn't care, he detested these symbolic tales.

He also detested Joelle for persuading him to come with her – he didn't want to be in a cinema, he wanted to be with Claudia. He was tormented by images that his mind insisted on presenting to him. The thought of her being touched by someone else was an agony.

If he thought about it logically, it was obvious Janine would make love to Claudia more often in bed than anywhere else – now that Claudia had moved in with her. Claudia lying naked on her back, her long legs spread wide, and Janine lying between them to kiss her pretty *joujou*. Logic informed him that was the nightly scene.

But logic has nothing to do with emotion – especially not the emotion involved when lovers kiss and touch each other. Pierre-Raymond was haunted by one particular image, Claudia and Janine in the department store dressing room. Janine pressing Claudia back to the wall, mouth on mouth, small hand up Claudia's skirt to arouse her . . .

The last time Janine Bonnard was in his studio for a portrait photograph she had painted her fingernails crimson. The deepest red, matching the colour of her lipstick. It was very striking, Pierre-Raymond had been fascinated by it. While he was working, arranging Janine and looking at her through the viewfinder, he had imagined those fingers with crimson-nails gripping his hard and upright flesh.

What a desperate pity Janine was not interested in men –

that had been his thought at the time. Now he was tormented by the memory of those red-nailed fingers touching Claudia, baring her pretty breasts and stroking them. Pulling her knickers off and feeling between her perfect thighs. Crimson-painted fingernails combing gently through Claudia's blonde fleece. It was intolerable.

Lost in these miserable thoughts, Pierre-Raymond continued to caress Joelle. She'd given up watching the movie – her head lay heavily on Pierre-Raymond's shoulder. Those unblinking eyes of hers were closed and she was sighing continuously.

Her hand was clasped over the hard pride in his trousers, but it was only a reflex action – she was too lost in her emotions and sensations to do anything to him.

Pierre-Raymond hardly troubled himself to watch the action on the screen or listen to the absurd dialogue – he was too deeply engaged in his jealous speculations about Claudia for much else to impress his mind. The Widow and her friend were no longer in the dimly lit bar. They were dressed again and in the back of a taxi. The Widow was wearing a white pullover and a black skirt.

Their destination was the Eiffel Tower, so the dialogue made clear. That must have a deep significance, but to guess it was beyond Pierre-Raymond. He knew there were many who saw Monsieur Eiffel's cast-iron erection as a gigantic phallic symbol but he had never been impressed by the likeness himself.

The taxi driver was a woman – she was wearing a short leather jacket and a cap with a shiny black peak. The Widow talked with her in doom-laden tones. 'This is the appointed place,' she said, and the taxi stopped under a stone arch in a deserted street.

The driver got out of the cab and showed that she had

nothing on below her jacket except her shoes. No skirt, no trousers, no knickers, no stockings. She was bare-bottomed. She got into the back with her passengers, her legs moving apart to display pale curls up her belly.

At this Pierre-Raymond's interest was captured. Though not by the screen action. Suppose women like the one in the movie were permitted to drive taxis around Paris – wearing only black leather jackets and otherwise naked? Taxi rides would be more interesting. Every traveller would peer in for a glimpse of the driver's charms while explaining where he wanted to be taken.

Such a driver would slide her thighs apart on the seat to let her passenger have a good look. The tip would be generous.

It need not end there, this more interesting travelling, with just a look and perhaps an arm thrust in the window for a rapid feel. Enterprising women drivers could perhaps be persuaded, for a suitable consideration, to get in the back of the cab with the passenger – as the one up on the screen had done.

She sat on the other side of the man from the Widow, her legs parted to reveal the thick lips that pouted between like a mouth waiting for a hot kiss and a tongue to be pushed into it. She and the Widow spoke across the man as if he wasn't there at all. He continued to say nothing, perhaps he was beyond words.

The Widow undid his trousers to display his advantages to the female cab driver. There followed more pretentious dialogue as the two women handled and commented on the thick and heavy male part that pointed up at them.

The driver unzipped her leather jacket. It was no surprise to observe that she was naked underneath it. Out spilled two plump white breasts, as good as the Widow's. The driver straddled the silent man's lap, her legs doubled and her knees on the seat.

She put her hands on his shoulders and waited while the Widow steered her friend's flesh up into her. 'We are beyond illusion,' said the Widow – and, as if the words had a meaning of some sort, the driver slithered up and down the hard shaft, her head back, her eyes sightless.

Her breasts were rolling deliciously to her movements and for a moment the sight brought Pierre-Raymond out of his gloom. The simple truth was that he adored round heavy breasts. Valerie's, for instance, he played with them whenever he had the time. But, his memory insisted – superb though Valerie's were, they were not as magnificent as Monique's the day she came with her mother to have her photo taken. Ah, beautiful Monique, seventeen years old and slim, but with such bountiful breasts. He had stared at them so hotly he was amazed her white silk blouse didn't scorch and burst into flames!

Monique's mother was beside him now, here in the cinema she'd brought him to. Slumping against the thickly padded back of her seat, her skirt halfway up her thighs, her eyes shut, her mouth hanging open. She was sighing and trembling in the aftermath of the fourth or fifth orgasm induced by his manipulating fingers.

Well, chérie, you wanted to come to the movies, Pierre-Raymond thought, *now you must accept the consequences. It amuses you to nickname me Monsieur Ten-times – now you are finding out how it feels to do it ten times. That's if you last that long, chérie, but more likely you'll collapse and faint after seven or eight. And then you'll find yourself alone in a taxi on your way home.*

For the first time since the movie started he became aware of the little noises around him. There was the inane dialogue from the screen, of course, and the soundtrack music. But there was also a continuous background of more interesting sound from the audience.

The tiny rustle of nylon and silk and satin caused by eager hands up skirts and in flimsy knickers. Now and then the little rasp of a zip or the almost inaudible pop of buttons. Sighs and soft breathing like a distant sea on an exotic shore. Evidently Joelle was not the only one in ecstasy – Pierre-Raymond grinned to think orgasms were taking place all about him. A mass secret orgy was under way.

These twenty couples in the cinema, entwined in the capacious plush seats, hands inside knickers, hands inside flies, tongues in each other's mouths, sticky fingers bringing orgasms to each other – once Pierre-Raymond thought of it like that he couldn't rid his mind of the concept.

'Oh, oh,' Joelle was murmuring faintly, 'oh, *chéri.*'

Her mouth was close to Pierre-Raymond's ear and he could feel her hot breath. Down between the legs she was slippery wet, her *joujou* was loose and open, her belly quivering. She had reached a condition of advanced sexual hysteria. Pierre-Raymond hadn't counted how many climaxes she'd had.

On screen the Widow had put her fingers in the man's mouth as the bare-bottomed driver bounced up and down on him. Her peaked cap had fallen off, the Widow had stuffed it up between her own legs, under her skirt, and seemed to be crushing it between her sturdy thighs.

The man had sat passive until now – the drive and energy he'd shown at the beginning when he climbed the circular staircase to ravage the Widow over the bannister, that seemed to have been dissipated when she sat over his face on the zinc-topped bar.

Now suddenly he cried out and bucked his loins sharply upward to force himself into the driver's pale-haired belly. Or was he struggling to break free of these women exploiting him – it was impossible to say what his heaving and jerking signified.

Pierre-Raymond's attention was torn away from the screen by a desperate moan beside him. He turned to see Joelle's body going into spasms of urgent ecstasy. Her shuddering lasted so long he guessed it was her final time that day. He didn't think she had managed ten, but it was enough.

'*Chérie*, how marvellous for you,' he murmured insincerely.

An Unforeseen Inconvenience

In the event, Pierre-Raymond was wrong to imagine he'd finished Joelle off in the Cinema Drapp. The sequence in the parked taxi didn't end when the female driver straddling the man's lap rode him to a whimpering standstill. After she dismounted, the Widow sprawled sideways across his lap to press her head between the driver's bare thighs and use her tongue. After that Joelle laid her head on Pierre-Raymond's shoulder and dozed off.

That amused him. And pleased him. He had scored over her this time. Too often it had been the other way round.

It annoyed him still to recall that Saturday morning she came to his apartment. He had pushed her face down on the arm of his grey sofa and flipped her summer frock up over her bare bottom. She squealed when she felt him penetrating her – he slid all of his fifteen centimetres in and pressed his belly tight to the cheeks of her bottom.

She'd been so furious, outraged and astounded to find herself used without her consent. But there was no way she could escape his impudent attention. She beat her clenched fists against the sofa cushions – she was at his mercy. He was ravishing her.

Even then, helpless and bare-bottomed as she was, spiked

upon his probing part, this damnable Joelle had managed to spoil his triumph – she reached a sudden and unexpected climax. Her belly squirmed on the sofa arm, she sobbed and bucked her bare bottom up at him to drive him in harder. In effect she'd turned defeat into victory at his expense. Even now, the memory of that day made him grind his teeth together.

But this evening, watching the strange movie with her, he had reduced her to whimpering passivity by his clever fingers alone – he'd pushed her further than her body or mind could tolerate. She was wrung-out and comatose and Pierre-Raymond was delighted to think he had achieved a notable triumph over darling Joelle. It was natural that having his hand between her thighs for so long had aroused him too – his condition was almost desperate. His dearest and most intimate friend was standing up staunchly. To be truthful, that had happened at the start of the movie when he slid his hand up Joelle's skirt and touched her warm and naked *belle-chose*.

After that, for the hour while he fingered her through almost continuous orgasms, his cherished part grew longer, harder and thicker, surpassing all reason. His trousers were strained over his belly, tight and hot and confining, uncomfortable – but the sensation was also delightful. After all was said, this was the state in which he preferred his fleshy length to be – stiff and strong and ready for action.

It was throbbing – and the movement caused the sensitive head to rub against his underwear – which aroused him more. Joelle's hand was on his thigh when the movie started, later she clasped him between the legs. But her welcome little attentions to him stopped when her own tremors grew insistent and demanding.

He had overloaded her nervous system with sensations until

it switched off and she fell into a trance-like doze. There was no prospect of her hand dipping into his trousers and bringing him to a merciful release.

Perhaps if he simply waited and allowed the rhythmical twitch against his underwear to carry him to its logical destination – which would be a sudden automatic release of these long-delayed emotions . . .

It could hardly be relied on to happen automatically. Better to arrange matters to his liking. Easy to open his trousers and push Joelle's hand in while she slept. Press her palm flat over his stiff and raging flesh and rub against it eight or nine times – in his present condition that would be sufficient. She would start awake to find her palm wet and sticky.

He grinned and wondered how she would react to the situation. Would she in her usual haughty way be annoyed to discover he'd taken advantage of her? Or would she accept it was his due, a small reciprocation for the hour-long pleasure she'd had in the dark from him – who could say? Joelle was too self-obsessed to be predictable.

The movie rolled on – Pierre-Raymond was too deeply concerned with urgent personal considerations to pay much attention – but he wondered vaguely where the woman cab driver had vanished to. And why the Widow and the man who had no illusions left were in a circus ring.

The man who had been pleasured forcibly in the taxi was naked and the Widow had changed her clothes yet again. She wore tight black leather trousers and riding boots with spurs. But nothing above the waist. Her heavy breasts bounced every time she moved – they were white as milk, the buds dark red and bold.

Pierre-Raymond's hard part jumped in his underwear and

almost brought on his release. He put his hand over Joelle's breast to squeeze it and wake her. She moaned a little, but she remained semi-unconscious.

The Widow's male friend was suspended upside down, swinging to and fro, attached by his ankles to a long rope that hung from a platform high up in the Big Top. His head was a metre above the sawdust and his wrists were tied behind his back. This exposure of his body revealed how hairy he was, his chest and belly were a mat of thick dark curls.

When he had been on his back on the bar, for the Widow to sit over his face, his open trousers revealed a curly bush between his legs as imposing as hers. But it was gone now – there was only pale flesh where he'd been shaved bare. Pierre-Raymond had to assume some deeply symbolic meaning, shaving him between the legs must express a significant concept.

Whether that was true or not, the effect was to make his male part look bigger. It was at full stretch – but as its owner was head-down, it pointed at the sawdust instead of skyward.

The young Widow stood up with her feet apart and her hands on her trousered hips, laughing at her friend swinging to and fro. But was he her friend? Pierre-Raymond had serious doubts when he saw the long thin whip in her hand. It was the type used by animal trainers to make a loud and intimidating crack.

She put her black-booted foot against his bare belly and gave him a push that made him spin on the end of his rope. She pushed at the small of his back with the same foot and sent him swinging in a long arc. When he stopped his babbling, she grabbed him by his male part and held fast until she had him motionless again.

'Even now you fail to understand,' she informed him when

he was quiet. She slid the whip handle between his thighs from the rear. There was no expression on her broad face as she drew the thong slowly through, trailing the whip-cord down over his bare shaven pompoms and the length of his down-pointing flesh.

Pierre-Raymond had lost touch with the plot of the movie – if there was so banal a feature as a plot. The upside-down man was babbling about something or other, there was no point at all in listening to idiocies about *Being* and *Non-being*. The woman went down on her knees in the sawdust to coil the whip-thong around his neck, as if she meant to strangle him.

She stood up again and took his downward-pointing part in her mouth. She was too occupied with that to listen to the nonsense her tied-up companion was declaiming – words to the effect that *Being* and *Nothingness* were the same as neither had validity.

Evidently he reached the end of his philosophical comments on the human condition. His head was hanging at the right level to kiss the Widow's *jouet*. But he couldn't – she was wearing black leather trousers. *Yes*, thought Pierre-Raymond, *that's symbolic*.

Undaunted, the head-down victim licked the black leather over the Widow's mound – the moisture his tongue left was visible on the smooth leather. Soon his licking became more frantic as the attention to his stiffness aroused him to an impossible degree.

In the dark Joelle stirred a little. 'Oh, oh,' she murmured, 'oh *chéri*.' Though her words were very faint, her mouth was so close to Pierre-Raymond's ear he could feel the warmth of her breath gentle on his skin. Between her thighs she was slippery-wet and the lips of her *joujou* were loosely open. She was in a state of sexual stupor – he couldn't guess how many climaxes she'd had.

On screen the Widow sucked at her friend – he was gasping and squirming so strongly that she wound her arms about his bottom to hold him still while she raised him to madness. When at last she stepped back, his stiff part slid wetly from her open mouth and she seized it and milked it briskly. He screamed and showered his creamy juice down over her bare breasts.

'Now I shall whip you until you faint,' she said, her fingers draining him of his last drops.

Joelle's body was rigid against Pierre-Raymond as she stifled a squeal, her hand clutching tightly between his spread thighs. Even through his trousers the grip was enough to drive him over the brink. His loins bucked sharply upwards, his desire gushed from him in quick spurts.

'Ah ah ah . . .' he moaned under his breath, unable to be silent, 'ah Joelle . . .'

She had lapsed back into a semi-coma the instant her ecstasy faded. Pierre-Raymond tucked his handkerchief down the front of his trousers to soak up the warm flood in his underwear. Had he been heard? he wondered, glancing cautiously round the darkened cinema. The pairs sitting to his left and his right were wholly engrossed in their own raptures – his involuntary little outcry had passed unnoticed.

Joelle was settled comfortably against him, head resting upon his shoulder, asleep again. He removed his hand from underneath her skirt and put his arm about her waist. Any more stimulation was out of the question, she had gone far past the possibility. He was pleased with his achievement.

And now his own intense pressure of emotion had been relieved so suddenly, he could watch the rest of the movie with more interest than before. From time to time he reached over to slip his hand into Joelle's unbuttoned jacket and fondle her breasts with sly pleasure. He had no urgent desire to do so, but that wasn't the point at all. Joelle didn't know he was doing it – which was why it pleased him.

Nevertheless, one single unintended and instant climax in his own underwear wasn't enough to content Monsieur Tentimes, that went without saying. When the movie ended he shook Joelle awake and led her out into the street and up to the boulevard and the nearest bar. She looked pale, and so she should. Tomorrow she'd stay in bed and sleep all day, he guessed.

A little glass of cognac livened her. She asked if he'd liked the movie – it was extraordinarily perceptive, she insisted, in its symbolic representation of relationships.

Pierre-Raymond agreed at once, that being easier than arguing with her about something he was sure he hadn't understood.

'The insights it provided were devastating,' he said, keeping his tone serious, 'you look perfectly devastated, *chérie.*'

Joelle glanced at her little diamond-studded wristwatch and he assumed she wanted to go home. The cognac had put a touch of colour in her pale cheeks, but she looked fatigued. They walked arm-in-arm to the taxi rank at the corner. He kissed her cheek and was about to wish her goodnight when she seized his arm and dragged him into the taxi with her. She gave his address on the rue de Sèvres.

'I feel most marvellously exhausted,' she said as the driver headed west, 'but I cannot leave you yet. I must come back with you, even if only for half an hour.'

When they arrived at his apartment she went straight into

the bedroom – with no pretence of waiting to be asked. It was as if she owned the apartment and Pierre-Raymond with it. *But this is absurd*, he thought, *I am not a paid lover, I am not a gigolo, I am Pierre-Raymond Becquet, the greatest lover in all Paris*.

He followed her into the bedroom – astonished and displeased. In the cinema he'd been fool enough to think he'd won and that he'd shown her which of them was in charge. Now she was demonstrating that nothing had changed between them.

She was standing by the side of the bed to undress – off came the jacket of her chic little cream linen costume, off came the skirt. Naturally, she was wearing no knickers, just a lace belt to keep her stockings up.

She took off her pink silk blouse and her bra – she sat naked on the bed and smiled at him.

'Take your clothes off, Pierre-Raymond,' she said, 'I want to sit on your face, just like the woman in the movie.'

His annoyance at being given orders was no protection against his natural urges – at the sight of her slender pale naked body *Grandjean* stirred and raised his head. It was as if he murmured secretly into Pierre-Raymond's ear, the stiff thick impudent fifteen centimetres of flesh in his underwear.

Look at those elegant little breasts, he seemed to be saying, *put your hands on them and give them a good feel – just look at those long thighs – you can put your head between them and lick the soft satin skin – and that pretty tuft of brunette curls on her belly – touch it, feel it – run your hands over her flesh – sink your fingernails into the cheeks of her bottom* . . .

And many more of the same enthusiastic suggestions, insidious and irresistible. Pierre-Raymond's resentment drained away from him as he stared at Joelle sitting naked and smiling on his bed and he stripped in silence.

'*Ah bon*!' she said, eyeing the strong stiff part standing up from between his thighs.

He got on to the bed and pushed her down on her back.

'But I want to sit on your face, *chéri*,' she said.

'Later,' he said, 'when you have rested a little. For now lie still and let me adore you.'

The instant Joelle's back was on the bed her legs slid apart. It was an automatic reaction with her – one he had noted before in their private encounters. He wondered if she slept like that at night, her legs parted and waiting hopefully. Did she dream there was a man lying on her belly, sliding his hardness in and out of her to the regular rhythm of her breathing?

Or did she sleep on her side more modestly? He stretched out beside her to kiss her soft little breasts and stroke her belly firmly.

His stiff part was against her thigh and twitching. The scent of her warm flesh mixed with the expensive perfume she sprayed on herself – three or four deep breaths made his head swim with desire. *Ah oui*, the time had come for her to repay the pleasure he'd given her in the cinema.

Whatever fanciful ideas she had in her head about playing the Widow and sitting on his face – or hanging him upside down from his own light fitting – it was time for him to slake his raging desire on her body. He was not nicknamed Monsieur Ten-times for nothing, he intended to use her warm naked body to the limit.

She was already open and slippery when his fingers eased into her – one finger, then two fingers, then three together. The tip of his longest finger touched her swollen little bud.

'What are you doing to me?' she gasped as her legs slid even further apart on the bed.

The answer to that was too obvious, and so he decided to make use of some of the absurd dialogue from the movie. As far as he could remember it.

'Each step that we take,' he said solemnly, 'brings us closer to realisation and a step nearer to nothingness. Do you dare?'

'I dare anything and everything,' Joelle sighed – and he knew it was true.

'*Being* and *Nothingness* are the same,' he said, wondering what it could possibly mean, 'neither has any validity.'

'You can't intimidate me,' she said, her beautiful dark brown eyes opening to stare at him.

'I shall destroy you,' he said, and meant it – or imagined he did. He could feel her legs tremble against him as his fingers played in her warm and wet *joujou*.

'You threaten me with this monstrous thing,' she murmured, 'I can feel it throbbing against me, you intend to destroy me with it.' Her fingers groped blindly up his thigh to grasp his stiff flesh.

'Oh yes, Pierre-Raymond, deprave me,' she pleaded, 'use me as you wish – ruin me, violate my body without mercy – I insist on it!'

Her fingers stroked up and down in a nervous little movement. Pierre-Raymond was hardly able to speak for the sensations that surged through his body. But he had no fear for the outcome, he was certain he had Joelle at a disadvantage and he was going to make every possible use of it. The little phrase *I insist on it* had reminded him it was very necessary to lower her absurd self-regard a notch or two.

His fingertips skimmed over her slippery bud in a profoundly sensual caress that paralysed her will. She made little gasping sounds, the fluttering of her chest causing her breasts to rise and fall in an enchanting manner. Her eyes were half closed and the whites were showing between her eyelids – he saw she was on the threshold of a climax. He slowed his caress, he intended to hold her suspended there.

In his mind it was like the circus scene in the movie, except that it was Joelle suspended upside down and naked, begging him for release. *Yes*, he thought, *that's what I want to do to her, hang her upside down naked and tease and torment her front and back, until she is screaming hysterically* . . .

. . . How marvellous, to see that slender elegant body dangling on a rope by her ankles, her hands bound behind her back, those tender little breasts lolling toward her chin . . .

How delicious it would be . . . to bite the small round cheeks of her bottom. To rub *Grandjean* against the satin skin between her upside down breasts. But how could this be arranged – this sexual torture of Joelle? To torture her body with unrelenting caresses and make her confess all her secrets . . .

'That day you brought your daughter to my studio, Joelle,' he said, 'when I'd finished taking her picture you sent her out to phone someone or other – you remember?'

'Yes,' she sighed, 'you cheated me that day.'

So that's her version, he told himself, not really surprised, even though the memory of the events of that day still made him uncomfortable. The studio door had hardly closed behind Monique when Joelle flipped his trousers open and slid her hand inside. He was stiff as a steel bar from his contemplation of Monique's massively beautiful breasts. He was hot and throbbing already – and then Joelle's long cool fingers clasped his swollen flesh.

She wanted him to take her hard and fast with her back to the wall and her skirt up around her waist. And he wanted the same, he was ready to push up into her. But matters had gone too far, he was excited by his long fantasies of playing with Monique in the darkroom – the instant Joelle's hand clasped him he spurted in his trousers, swaying on suddenly weak legs.

'It was you who cheated me that day, Joelle,' he said slowly and carefully, so that she would understand him even in the shaking throes of her incipient orgasm. 'You were too impatient and you made me do it before I had time to pull your skirt up.'

'I couldn't help myself,' she babbled, 'I was desperate – I'd been watching while you were photographing Monique. I could see the bulge in your trousers, I knew you wanted me.'

'Did you?' he murmured, amused by how she deceived herself.

'All the time you were taking pictures of Monique I knew that you were looking up my skirt,' Joelle sighed. 'I was sitting on the wickerwork settee behind her, so she couldn't see me when I pulled my skirt up over my knees and opened my legs, to let you look at me while you were working . . .'

This came as a surprise to Pierre-Raymond. At the time he had been enmeshed in his fantasy about Monique's breasts and hadn't noticed Joelle raising her skirt for him to view her dark brown curls. Naturally, she hadn't been wearing knickers that day.

If he had noticed her little display, it might well have been more than he could bear, that and the fantasy of Monique in the darkroom with him, baring her breasts for him – there had to be a limit to how much stimulation a man could stand.

'Yes, I was excited,' he said, which was true, 'the bulge you saw in my trousers testified to my state of mind.'

'In my imagination you stood in front of me and I opened your trousers wide to pull that long stiff thing out and kiss it and take it into my mouth,' she gasped, her body writhing under the slow caress of his fingers between her legs.

'I became impossibly aroused by looking up your skirt while I was taking pictures of your daughter – what you showed me drove me almost mad with desire,' said Pierre-Raymond.

That part wasn't true at all, but she couldn't know.

'Are you surprised that I did it in your hand?' he asked. 'You had driven me almost insane by parting your legs while you were watching. When it happened you were angry – you said I insulted you. But there was no insult.'

'I was wrong,' she sighed, 'it was a compliment, I understand that now, Pierre-Raymond – forgive me.'

'No never,' he said, his fingertip moving expertly inside her slipperiness. She shrieked as a climax struck her like a fist – her back lifted off the bed.

Now I have you dangling upside down on my rope, said Pierre-Raymond to himself, while he observed her spasms, *you are bound and helpless, Joelle, I shall torment you all I wish.*

He leaned over her squirming body, intoxicated by this power he had over her for the moment, determined to exercise it to the uttermost. One hand was busy between her thighs, keeping her shrieking in orgasm, his other hand searched over her body, up and down – his fingertips were rubbing pinching and probing, squeezing, tickling. Her breasts, her armpits, her open wailing mouth, his urgent fingers violated them all.

Her spasms seemed to go on forever, heels drumming on the bed and arms flailing. At her final gasp, she jerked upright to a sitting position, her eyes staring blindly. She was in a sort of sexual seizure, he realised.

'Time to destroy you,' he said, but she was beyond hearing or understanding his words.

He slammed her down on her back and hurled himself on top of her, his belly on hers and his legs between her legs. She still moaned and babbled as her body rolled from side to side and her legs kicked. He used his weight to hold her to the bed while he pushed deep into her very wet and warm entrance.

'I'm dying!' she shrilled, and her perspiration-wet body was heaving and squirming under him.

Ten short sharp jabs, no more, and he spurted into her belly. She convulsed under him so frantically she almost dislodged him – then by stages the spasms lessened until she lay still. He raised his head to stare into her face. Her eyes were shut and her cheeks were pale. He kissed her open mouth and murmured her name, but the only response was a faint moan. She was fast asleep before he rolled off her.

It seemed unkind to shake her back to consciousness and tell her she must get dressed and go home. He pulled the covers over them and went to sleep beside her, his hand resting her belly. He was very satisfied now he had destroyed her.

Sometime during the night he woke up aroused and stiff again. He had been dreaming about Liliane, and this was surprising. To fall asleep beside Joelle after ravaging her so thoroughly and then dream about doing it to a different woman – the mind plays strange games, he thought.

He had dreamed of Liliane naked in her bedroom, standing with her back to him. She was bending over to put her hands

202

flat on the bed – that absurd construction of wood and gilded ironwork, decorated with fake brocade curtains and long gold tassels.

He was close behind her, his trousers down around his ankles. The swollen head of his long stiff part touched her pretty rump and in another moment he would push it into her. His hands were between her thighs, stroking the tender insides while she moved her feet wide apart. Her *joujou* was a plump fleshy mound with a long split, the dark brown hair was sparse here underneath.

He held her hips to steady her while he mounted – and heard a furious knocking at the door. By great good fortune the bedroom door was locked – it was her boyfriend Roland out there, trying to break in and stop him doing it to her.

'*Be quick*, Liliane said calmly, *you can do it before he forces the door. By the time he breaks in he'll be too late.*

Pierre-Raymond pushed up into her wet softness. The rhythm of his thrusts matched the hammering on the door. The pace was set by Roland and this comical situation was turning into a race to see what happened first – would Roland break in and drag him off Liliane – our would Pierre-Raymond spurt in her clinging *joujou* before the boyfriend got there.

The race was not settled, there was no winner, because as the competition grew keener Pierre-Raymond woke up. He was in his own bed with Joelle. The light was still on because it had been too much trouble to switch it off before he fell asleep an hour to two before.

Joelle lay on her back beside him, she had one arm bent under her head on the pillow. Her breathing was slow and regular, she was deeply asleep. When he lifted the sheet to look at her body he saw that her legs were apart and her other hand lay over the brunette curls between them.

He reached down between her thighs to lift her hand carefully out of the way and clasp her *joujou* in his palm. Warm and soft, the feel of fleshy lips and curls was very pleasant. He decided to play with her and make her excited, then she'd wake up ready for him. His fingertips eased into her to find her secret bud.

Joelle was helpless, he had her completely at his mercy – for the third time that evening, he realised with real astonishment and shaking excitement. The first was in the Cinema Drapp, when the half-naked female taxi driver was bouncing up and down over the man's lap and the Widow slid her fingers into his mouth.

That was when Joelle had moaned and shuddered in her urgent need. And Pierre-Raymond knew he could do anything he wished to her – even stripping her naked in the cinema and folding her over the back of the seat in front and taking her from behind.

The second time was in his bed, when she jerked bolt upright, as if on a spring, her eyes staring blindly. He pushed her down flat on her back and ravaged her brutally – and she was too far out of her senses to know what he was doing to her. That was an extraordinary moment of delight – taking advantage of Joelle.

And now this time, the third time – she was profoundly asleep and almost impossible to wake. He threw the bedcovers right off and balanced over her on straight arms, gazing down between his belly and hers, savouring the never-to-be forgotten moment.

Joelle was his to use as he wanted. She could make no demands on him, none at all. She could only lie unconscious on her back while he ravished her in every way he could think of.

His stiff part was quivering, pointing at the smooth lips between her spread thighs. She was open and wet, he had seen to that. He edged forward a few centimetres and watched the purple-plum head of *Grandjean* touch those pouting lips.

You treat me as if you owned me, Joelle, he said in a whisper that only he heard, *but tonight I own you and I am going to use your body as no one else has. Or perhaps they have, who can say how far your little depravities have taken you, chérie?*

But I am Monsieur Ten-times, and before morning I shall do it in every opening of your pretty body. And you will lie there in a coma of fatigue and not know what is being done to you.

With a strong steady push he drove into her unresisting body. His hot belly was on hers and he began a firm rhythmic thrust. His ravishing of Joelle Marot was now beginning in earnest.

Eventually he slept, very contented. He was woken hours later by a hand on his shoulder shaking him. It was Joelle, naked and kneeling beside him, panic in her voice. It was broad daylight.

'What's the matter?' he asked, staring fondly at the slender body he'd ravaged very comprehensively.

'It's gone ten o'clock,' she said shrilly, 'I've been out all night – what am I going to tell my husband! Why did you let me fall asleep?'

It wasn't a question, it was an accusation. And the alarm she felt was clear in the sharpness of her tone. But Pierre-Raymond refused to let his unfamiliar goodwill toward her be dispersed. He told her he had fallen asleep himself. He almost apologised.

Joelle was off the bed, muttering and fuming while she picked up her scattered clothes from the floor and dragged them on. He offered to make coffee before she left but she scowled and said there was no time for that. So he stayed comfortably in bed and watched her dressing.

After all he'd done to her in the night he felt he owned her. He owned that smooth-fleshed *joujou* into which he'd jetted his passion. Her mouth – now set in a grimace of dismay – that too had been used for his delight, he had left a claim of ownership in it while she slept. And that round-cheeked bottom, delectable as a peach, that had also received evidence of his desire after he rolled her limp body over on to her belly.

Joelle was putting on her lacy bra – she raised her arms high to stare suspiciously into her smooth-shaven armpits.

Yes, they have become mine by right of conquest and despoliation, Pierre-Raymond thought with amusement, *but you know nothing at all of this, chérie, you slept through it and so you will never really understand why I won you.*

'It is impossible to go home like this,' Joelle said angrily, 'I smell of sex from head to foot. What am I to do!'

Pierre-Raymond lay on his side, gazing at her fondly. She had no knickers to put on, only her stockings and skirt. He slipped his hand down under the sheet to hold his stiffening part while he enjoyed the spectacle. In spite of his repeated activity in the night, *Grandjean* was vigorous again and enjoyed being held.

In the circumstances it was out of the question to ask Joelle to get back into bed. It would be extremely interesting – apart from being desperately exciting – to repeat the night's acts of possession and see if *déjà-vu* memories were stirred in Joelle's mind. Perhaps at the moment of orgasm there would be a flash of realisation that made her understand her body was owned by him.

'The bathroom is at your disposal,' he said hopefully, 'need I say that it would give me immense pleasure to sit with you in the bath and wash you from nose to toe.'

'Don't be absurd!' she said, sounding very unfriendly. 'I've no time for that now. You've put me in an impossible situation. I've got it – I'll take a taxi to Giselle Picard's. I can phone from there and tell my husband we had a little too much to drink and I stayed the night at her place. And I can bath there while Giselle's maid presses my clothes.'

A Dream Comes True – Almost

After Joelle dashed off in a bad temper, slamming the apartment door behind her, Pierre-Raymond had to laugh. He had never seen her so flustered in all the time he'd known her.

He was reluctant to get out of the bed on which he had scored so notable a victory over her but eventually he put on his silk dressing gown and went to the kitchen to make coffee. When he'd drunk it he soaked himself in a hot bath for twenty minutes and shaved.

'What a night,' he said to his grinning reflection.

It seemed to him as he stood naked before the mirror, shaving cream all over his face, that there was a contented look – one could almost go so far as to call it smug – about his dangling part. True, it was hanging down in front of him, and true it was half as long and thick as when it was performing for the pleasure of its owner, but it had a certain look of self-satisfaction about it, nobody could deny that.

And rightly so – last night he had taken possession of Joelle and probed and loved every centimetre of her smooth body while she lay motionless in a deep swoon of sexual fatigue. The proud and haughty Madame Marot had been exploited far beyond anything she herself could have imagined – and she knew nothing of it.

'Life being what it is, one dreams of revenge,' said Pierre-Raymond, although he couldn't recall which philosopher had said it first. 'Madame has been well served, and it is my secret.'

That was the best part of it, Joelle's total ignorance of how her body had been abused for Pierre-Raymond's pleasure. Perhaps a faint suspicion flitted through her mind as she was dressing. She had raised her arms to examine her armpits, a puzzled frown on her face.

In the night, while she slept so deeply, her armpits had been wet and sticky with Pierre-Raymond's passion. Both the left and the right, his body poised above her while he thrust into those smooth-shaven and delicate pockets.

He had spared no part of her sleek, well-groomed and pampered body. He'd straddled her and done it between her elegant little breasts, that went without saying. When she woke in the morning the sign of his slaked desire was dry, but it might be possible that she detected some lingering trace or scent on her skin.

'What a pity she jumped out of bed as soon as she was awake,' Pierre-Raymond said to his reflection, 'it could have been very enjoyable if she'd stayed with me this morning. I am completely refreshed and ready to stage a rerun of the night's adventures, this time with Madame fully conscious and participating.'

Of all the ways he'd had her in the night, which was the most exciting? he asked himself, gliding the razor over his face. In her mouth was particularly pleasing, lying on his side with her facing him but further down the bed so that her nose was level with his bellybutton.

His left hand on the nape of her neck to hold her head steady while the swollen head of his male part went between her lips – and he had massaged the long stiff shaft with busy fingers until he made himself spurt into her mouth.

'Ah yes, Joelle,' he sighed, 'what do you think of that? You never took me in your mouth when you were awake – but now, what choice do you have, *chérie*?'

And then for a heart-stopping moment he feared he'd woken her by this delicious abuse. She made gurgling sounds to the jet of his desire. Pierre-Raymond was aghast – was this damnable woman again going to spoil his little triumph!

It was impossible to halt the process of his climax, his hand flew up and down his straining shaft, his essence squirted into her mouth – and her eyes opened.

He gasped in dismay and shuddered. But even in the throes of his pleasure he realised she saw nothing, her eyes were vacant. It was a blank stare, uncomprehending, mindless. He pressed her face closer to his belly until her nose touched him, while with busy fingers he milked himself into her wet mouth.

It was finished! He released her neck and rolled over on his back, watching her face carefully for any sign of intelligence. But her eyes were empty and in a moment or two they closed.

'So which was the most gratifying of the many ways I enjoyed dear Joelle?' he asked his reflection again. 'An enchanting – but impossible – question.'

The face in the mirror assumed a thoughtful expression – with one eyebrow raised.

Perhaps the best of all was when he rolled her over face down and pushed a pillow under her loins to raise her bare bottom up high enough for him to approach her from behind. This was truly when he got his own back for the Saturday morning when she came to his apartment uninvited. She had treated him like a gigolo, then spoiled his little triumph by reaching a climax while he tried to humiliate her.

Then she'd been face down over the sofa arm with her frock up to expose her bottom, his hand on her back to stop her getting up while he ravaged her. And in the night she'd been face down on the bed while he arranged her thighs and opened her slippery *joujou* for easy penetration.

No complaining or squirming about this time. She lay limp and unconscious while he pushed into her.

'*Et voilà, chérie,*' he said when his belly lay on the bare cheeks of her bottom – the same words he'd used that Saturday morning. Words he hadn't forgotten, because they'd returned to annoy him whenever he recalled that day. Until last night – the moment of paying her back.

Naked in his bathroom at the basin, staring at himself in the mirror, it was no surprise to observe *Grandjean* had grown thick and long and hard at the pleasing memory.

'Yes, my dear friend,' Pierre-Raymond said aloud, 'be strong and brave, and we shall this very day arrange delightful little episodes for you, I promise faithfully. Beginning with dearest Valerie when we arrive later this morning at the studio.

The reflection in the mirror jumped and seemed to grow bigger still. Pierre-Raymond grinned and finished shaving. In his mind he was rehearsing what he was going do at the studio. He would say *bonjour* to Valerie and kiss her on both cheeks.

And while she returned his greeting he would slide both hands up under her pullover or into her blouse or whatever she had on and squeeze those superb bouncing breasts of hers. Then he'd reach around her back to undo her bra and feel their naked magnificence. The effect on *Grandjean* would be immediate, he'd stand up stiff and quivering in Pierre-Raymond's trousers.

Valerie would open them and pull him out and massage him, she did that very satisfactorily. And then? Perhaps Pierre-Raymond would sit her on the chaise longue and slip her little knickers down so he could kneel between her spread thighs.

But perhaps he would stand her against the wall with her feet parted and slip his hand down inside her knickers and play with her till her legs were trembling. Fingers fluttering inside her wet and slippery *joujou* until her knees gave way so he had to hold her tight to stop her sliding to the floor. And all the time his upstanding friend would be jerking and shaking in anticipation.

Or should he make Valerie lie over the desk with her skirt up round her waist so he could lean over and slide into her – hands under her clothes and roaming over her bare breasts?

'You will have to wait to find out how I choose to do it, my dear friend,' he said with a wink to his stiffly jerking flesh.

He recalled the time he had Valerie at the office window, the day he went back to work after his break with Claudia. He stood there that strange day, only an hour or two after leaving Liliane. He had been thinking about her while he stared across the Quai St Michel to the Seine and Nôtre Dame cathedral.

Valerie was at her desk typing and he suggested she should join him at the window.

She'd imagined there was something of interest to see outside, but everything of importance was inside the office. He'd closed her mouth with a kiss and put his hand up her skirt. The flesh of her thighs felt like silk – he slid his hand in her knickers and touched her thick bush of curls.

Then there was no question of going back to her desk. '*Ah*

oui,' she murmured as he turned her so her back was to the window. By then his fingertip was gliding over that little bud between her fleshy folds. She had his trousers gaping open and her hand was pumping firmly.

The bathroom mirror reflected the strong bounding of Pierre-Raymond's upright part at this recollection of Valerie standing with her back to the office window. Whoever was passing outside and looked up would have observed a brunette, flattened against the glass, and a man pressing himself tight against her.

All these thoughts and imaginings were very pleasant. And the anticipation was keen indeed. But life only rarely works out as planned. When Pierre-Raymond got to his studio an hour later Valerie was not there. He'd stopped for something to eat on the way and the time was well after midday.

There was a note left in the typewriter for him. It said that she'd gone to lunch. He was trying to make up his mind if this terse little message meant she was annoyed. Perhaps he ought to have phoned her when he woke up so late and made an excuse.

Pierre-Raymond did not want Valerie to be angry with him – he adored her, he desired her friendship during working hours. Her intimate friendship. He never tired of watching her heavy round breasts bounce when she moved about or got up from her chair or sat down quickly. He wanted her to be here with him now so that he could slip his hand up her pullover and caress her.

If this train of thought had continued it is very possible he would have become melancholy. But fortunately for him there was a tap at the office door. Before he had time to speak it opened and in came Monique.

'*Bonjour*, Mademoiselle Marot,' he said, astonished. 'Is your mother with you?'

He couldn't imagine how Joelle could possibly have gone home, made her excuses to her husband, bathed, done her hair and her make-up, dressed and brought her daughter here. And she hadn't, as Monique quickly made clear.

'*Bonjour*, Monsieur Becquet,' she answered prettily. 'No, I am alone and I've come to see the proofs of my pictures. Are they ready?'

Whereas Valerie – receptionist, secretary, book-keeper, sexual plaything – often wore close-fitting roll-neck pullovers to draw attention to her heavy breasts – quite unnecessarily – Monique had been taught by her mother that oversized breasts were simply not elegant – the best thing to was hide them.

'Your receptionist has breasts like water-melons,' that's what Joelle had said about Valerie. But her own daughter's were just as big. Naturally, Joelle made no reference to that unfortunate truth, although it was obvious that she'd done all she could to minimise her daughter's abundance.

When Monique first came to the studio with her mother she was wearing a white silk blouse that was loosely cut. In theory her natural bounties were lost in the silk. But the blouse couldn't really disguise the seventeen year old's beautiful fleshy mounds – not from a connoisseur of women like Pierre-Raymond.

Today Monique was not under her mother's eye. She was wearing a white blouse with a high neck fastened with black jet buttons – this blouse fitted snugly over her breasts, clearly outlining their impressive size and shape. It was tucked into a swirling black skirt and, to be sure that her natural beauties could not be missed, she had a black leather belt tight around her waist.

Pulling in her waist made her bouncers appear bigger. And

the little grey-and-white check jacket she wore over the blouse was unbuttoned, drawing men's eyes to her outstanding features. And certainly Pierre-Raymond's attention was engaged – so strongly that it required a great effort of will not to stare or to slip his hand in his pocket and comfort his quivering part.

To say the very least of it, Monique was lusciously young and desirable. A very familiar and always very welcome sensation of stiffness and of bulk in Pierre-Raymond's trousers made itself apparent. He gave a half-suppressed sigh of wonder – he wanted to get his hands on those substantial delights of Monique's.

By this time his brain was speculating out of control. This was his opportunity to undo Monique's pretty blouse and strip away her bra and handle her – to feel the warmth and weight of her bare bounties. *Ah Dieu*, how unbelievable a pleasure to kiss them and lick his tongue over their tender young buds!

He smiled amiably at her and told her the proofs were ready. It would be an honour to display them to her in the darkroom.

But there was also much more he hoped to see displayed in the privacy of the darkroom. He knew it was impossible for him to be alone with any pretty female over the age of sixteen and not make advances to her. He was Pierre-Raymond Becquet, therefore he had a right to expect his advances would be welcomed.

He never missed an opportunity to demonstrate how he adored women – in the most practical way he knew, by slipping his hand into their knickers. Monique had come alone to the studio, this must mean she wanted him to make love to her. That was logical.

In spite of his urgent arousal he tried to be sensible and to move cautiously. Monique's body was lush but she was only seventeen he reminded himself, most probably a virgin. If he offended her by moving too fast, she might complain to her Mama. Which could be very disastrous.

Move with a little caution, he advised himself, and he turned on all the lights in the darkroom, not just the dim red light. He kept his hands carefully to himself and spread the photos on the workbench for her to look at.

Good intentions are one thing, deeds quite another. And as an ancient proverb advises, a hardness in the trousers brings on a softness in the brain. He was standing beside Monique while she examined he proofs and it was not long before his hand lightly touched hers as they discussed the pictures.

When that passed without comment by her, a natural progression led his hand to rest gently on her waist.

He was clear about what he wanted to do next. In his feverish mind he envisaged sliding his hand down to her bottom to stroke it a little. And then he would be committed. If she objected he would find himself in an awkward situation. But risks had never stopped him in the past.

His hand was not even halfway in its glide down to her bottom when events took a different turn. Monique moved around to face him, leaning a hip against the high bench. She regarded him in an innocent manner while he was staring in speechless adoration at her delightful protuberances.

'Monsieur Becquet,' she said conversationally, 'I've heard my mother talking about you to Madame Picard and her other friends when they thought I couldn't hear what they were saying.'

'Truly? What do they say about me?'

'They all like you, mother's friends. And from what they say, it seems that you like them. They love to gossip about who

217

will see you next and who saw you last.'

'It is pleasing to be appreciated by friends,' he answered.

His hand still rested on her hip – a little below it – and he was wondering how to proceed gracefully. Slide his hand up her side toward her longed-for beauties?

'There is something I don't really understand,' Monique said, 'why are your women friends older than you? Even my mother. Do you feel a particular sympathy toward middle-aged women?'

'Madame Marot and her friends are beautiful and sophisticated ladies,' Pierre-Raymond said, uneasy at the question. 'They are stylish, they take the greatest care of their appearance, their clothes are beautiful.'

'So a stringy middle-aged body in expensive silk underwear is attractive – I must remember that,' said Monique, sounding very guileless, although Pierre-Raymond realised that she understood more than he had guessed at first.

'Age is of no importance – I adore beautiful women,' he said.

He put a hand on her other hip and took a half-step closer to her. Her perfume was delicious, fresh and flowery – very young. She didn't pull away – but her voice was cool and so was the look in her brown eyes.

'It was very amusing when I heard the nickname they have for you,' she said with a little smile.

'Nickname? What do you mean – what nickname?' He was trying to sound sincere.

'Mother and her friends call you Monsieur Ten-times. I'm sure you know that. At first I didn't understand what it could mean, but then it dawned on me.'

Naturally, Pierre-Raymond couldn't help looking proud when

he heard it from Monique. He no longer believed she was a virgin, if he ever really had.

'You find it impressive, this nickname?' he asked silkily.

'Impressive? To be truthful I found it slightly comic. But I suppose women of a certain age concealing their sagging bellies in silk knickers are impressed if a man wants them twice.'

'You are cruel, Monique,' he sighed, 'but you are beautiful – and so I adore you.'

'But surely you only adore women who pay you to adore them?' she said, her clear brown eyes gazing into his. 'Isn't that so, Monsieur Ten-times?'

'Please don't call me that,' he gave her his charming smile, 'I am Pierre-Raymond. I find *you* adorable, Monique.'

His hands were inside her open jacket – he'd been holding her by the hips – but, now she was mocking him, his hands had slid up above her belt to rest just below the ribs. Through her blouse the warm feel of her flesh excited him till he hardly knew what he was doing – his palms continued to slide slowly upward.

'If our conversation is to continue,' Monique said firmly, 'I insist you put your hands in your pockets. I hate men trying to maul me.'

'Ah, a thousand pardons,' he said, taking his hands away from her. Whether she intended jacket pockets or trouser pockets was not a consideration – he put his hands into his trouser pockets where *Grandjean* stood fiercely upright, demanding attention. He touched him with a fingertip and felt the sudden leap.

Monique smiled. He wondered what the reason was – because she was pleased he was no longer touching her? Or could it be that she was amused by the movement of his concealed hand?

Deep in his pocket he was holding his jerking length and rubbing it.

'Something very inconvenient will happen in your underwear if you do that,' she said with another smile. 'I know about men, I know what you want. You're all the same, young or old, you want to feel my breasts.'

'But of course,' Pierre-Raymond murmured, 'every man who ever meets you is desperate to get your clothes off and admire those marvellous breasts of yours. If I were permitted to touch them, only for a moment or two, I'd fall in love with you. I wouldn't be able to stop myself. They are superb, and you are adorable.'

'But I see no advantage if you fall in love with me,' Monique said thoughtfully. 'You're not bad looking, but you're much too old for me. So I shall not allow you to touch me.'

'Ah,' he said sadly, certain in his secret thoughts that he'd persuade her to change her mind before she left.

'Since we're talking about this absurd subject,' she went on, 'you can satisfy my curiosity – show me this thing my mother's friends are so madly enthusiastic about.'

'Do you mean what I think you mean?' He was amazed.

She nodded. He ripped his trousers open and let his distended part jump out. It stood very proud – glossy plum-purple head on a stiff and thick-veined shaft, pointing upward eagerly at her.

'*Mon dieu – c'est formidable*!' she exclaimed.

'*C'est maqnifique*,' he told her arrogantly.

Would she be horrified, he wondered, if he informed her these fifteen centimetres of hard flesh had been inside her mother several times during the night just past? Not only in her *belle-chose*, but inside her other bodily openings.

'Because of you,' he said dramatically, ' it is in this condition that you see.'

'I know that,' she said calmly, 'I'm not an innocent fool.'

To his delight she slipped off her little jacket and threw it onto a chair. She undid the jet buttons at the high neck of her blouse and opened the entire front, pulling it out of her skirt waist. She looked into Pierre-Raymond's eyes with an expression of amusement while she reached behind herself to unclip her bra – this attitude of hands behind her back pushed her breasts out further, making them seem even more massive.

She was holding his gaze – commanding him to keep his eyes on her face. But it was impossible, his natural male reaction took over. He lowered his eyes, to stare with sincere longing at her plump delights – they were so heavy that they already drooped a little, though she was only seventeen.

Their tender buds rose from large terracotta-red rings – they were so enchanting that Pierre-Raymond's hard male part bounded strongly and Monique smiled into his flushed face.

'Now you have what you want,' she told him, 'I am letting you see my breasts.'

He was involved in frantic emotions and he totally missed the amusement in her voice.

'They are superb!' he sighed, casting around in his mind for a better word than that to praise those tremendous bouncers.

Superb sounded banal. But what else could he say? Certainly not her mother's term for Valerie's pair – she'd dismissed them as water-melons. Which seemed appropriate for Monique's, but it would not please her to hear them described like that.

Uppermost in his whirling thoughts as he stared at those bare plumpnesses was the desire to press *Grandjean* between them and squeeze them together into a soft pocket for short fast thrusts – he was so aroused that it would take only a few seconds until be jetted his torrent on to her satin skin.

'My mother lets you do it to her, of course,' Monique said in an offhand way, 'and Madame Picard. And all their friends. How much do they pay you, Monsieur Ten-times?'

'You mean to insult me,' Pierre-Raymond said sadly, 'I am not a gigolo, I do not accept money from women.'

'Ah really?' said Monique, raising one eyebrow in a way that indicated she didn't believe him. 'You do it for love?'

'I adore beautiful women,' he said with as much dignity as he could – an almost impossible attitude to achieve standing there with his trousers undone and his hand stroking his stiffness up and down under the quizzical gaze of a seventeen-year-old girl.

'But of course you adore them,' said Monique, she was smiling as if he'd made a joke, 'and they adore you too. Certainly, the middle-aged ones adore you, from what I've heard.'

Pierre-Raymond stared fascinated as she cupped her breasts in her long-fingered hands to bounce them up and down a little. It was too much, he reached out to touch those fleshy rotundities.

'I think you'd better not do that,' she said at once, but she didn't pull away from his caressing hands. 'You said you'd fall in love with me if you touched me and that would be boring.'

'Boring for you, not for me,' he sighed, stroking them.

'Of course boring for me,' she said, 'and for you too because it would ruin the way you earn your living – you couldn't carry on doing what you do for so many middle-aged ladies if you were in love with me.'

'You persist in misunderstanding me,' he said in a melancholy voice, 'that is not how I earn my living. I am a photographer.'

He moved closer to Monique while he fondled her bare breasts. His mutinous male part pressed hard and heavy against her skirt over her soft belly.

'*Je t'aime*, Monique,' he murmured, 'do not laugh at me.'

'So quickly?' she said. 'I only came to see my proofs.'

The fine smooth wool of her skirt felt very pleasant against the length of hot hard flesh pressed firmly to it. He rubbed up and down slowly, his hands playing over her breasts. He was now so close that he could put his cheek against hers.

He wanted to kiss her and he made a start by kissing her ear. She was wearing gold studs in the lobes. He touched the tip of his tongue to one and tasted the metallic savour of the gold and then the warm flesh around it.

The taste of Monique was delicious. And that was only her ear – how marvellous must be the taste of her breasts if she would let him kiss them. When he got her knickers down and licked her belly, the taste would be incredibly arousing.

And then between her legs – his mouth on the sweet young lips there! That would be totally overwhelming, he was sure that he would explode instantly into ecstasy and spurt on her stocking.

He reached down to get his hand under her skirt. She breathed in quickly when his fingers slid up between her thighs.

'This is not what I came for,' she said.

She didn't sound very interested one way or the other. He was intrigued that so young a girl was able to remain so very self-assured. But she was Joelle's daughter, one ought not to forget that. Or so he told himself as his fingertips found thin satin between her legs and the soft warmth of her *joujou* through it.

'Listen – I heard a door close,' she exclaimed, 'did you hear it? Someone's come into the studio.'

Pierre-Raymond kissed her neck and he slipped his hand into her little knickers.

'It is only my receptionist returning from lunch. There is no cause for alarm,' he told her.

'But she'll come in and find us – then what will you say?'

'The red warning light is on outside the darkroom door. Have no fear – she won't come in.'

Monique considered his words, then she put both hands against his chest and pushed him gently away.

'You've touched me long enough to fall in love with me,' she said, ' hands off, Pierre-Raymond.'

He was pleased she used his name and not his absurd nickname. But he wasn't pleased to be ordered off. He glanced down at his hands, the clever hands that had felt Monique's breasts and her girlish *joujou*.

He raised his hands to his mouth and kissed his fingertips in reverence.

'It is impossible to stop,' he murmured, 'you must not refuse me now – *je t'adore*, Monique.'

'Ah, how interesting that you are already suffering the agony of unreturned love,' she said. 'I warned you it would not be to your advantage to fall in love with me.'

She reached out and clasped his twitching part between finger and thumb, just below the swollen head. He thought he would die of sheer pleasure, just because Monique was holding him. As for what it would be like to feel *Grandjean* slide into the softness of her *jouet*, there were no words to describe it, none.

It was urgent that he get her knickers off and lift her up to sit on the workbench so that he could stand between her thighs and push up into her girlish belly.

'Thank you for letting me see this thing that my mother and all her friends think so much of,' Monique said with a grin, 'that's the reason I came here, curiosity.'

She was jerking his stiffness rapidly up and down, staring at it with an expression of intense interest on her face.

Pierre-Raymond wasn't listening to what she said. Feeling her grandiose breasts had aroused him so furiously that his crisis was imminent.

'I suppose middle-aged ladies get a thrill from it,' she said thoughtfully, her hand very insistent now, 'I don't believe you do it ten times. Mama and her friends are too feeble and used-up – they'd die underneath you.'

He sighed her name. At the instant he spurted she slid to the side and jerked him to the right – his desire splattered on the proofs of her pictures laid out on the workbench.

'*Au revoir*, Pierre-Raymond,' she said casually, letting go of him, 'choose the best one yourself and send me six copies.'

There Is More Unwelcome News

Two days after the little episode with Monique in the darkroom Pierre-Raymond phoned the Marot residence. He hadn't been able to stop thinking of Monique by day and by night – specifically he couldn't stop thinking of the magnificence of her breasts.

He'd seen them bare, those fleshy delights – seen her bounce them in her cupped hands. She'd let him touch them – *bon Dieu!* He'd felt those sumptuous playthings under his palms. And more, he'd had his hand up her skirt. He'd touched her, he'd caressed her soft young *joujou*.

The memory gave him no rest – it was of the utmost urgency he meet her again and get her knickers off. Not in the studio this time, because of Valerie, but here in his apartment. On the bed or on the sitting-room sofa – preferably on both. Strip off her little knickers and get on top of her . . .

After his curious little adventure in the darkroom with this delicious seventeen year old, when she had handled him so intently, it was impossible to sleep peacefully again until he achieved his aim, the supreme goal. Monique naked on her back and he naked on her – it would be one of the unforgettable moments of his life.

Madame Marot herself answered the phone. Pierre-Raymond

spoke cautiously, not knowing if she was alone in the room, or if her husband was present. In the late afternoon Monsieur Marot ought to be attending to his business, whatever that was. Or in bed with his girlfriend, if he had one. He ought not to be at home – but with the very well-to-do one could never be sure.

Another awkward point was whether Monique had told her mother she'd called in at the studio to see the proofs. Perhaps in the light of the intimate moments in the darkroom Monique had said nothing about seeing him. Certainly she'd have kept quiet about displaying her bounties to Mama's lover. And about handling the fifteen centimetres which Mama made use of for her delight.

'I'm glad you phoned,' Joelle said briskly, 'you've caught me in the very nick of time – I'm going away for a few weeks.'

'A holiday?'

'My husband thinks I've been doing too much recently – all my charities and committees and social events – I'm hardly ever at home, he says. He's determined that I must have a complete rest from it all. We're off on a long cruise – we catch the train to Le Havre this evening and sail tomorrow.'

'I wish you *bon voyage*,' said Pierre-Raymond, his mind was in a whirl of speculation.

It was evident to him this sudden decision to leave Paris for a long cruise was to do with the night she'd stayed out because she fell asleep in bed with him. And had been spectacularly molested while she lay unconscious. Possibly Monsieur Marot hadn't been absolutely convinced of the reliability of her story of staying overnight with Giselle Picard.

'The pictures of your charming daughter,' Pierre-Raymond said warily, 'shall I address them to her in your absence? Or is she going with you?'

'No, my husband is a romantic,' Joelle said chuckling, 'it is another honeymoon, this tropical voyage. We shall be staying in Martinique and Guadeloupe and other exotic spots. Daughters are not required on the voyage, you understand.'

'Yes, I believe I understand you.' Pierre-Raymond was amused by the prospect of middle-aged Monsieur Marot trying to compete with the exploits of Monsieur Ten-times.

He was sure now that Marot had put his foot down hard. Joelle was being uncharacteristically deferential – she must be afraid that her husband might dump her unless she changed her ways.

What she said next cast doubt on the possibilities of serious change on her part, whatever her husband might be led to think.

'I'll have a marvellous suntan when we get back to France in about six or eight weeks,' Joelle said, her voice dropping down a tone, 'a golden tan, all over my body, Pierre-Raymond.'

'Enchanting,' he said, his imagination suddenly stirred.

'I shall want you to take pictures. Not portraits this time – poetic studies showing all of me. My all-over suntan. Have you taken many photographs of nude women?'

'None at all,' he said, which was not entirely true.

It had to be admitted that the thought of Joelle's smooth and pampered body stretched out naked – on the wickerwork settee in his studio perhaps – this picture in his mind caused a pleasant stiffness in his underwear.

The assignment had enormous interest, Joelle's all-over tan. The photos and what they would inevitably lead to. Joelle from front and back. Standing, sitting, lying down. Pictures before and after to show the change in how she held her body and what and what her facial expressions revealed.

'I shall begin to plan the session right away,' he said. 'The poses will require much thought and attention to show your tan to greatest advantage. In the meantime, I'll send the photos of your daughter to her, yes?'

What he really had in mind was to phone again tomorrow, after Monsieur and Madame had departed and suggest to Monique a visit to his apartment to collect her pictures. And then – ah, then he would educate this delicious young girl in the delights of lovemaking – ways she hadn't even dreamed of. Monique naked on his bed, her beautiful body at his disposal. That same bed he'd violated her sleeping mother on.

But it was not to be.

'She's not here,' said Joelle. 'I packed her off this morning to Nice to stay with my husband's sister while we're away.'

'I see.'

'Keep the photos till I get back and I'll collect them when I come to show off my beautiful suntan.'

'I shall look forward to that with great eagerness,' he said, putting the phone down with a brief *au revoir*.

All this was infuriating. With Joelle dragged to the Caribbean by her suspicious husband, what an opportunity to get close to dear little Monique! Perhaps *little* wasn't the best word, some of her was far from little. But what use was Joelle's absence if Monique was hundreds of kilometres away on the Côte d'Azur?

The image that intruded immediately into his mind was Monique on the beach – Monique in a tight swimsuit. '*Oh mon Dieu*,' Pierre-Raymond exclaimed aloud, still clutching the phone in his hand. Monique's bouncers in a swimsuit – every man on the beach would have a big bulge in his shorts.

He considered the idea of taking a few days off and flying to Nice to look for her. The problem was that he'd been away from work a lot recently, what with his heart being broken by Claudia and other annoyances. And if Joelle got to know he had been to Nice she'd guess why at once and that would cause trouble.

Sad to say, the sensible plan was to be patient and wait till the whole Marot family came back to Paris. Monique had shown an interest in him – to the extent of taking his pride in her hand and putting it through its paces.

'Next time, Mademoiselle,' he murmured to himself, 'next time it will not be in your hand but in your charming *joujou.*'

When he locked up and left the studio that evening he put the proofs of Monique's photos in his pocket to take home with him. He had dinner in a small restaurant he liked – a simple meal of Strasbourg *pâté de foie gras*, a moderate helping of *agneau rôti* accompanied by a dish of mixed wild mushrooms, then a slice of Roquefort cheese – and he drank a half-bottle of Burgundy.

By eleven he was ready for bed, pleased to have an evening to himself for once. An early restful night. He was undressed and enjoying a last glass of cognac in the sitting room, looking at the proofs of Monique's pictures.

It was not easy to decide which was the best. Of course, he'd been compelled to wash and dry them after the comic accident in the darkroom.

In his mind's eye he stripped Monique of the loose white silk blouse she wore for the sitting and he imagined her in a close-fitting swimsuit. A white one? A black one?

He was giving this vital question his complete attention when the door bell rang. Who on earth could it be? he asked himself. Not a neighbour complaining about noise – his radio was playing soft dance music. Not Joelle, she was in Le Havre on a ship, or on a train on her way to it.

Not Monique, she was in Nice with her aunt. Not Claudia – she was in love with that damnable actress.

He pushed the photos behind a cushion of the grey suede sofa, just in case, and went to the door. To his astonishment Liliane stood there, wearing a light summer raincoat. Without a word of greeting or explanation she hurled herself into his arms – hard enough to make him stagger back into the apartment.

'He's going to kill me!' she gasped, clinging to him. 'I'm so terrified – save me, Pierre-Raymond!'

There was a look of terror on her long and pretty face – or a convincing facsimile of terror.

'Who do you mean?' Pierre-Raymond asked. 'Roland?'

He pushed the door shut with his free hand – his other lay on her neat little bottom to press her close to him. It felt good, even through a raincoat, the softness of her body against him. He was wearing silk pyjamas and his beautiful dressing gown and he felt his ever-ready male part stiffening.

Liliane unwrapped her arms from his neck and darted into the sitting room.

He followed her at a more relaxed pace and found her standing at the window, looking down at the street below.

'What are you doing?' he asked, craning his neck to see what she was staring at. The light summer rain had stopped some time before and the pavements gleamed under the streetlamps.

'He followed me here,' Liliane said. 'He managed to keep well out of sight every time I turned round to look. But I'm certain he was behind me. He's down there watching the building now.'

Pierre-Raymond couldn't see anybody. Not walking past, not on the pavement opposite, not hiding in any doorway. It wasn't far to the corner of the rue de Sèvres. There were cafés to hide in there, but they were out of sight of his apartment building.

'You're in a very nervous state,' he said, 'it's possible you imagined you were being followed, my poor darling.'

'It's true!' she said, 'I know he's down there somewhere.'

Her pretty nose was touching the window. Pierre-Raymond was behind her looking out over her shoulder – his hands lightly on her hips. There was nobody in sight below, not even a dog lover walking a pet.

'*Chérie*,' he murmured while he undid the belt and the buttons of her raincoat and eased it off. Without looking, he flung it in the direction of a chair. She seemed too preoccupied to even notice when he put his arms around her again and felt her spiky little breasts through her thin summer frock.

'He is an animal, Roland,' she said. 'I'll never speak to him again after what he did to me this evening.'

'Ah,' said Pierre-Raymond, suddenly interested, 'and what did he do to you?'

She explained that Roland had been out since noon with his friend Lemall from the neighbouring apartment. When he came back about ten it was evident they had been drinking together. Roland was in a hostile mood – it was equally evident the conversation had been about her. Lemall had slandered her. Roland accused her of infidelity the moment he was inside the door.

She had been washing her hair and painting her toenails. She was in a half-transparent slip and she was barefoot, with a bath towel wrapped round her head. Roland grabbed her wrist and sat heavily on a chair and pulled her across his lap, face down.

Unbelievable as it must sound to a civilised person, she told Pierre-Raymond, Roland dragged her thin slip up over her bottom and ripped her knickers off completely – but actually *tore* them into pieces, can you believe! Naturally she shrieked at him to let her go and she kicked and struggled.

He didn't let her get up, he pushed his hand down between her thighs and pinched her *joujou* cruelly. He called her a slut and said he knew very well that she opened her legs for that damned photographer and she was just like a tart on a street corner.

'*Mon Dieu*!' said Pierre-Raymond, worried the boyfriend might indeed come to his apartment and beat him senseless. 'This is a desperate situation.'

Fortunately for him, Liliane took his exclamation to mean her situation face down across Roland's knee was desperate, not the question of Pierre-Raymond's personal safety.

She burst into angry tears while she told how she'd struggled against Roland's grasp and had beat her fists against his shins.

'I hate you,' she screamed.

'I hate you,' Roland snarled.

That was how she related it to Pierre-Raymond. And then – can you believe it – the monster pried her open and put his fingers in her.

'You betrayed my love with this man when I wasn't here,' said Roland in his rage.

'I love Pierre-Raymond,' she shrieked, hoping to stop him in his tracks by telling him her affections lay elsewhere. She lay slumped over his lap, waiting for common sense to assert itself and his brutal treatment to reach an end. Or so she said.

The bath rowel had fallen from her head during her struggles. Roland seized a handful of her damp hair and pulled her head up to make her look at him while he glared into her eyes.

'I'll get my own back on both of you, your fancy photographer as well as you,' he said. That was what she told Pierre-Raymond while she stood at his window and he felt her breasts.

'I see,' Pierre-Raymond said thoughtfully, 'he made threats – I don't like the sound of that. He knows where my studio is. He turned up there asking for me. I told you about it.'

'He is an animal,' Liliane said breathlessly.

'Fortunately I was out,' Pierre-Raymond murmured thankfully. 'Valerie got rid of him. Does he know where I live – if not, he would have a reason to follow you.'

'Who can say?' Liliane said, seeming calm again now her tale of terror was told. 'I do love you, Pierre-Raymond, it wasn't a lie to bring Roland to his senses.'

'But of course you love me,' he said, 'it was brave of you to reveal it at so desperate a moment.'

To him it was natural that pretty young women should love him – he was Pierre-Raymond Becquet, a man of distinction.

'You are in pyjamas,' she noticed at last, 'I got you out of bed – forgive me, but I have nowhere else to go.'

'There is nothing to forgive,' he assured her, not believing it himself.

They stood watching the rain-wet street. He was very close to her, his loins pressed against her bottom. He reached round her and down to slip his hand under her frock at the front and feel up between her stockinged thighs.

'Was any harm done when you were mistreated so barbarously?' he asked, his hand stroking her belly inside her knickers. 'Are you bruised or scratched, *chérie*?'

'It was frightening,' she said, 'he wanted to rape me, but he doesn't want to admit that he still desires me. That would have given me an advantage.'

Pierre-Raymond didn't understand what she meant. In any case, he was losing interest in her row with her boyfriend for a most obvious reason – his fingertips were roaming between her thighs and over her *joujou*. In his pyjamas *Grandjean* was standing bold and hard. He pulled his dressing gown belt loose and opened it to let his pride leap out, quivering happily in sudden freedom.

'But this is how it all began,' said Liliane.

Her plan was advancing well – Pierre-Raymond had acknowledged that she loved him. What she wanted next was the suggestion to move in with him. *Slow and sure*, she said to herself while his clever fingers caressed between her legs, *don't try to rush it, let him think that he's in control.*

He lifted her skirt at the back and she felt him lay his hard part upright along the crease of her bottom. It felt hot and it throbbed through her flimsy knickers. She pushed against him to make him conscious of the feel of her taut round cheeks.

'Move your feet apart a little,' he murmured, his mouth close to her ear and the sweet perfume of her hair in his nostrils.

'Look, there he is!' she exclaimed. 'Across the street, he's staring up at us.'

'That's not him,' Pierre-Raymond assured her, 'that's someone who lives on the top floor, I know him by sight. Come away from the window, *chérie*, you are nervous and overwrought.'

He was gently sliding his thickness against the smoothness of her knickers. His dressing gown hanging open got in the way so he shrugged his shoulders out of it and let it slide to the floor.

'Are you certain it's not him?' Liliane demanded.

'Entirely,' and Pierre-Raymond kissed the back of her neck as he pressed the tip of his middle finger into her.

Nervous she might be, but she was also sexually aroused and didn't want him to stop. Her little bud was swollen and wet underneath his fingertip. She put a hand behind her, between his belly and her bottom to feel the hard flesh pressed against her.

'If we are truthful,' she sighed, 'we must admit we deceived Roland. I should have known he'd never forgive me after what he did to me the first time.'

'The first time? When was that?'

'After you came to the apartment and stayed. I told you about Lemall seeing you at the door.'

'But you made up a story to explain my visit, you said.'

'Roland only pretended to believe me. He is a suspicious man. He went to your studio to confirm his suspicions about us. When he didn't find you there he came back in a rage.'

'*Bon Dieu* – you never told me this. What did he do?'

'I was in the kitchen preparing lunch when he got back to the apartment – he burst in shouting and dragged me by the arm into the bedroom. I thought he'd gone mad or was drunk.'

'What did he do – did he beat you?'

Liliane said she'd been flung roughly on the bed and lay limp and terrified while Roland ripped her clothes off. She shut her eyes and bit her knuckle when he spread her legs – she felt the bed dip under her as his weight came on it. He was on his knees between her legs.

'No, no more . . .' she moaned, 'I beg you . . .'

Roland lay heavily on her, she felt his thumbs pull her open, then he pushed in. 'No, Roland, no,' she'd cried, but he was already riding her fast. And sooner than she thought possible he was in the grip of ecstatic convulsions – he gushed his fury into her.

Two minutes later he was off her and standing by the bedside, zipping his trousers and buckling his belt. He told her that if she went with the photographer again he'd give them both reason to regret it. Then he flipped her over on her stomach and gave her a resounding slap on her bare bottom. She squealed. Roland said he was hungry and ordered her to the kitchen to get his lunch.

Pierre-Raymond listened with great interest to these revelations and tried to visualise the scene. He could see Liliane lying on her back with parted legs and the tatters of her torn clothing hanging from her. He could see the boyfriend with the moustache like a Mexican bandit kneeling over her, face furious and stiff part ready to jab into her.

At this crucial point in Pierre-Raymond's thoughts the memory of the actual bed intruded – that bed on which Liliane had been abused and ravished. That strange construction of dark wood and gilded iron with the fake brocade curtains and gold tassels. It was impossible to imagine any act of passion being staged there on that tasteless horror, whether of love or of hatred.

Nevertheless, that was what Liliane wished him to believe had taken place. And she wanted him to understand it was his fault. The smacking and ravaging were because he had been permitted to stay all night while Roland was away.

'The man is a barbarian,' he said, 'you must never go back to him, I forbid it!'

He stooped for a moment to get his arm around her thighs and pick her up. She was slender and light as he carried her across to the sofa.

'That's enough of staring out of windows for monsters who are not there,' he said, stripping off her clothes.

He arranged her full-length on the suede, he knelt beside her and kissed her pointed little breasts and her belly. She parted her thighs gracefully and raised one knee to let him admire her pretty *joujou*.

For a brunette she had little body hair. There was an upright and narrow strip of curls between her legs, neatly clipped, the lips of her *trésor* and her groin were smooth and bare. Pierre-Raymond bowed his head and rained kisses on her prettiness and explored with the tip of his tongue.

'I feel you truly adore me,' she sighed, her hand holding his nodding part which stuck stiffly out of his pyjamas.

'But of course,' he said, raising his head and straightening his back while he shed his pyjamas quickly.

Liliane's slender naked body was furiously exciting – however many times he'd seen it before. In the days when she worked for him he'd seen her naked every day. And caressed her pert little breasts and her neat round rump. Times without number he'd slid up into the long split of her fleshy mound.

Those days could come back again. He need only say yes – that was the message she was conveying to him. He stroked her slowly with sensitive fingertips and opened those pretty lips between her thighs. He was thinking hard about her unspoken proposition while he made her so wet that his fingers slid easily into her. She shook in little tremors of pleasure as he played with her.

'I've never been able to get you out of my mind,' she

sighed. 'I was insane to leave you, Pierre-Raymond.'

'*Je t'adore*, Lili,' he murmured.

'Why did I ever leave you?' she said. 'I've asked myself the question a thousand times. Was I ever in love with Roland? Was I deceiving myself?'

She was making it sound as if she and Pierre-Raymond had been desperately in love. This was starting to trouble him. The fact was she'd been his receptionist and secretary for a year or so, only that. Naturally, he had her knickers off when the occasion served – he was a man who could never resist a pretty woman. To tell the truth, he could never resist any woman, pretty or not.

Women are always beautiful, that was Pierre-Raymond's belief, *even when they're plain they're beautiful*.

At this instant, when his cherished part was standing up hard as a steel bar and his fingers were caressing Liliane's *joujou*, this was no time for a discussion of her feelings or her future affections.

He slid on top of her and she moaned and spread her legs wider. With well-practised fingers he steered the head of his pride to her waiting *joujou* and pushed strongly in. He was well mounted and his hands gripped her shoulders while he thrust in and out to a stately rhythm that made her squirm and gasp with pleasure.

The act of doing it to her brought back a memory. Or rather a dream he had forgotten. That night Joelle stayed with him after they'd been to the cinema. After he'd ravaged her thoroughly, he fell asleep and dreamed of Liliane.

It was the dream that was really a memory – of being with her in her own bedroom. More precisely, Roland Leduc's bedroom. She was naked and bending over with her hands flat on that bed with the fake brocade curtains and gold tassels. He was close behind her, trousers down around his ankles, hands on her hips.

As he slid into her he heard violent knocking at the door. It was Leduc trying to break in and stop them doing it. *So strange a dream*, Pierre-Raymond thought when he woke up. It seemed that he'd suffered an unconscious trace of guilt toward Leduc in the matter of enjoying his girlfriend. Which was surprising – guilt was not an emotion with which Pierre-Raymond was acquainted.

Here on the sofa there was no such consideration. Liliane had left Leduc, who was a brutal monster, and had rushed to him for aid and comfort. Just as he'd gone to her for solace and comfort in his heartbreak. And as all the world knows, there is no better way to comfort a woman than to make love to her. The ecstasy of orgasm dissolved sadness. Especially if it was repeated several times. Which he fully intended.

He heard the arousal in her voice as she moaned his name over and over again. Her slender legs were locked around his thighs, her loins were jerking up at him.

'*Je t'adore*, Pierre-Raymond,' she gasped, her mouth squashed against his mouth.

Her words pleased him. Although adoration was his due. He was Pierre-Raymond Becquet and every woman fell desperately in love with him when she felt his fifteen centimetres of stiff flesh inside her. He slid in and out confidently, this was what he did best, better than anyone in Paris – reduce women to whimpering ecstasy that made them adore him for ever.

He ignored a certain uneasiness in his mind – the question of what he would do about Liliane tomorrow morning.

He felt the climatic moment arrive in his belly and he thrust hard and fast. Liliane responded at once, pushing her smooth belly up at him, clawing her nails down his back and shrieking in her orgasm.

One in the eye for you, Roland, he said silently in his head, *what a pity you aren't really standing outside the building in the rain and gnawing your fingers in jealous pangs.*

The idea amused him, the brutal and deserted lover out in the street all night. Only a deranged animal would do what he had done – fling Liliane over his lap and rip away her knickers and thrust a hand between her thighs and probe her with harsh fingers. But it must be admitted the idea was not without interest.

There was that unforgettable morning he'd pushed Joelle Marot over the arm of this very sofa – on which he had just pleasured Liliane. The elegant Joelle face down over a sofa arm, with her frock up over her bottom. Without knickers, of course. Pierre-Raymond standing between her legs and keeping them apart while he felt her and gave her a good tousling – to cries of outrage.

Perhaps Roland Leduc had not been entirely bestial – but very clearly he was stupid and he had lost Liliane's affections. Not surprising, he was an ordinary sort of person, Leduc – and that bandit moustache was only an empty boast. Persons like him were totally unable to compete with Monsieur Ten-times.

By morning, Monsieur Moustache, Pierre-Raymond thought, *I'll have given more pleasure to this pretty woman with the charming little breasts than you've given her in the past twelve months. And I shall take more pleasure from her than you can imagine. I am Monsieur Ten-times. Adieu, Roland.*

When Liliane at last stopped kissing his face, he carried her naked into the bedroom. He left her for a moment while he went back for the bottle of cognac and then sat on the side of the bed to toast her. She looked delicious propped up on the pillows, her slender body fully revealed for him. Between his legs *Grandjean* lay limp, but not for long. He would leap upright again as soon as Pierre-Raymond ran his hand over Liliane's thigh.

'There is something else I must tell you about Roland,' said she. 'He'd already started to get his own back on you before he assaulted me tonight. He started after he became suspicious of us. When Lemall told him you'd been to see me.'

'He slapped you and ravished you, my poor *chérie* – the man is an animal.'

'He's a brute,' she agreed, 'and there's a lot you don't know about him – he's been to your studio more than once. When you weren't there. He made friends with your receptionist.'

'Impossible! She wouldn't have anything to do with him.'

'You are mistaken, *chéri*. Roland can be very charming when he wants to. He took delight in tormenting me by telling me how he took her to a bar and won her confidence.'

'No, he was lying. Valerie adores me,' he said confidently.

'He turned her against you – I'm amazed you haven't realised it yet. He told her that we broke his heart, you and I.'

'But this is ridiculous,' Pierre-Raymond exclaimed, 'I don't believe it – he invented this nonsense as psychological torture for you.'

Liliane shook her head.

'He was telling the truth,' she said, shaking her head. 'When he bragged about taking your Valerie to a hotel I held my hands over my ears – but he pulled them away and made me listen.'

243

'A hotel – now I'm absolutely certain he was lying!'

But there was a chilly sensation inside Pierre-Raymond's belly.

'She wouldn't go with him, the idea is absurd!' he said.

He didn't want to say it to Liliane but he was convinced that Valerie would never allow herself to be loved by a fumbler like Roland Leduc, not after the embraces of Pierre-Raymond Becquet. It was too preposterous to consider.

'He was gloating when he made me listen.' Liliane twisted the knife in the wound. 'He said she was a real woman with proper-sized breasts, not two peas on a plate. Oh, Pierre-Raymond, are my breasts too small?'

'They are delicious,' he assured her, kissing each of them in turn, 'what other lies did this madman tell you?'

'Were they lies ? He was very convincing. He said Valerie has dimples in her backside. And an oval mole on her belly. Is this true or did he make it up?'

'Lies, idiotic lies,' said Pierre-Raymond.

He hid his face in between Liliane's thighs, his hands under her to grasp the small round cheeks of her bottom.

The brutal monster with the Mexican moustache had carried out his threat to get even – he had defiled Valerie. Pierre-Raymond moaned at the thought of this animal kissing her heavy breasts, clumsy fingers groping between her thighs.

Why had Valerie permitted this atrocious person with the ugly moustache to lie on her belly and jab his vile *thing* into her? *Ah Dieu* – it was a betrayal as bitter as Claudia's desertion of him for the actress!

'He lied to you – he hasn't seen her naked,' he insisted.

But he knew different. He was desolate, his voice was muffled between Liliane's thighs. Nobody was going to get the better of Monsieur Ten-times, that was unthinkable. He flicked his tongue into Liliane's smooth groin – he was going to prove he was the *Seigneur*, the supreme overlord of the bedroom.

Lost Confidence Is Restored

At nine in the evening every table was taken on the terrace of the Deux Magots – and Pierre-Raymond strolling on the Boulevard St Germain saw Claudia sitting there with Janine Bonnard.

They had small cups of black coffee in front of them and they were chatting and smiling and touching hands from time to time. Some observers might have said they were an interesting couple, dark-haired Janine and yellow-blonde Claudia. Attractive women, one over thirty and the other under twenty. If a man could have them in his bed, both at the same time, it would be the supreme moment of his entire life!

Pierre-Raymond found the scene atrocious. To see Claudia with that woman reminded him of his suffering when she left him. His heart had been broken. For a moment, the night she came back to his apartment, he'd hoped she was his again. She told him about Janine and eventually, after endless absurd evasions, she'd let him make love to her.

But she was using him because of a quarrel with Janine and in the morning she'd left again. He hated her now for all the misery she'd caused him. He stared bleakly at the pair of them sitting at their table by the pavement, turned on his heel and strolled back the way he'd come. He didn't know if they saw him or not – and he didn't care.

He was angry and depressed. Seeing them together brought into his mind an image he hoped he'd got rid of, the image that set his jealousy blazing – Claudia and Janine in a department store changing room. Janine pressing Claudia against the wall with a hand up her skirt. Janine kissing Claudia while she stroked her blonde-haired *joujou*.

And that other image that haunted him after Claudia explained she was in love with the actress. Claudia naked and on her back on Janine's bed. Her long slender thighs apart, Janine's dark-haired head between them. Janine's tongue touching that darling bud and sending flickers of delight all through her. Claudia in orgasm moaning *je t'aime* to Janine.

How well he knew Claudia's perfect young body, and adored it. And what was bizarre, he knew Janine's body too. Not as a lover, of course. No mere man was allowed to touch her. He'd photographed her for theatre publicity as he had other actresses. But there was more than that – he and Janine shared a certain secret.

He had also photographed her naked, that was the secret. Not for publicity – she was a serious actress, not a Folies Bergères showgirl. She ordered pictures of herself naked to give to her lovers – young women, that went without saying.

She swore Pierre-Raymond to secrecy. And she made him promise to keep his hands to himself. And not to comment on her charms because she felt insulted when a man desired her, she said. She made him lock the studio door – then she stripped naked to pose for the camera.

He found the session even more exciting than he'd imagined it could be. Janine was tall and well shaped – she had presence, as actors say. Whether standing or sitting, she posed to advantage without self-consciousness or embarrassment for her nudity. The bulge was huge in the front of Pierre-Raymond's trousers.

He gazed at her nicely rounded breasts, all the more exciting because he wasn't allowed to touch them. As he took pictures he secretly admired her broad belly with its deep-set button. And he gloated silently over her brunette fleece.

He visualised himself touching it. And separating those curls to kiss the *trésor* they covered. At the mere thought, *Grandjean* throbbed and grew impossibly thicker.

Janine guessed what he was thinking. There was a gleam in her eyes, a subtle air of superiority about her. A message for him. *Yes, I'm allowing you see how beautiful and desirable I am, you miserable worm of a man – you are frantic to touch me, stiff as a steel bar in your underwear – you are drooling and panting to handle me and caress me – you would give everything you own for the opportunity to stick your ugly male thing into me – but you never will, Pierre-Raymond. Never.*

She posed artistically with her back to the camera, turning a little to look back over her shoulder with a haughty expression – a pose that showed the beauties of her back and her bottom and the hint of a breast. She lay on her side on a fur rug upon the floor, a hand supporting her head, a half-smile on her face – and her thighs together. The pose displayed her breasts well, and it revealed the richness of her brunette fleece.

She sat on the Indonesian wickerwork settee with one foot on the floor, the other leg drawn up, hands clasped on her shin. A pose to spread her thighs and show off her plump-lipped *joujou* to perfection. A pose that very nearly caused Pierre-

Raymond to spurt his pent-up passion into his underwear as he focused his camera.

When he'd seen all of Janine's body he formed a conclusion as to how she would make love. She was very desirable, all of her, and her thighs were her best feature, in his opinion. They were strong, it was evident she exercised regularly and took dancing lessons to keep fit and healthy.

In bed she would be a vigorous lover, Pierre-Raymond was sure of that. He dreamed of those strong thighs of hers around his waist while he lay on her belly. A dream was all it would ever be, alas. Janine Bonnard was not for him. Or any other man.

Needless to say, he spun out the photo session for as long as he could. When it was finished, Janine dressed in front of him, not in the least concerned if he was looking at her or not. The devastating truth was that the great Pierre-Raymond Becquet did not exist sexually for her. He was a cipher, a nothing.

Happily for his peace of mind he didn't realise that. When at last she departed with a cool kiss on his cheek, he rushed into the darkroom, his fingers dragging his zipper open. Out sprang his fifteen centimetres of hard flesh, desperate for relief.

'Yes, yes, yes!' Pierre-Raymond moaned while his clasping hand raced up and down his straining shaft. 'Yes, Janine, for you!'

He stared wide-eyed and open-mouthed at his massively swollen part as the muscles of his belly clenched in sudden spasm – and he reeled a step backward to the spurt of his sticky passion.

'Janine – bitch!' he gasped. 'I want you!'

It was only a year ago, that unforgettable day that Janine Bonnard posed naked in his studio. Now a bitter irony had intruded into the situation. Darling Claudia, whom he'd loved to desperation, had the privilege of touching and kissing Janine's body and giving her shattering little orgasms.

And Janine now enjoyed what was rightfully his, the pleasure of embracing Claudia naked and doing delicious things to her.

His mind filled with rage, Pierre-Raymond wandered aimlessly, from the Boulevard St Germain to the Boulevard St Michel and on past the Luxembourg Gardens. He found a bar and sat for half an hour drinking a glass of marc and then a second glass while he pondered his grievances.

When he left the bar he decided he'd done enough walking and made for the nearest taxi rank.

There was nothing he could do about Claudia and his anger had now become focused on Valerie. She had betrayed him with a man who wished him harm. It was intolerable, she must be confronted at once and sacked from her job. He would have no traitors in his employ!

Valerie lived impossibly far away. He'd never had reason to go there, but he knew the address – it was in a street by the Parc Montsouris. *It would have been better to take the Metro*, he thought glumly, the taxi fare would be outrageous. But it was out of the question to worry about money at a time of crisis.

The taxi dropped him outside her building at last. The driver glared in contempt at the tip Pierre-Raymond added to the fare. But then, all Paris taxi drivers despise their clients, whether they tip them or not.

The apartment was on the second floor. Pierre-Raymond ran up the stairs and knocked dramatically on her door. Valerie opened it with a puzzled look on her face – without a word he put his hands on her shoulders and pushed her back into the apartment. Then kicked the door shut behind him.

The time was after eleven and she was in a pink dressing gown and flat slippers, evidently on her way to bed when he arrived. But that was lost on him, his mind was too full of grievance.

'What are you doing?' she gasped, resisting being pushed any further into the apartment.

Certainly she had cause for alarm – his face was flushed dark red and his mouth was set in a grimace of anger. Without saying a word he forced her back against the wall and pinned her there with his belly against hers. Without any consideration for what he was doing, he opened her dressing gown and got a knee between her legs to force them apart.

This wasn't what he'd come to her apartment for – it had been very far from his thoughts. He hated her because she had let herself be defiled by Leduc. But when he was alone with any woman his automatic reactions took over. He was furious with Valerie, he was almost incandescent with rage, he wanted to rip her clothes off and slap her bottom – as Leduc had done to Liliane.

But what happened was that his hand darted under her nightie. And up between her plump thighs.

She wriggled and twisted to escape, but couldn't. His fingers touched and felt the fleshy lips between her legs – then he was clasping her warm hairy *lapin* in the palm of his hand.

'You're drunk,' she accused him, pushing at his shoulders to get him away from her.

'I never want to see you again,' he said, 'I know everything. You are dismissed without notice or pay – you are never to show your face at my studio again.'

'Have you gone mad?' she said. 'What is the matter with you, Pierre-Raymond?'

'You've taken sides against me with that violent maniac Leduc. You went to a hotel with him and let him make love to you. This is a gross deception – it is unforgivable. I hate you.'

'Who has been telling you these wicked lies? I've been to no hotel with him, I assure you!' she said quickly.

'Next thing you'll tell me you've never talked to him – never been to a bar with him!'

'Yes, he bought me a drink and told me a story about how you turned his girlfriend against him – the one who was working for you before me. Liliane Bonchamp. They've lived together for two years, he said. While he was away you went to his apartment and made love to her on his bed. You told me you were ill.'

'The man is paranoid,' Pierre-Raymond said sharply, 'you were wrong to listen to these delusions. And it was worse than wrong to let him do things to you – it was shameful.'

'Someone has deceived you, and it wasn't me – he talked and I listened and that's as far as it went. There was nothing else.'

Could Pierre-Raymond believe her? She displayed anxiety, but there was that slight touch of mockery about her mouth and eyes that made him unsure of her. To be unsure was to be uneasy. And vulnerable.

'If I *had* let him,' she went on, 'not that I did, but suppose that I had, why should that concern you? You never wanted me, you use me for your pleasure when we're alone in the studio, it means nothing to you.'

The feel of her *joujou* in his palm was warm and comforting. A man would have to be a fool not to stroke it given the chance. Annoyed though Pierre-Raymond was with her, he had the distinct impression that her thighs had relaxed a little.

'Use you? But I adore you!' he declared. 'It's you who use me. I do not object to that – my destiny is to give pleasure to women. All I demand in return is a degree of loyalty – and this has been sadly lacking, Valerie.'

He was hardly aware that his fingers had separated the fleshy lips between her thighs – the action was automatic for him. She breathed a little faster and stared into his eyes.

'You adore everyone,' she said, 'it's worthless.'

She forced her hand behind his belt, down into his trousers to grasp his male part. It was stiff, of course – despite other matters on his mind, feeling Valerie had easily elevated him to his favourite condition of strength and readiness.

But she did not mean to submit without making her displeasure with his abrupt appearance known. She jerked his cherished part up and down so violently that his thoughts were concentrated on it uncomfortably. Everything else was sidetracked.

'All your adoration comes to is getting this *thing* inside any woman you happen to be with,' she accused him. 'Speak the truth for once – admit it.'

Pierre-Raymond had never considered candour a suitable basis for a satisfying relationship with a pretty woman. Even if they said they wanted to know the truth, they never really meant it. And anyway, too much truth put little wrinkles around the eyes. There was no point in continuing this discussion with Valerie.

His mouth found hers in a commanding kiss to silence her. It occurred to his conscious mind that she was almost naked – just a short and flimsy nightie. His hands slid upward over her

254

smooth belly, his palms on her warm skin made her sigh.

He clasped her heavy round breasts – he felt them and stroked them, he fingered their buds. She unzipped his trousers now and pulled out his stiff part. She massaged it firmly and rubbed it against her belly. And still they kissed, mouths open, a never-to-end kiss of lips clinging together, tongue licking tongue.

After a seeming eternity he took a half-step back and raised her nightie up to her armpits and stared at her heavy breasts – her naked body aroused him to the point where he scarcely knew what he was saying.

She understood this well – her feet moved apart so her thighs could open and let him see what lay between them. But it was at her breasts he gazed, his hands playing with their massiveness.

'Ah, Valerie,' he sighed, *'je t'adore, chérie.* But I can never forgive you for what you have done.'

'Does it matter?' she asked. 'You said you never want to see me again. It is pointless to talk of forgiveness.'

Pierre-Raymond murmured and sighed wordlessly as he bent down to kiss her breasts. He licked them, not just the dark red buds but the whole expanse of warm flesh, all that desirable springy female bounty. He began to moan faintly – Valerie knew then how to change the situation to her benefit.

She sank to her knees and shrugged off her dressing gown. She hoisted her nightie over her head and threw it aside – raising her arms high made her breasts lift and bob, eliciting sighs of joy from Pierre-Raymond as he watched them sway and bounce.

She was down on her knees offering him her breasts – they were just about the right height. He bent his knees outwards a little to place his long length between them and he pressed her sumptuous delights together with both shaking hands to contain *Grandjean* snugly.

'Valerie, Valerie,' he babbled, thrusting strongly into the soft fleshy pouch he'd formed.

She stared up into his flushed face, pleased by the response she'd provoked. She pulled her shoulders back and straightened her spine – she reached around to grip the cheeks of his bottom through his trousers and squeeze. She slid her fingers down the crease between the cheeks to find his knot and press it hard.

'That's what you want,' she said mockingly, 'you want to make love to my breasts. That's why you came here, isn't it? Nobody else you know has a pair as big and bouncy as mine. You need me – but why are you so angry with me?'

What she said was not entirely true. Monique Marot had a pair just as big, if not bigger, than Valerie's. Pierre-Raymond had been allowed the privilege of seeing them bare in his darkroom. And Monique's were bouncier than Valerie's – because she was seventeen and Valerie was twenty-five. But Monique's were not available to him and Valerie's were.

'Your breasts are magnificent,' he panted as his loins jerked quickly to and fro, 'you must never leave me, Valerie, never.'

The expression that made him uneasy was on her face while she stared down to watch *Grandjean*'s red-purple head popping out of the cleft of her plumpness and darting back down.

'One minute you say you never want to see me again – then the next minute you're begging me to stay – it's confusing,' Valerie said, her eyebrows raised, 'so what do you really want, Pierre-Raymond?'

He was too involved in his sensations to catch the mockery in her question. And a moment later he cried out and shook on legs turned suddenly rubbery as his hot desire spurted up her chest, right to her throat.

When he had control of himself again and his knees were firm, Valerie stood up and took his hand to lead him to her bedroom – his wet part hanging limply out of his open trousers. He stood silent, his thoughts confused, while she removed his jacket and sat him on the bed to take off his shoes and then his trousers.

He hated her for her deception with Roland Leduc. But she was so loving, so compliant with his desires. He lay on his back on the bed while she stripped him – shirt and socks and underwear. He was silent and quiescent, enjoying her attentions – watching as she used his silk underwear to wipe away the creamy trickle from between her breasts down to her belly.

'Which is it you really want, Pierre-Raymond?' she asked him again. 'Am I sacked or am I to stay?'

She was certain she knew the answer – she wouldn't have asked the question otherwise. He had this obsession with her breasts, he liked to watch them bounce under her clothes in the office. She moved about more than her work required just to make them sway and roll and jump.

By this simple action she could make Pierre-Raymond grow hard any time of the day. This she had discovered early on in their working relationship. It amused her, making him taut inside his trousers, glancing covertly at him to see that straining bulge under the cloth.

She could have wrapped her dressing gown around her when they moved away from the apartment door, but she'd deliberately left it lying on the floor. And sitting on the edge of the bed while he lay on it – this ensured he was unable to take his eyes away from her naked body and her oversized breasts.

At heart he was an uncomplicated person, she decided. For all his apparent worldliness and sophistication, the truth was that big breasts threw him into a condition of sexual frenzy.

Only five minutes had passed since he'd climaxed on her chest – yet seeing her naked and being undressed by her had made him stiff again. His susceptibility was comic, she thought – though it was extremely useful to know about.

She almost laughed to note his rapid progress from staring at her bare breasts to touching them – his hand was gliding around and over her rotundities. And it was no surprise that his other hand lay on her thigh, high up. Would he use her breasts for a second time, she speculated – or have her flat on her back with her legs apart? He was very predictable in that she knew what he'd do, but very unpredictable in how he'd do it.

What was it he really wanted, she'd asked. He hadn't answered her question directly. Not in words, but between his thighs his male part was answering for him, standing up hard and ready.

'I want to believe you, Valerie,' he said seriously, his hand sliding slowly up her thigh toward her brunette fleece, 'truly, I want to believe you haven't turned against me and betrayed me with the madman Leduc. Or in other ways – it would devastate me to think you could be disloyal.'

'Roland Leduc hasn't laid a hand on me,' she assured him, and she sounded very convincing.

But on the other hand Liliane had sounded convincing when she repeated Leduc's account of dimples in Valerie's bottom. And an oval mole on her belly.

That small brown mole – which Pierre-Raymond had the pleasure of seeing at that very moment. A beauty spot on the smooth skin of her belly. He did more than look at it, he touched it with a fingertip and he wondered and wondered about her and Leduc.

He had never seen Roland Leduc in person, only a framed photo of him when he went to his apartment for consolation from Liliane. The man with a Mexican bandit moustache – how absurd to imagine him lying with his head between Valerie's thighs and that silly moustache brushing her fleece.

Perhaps Leduc lied to Liliane about his success with Valerie. Perhaps Liliane made it up herself so Pierre-Raymond would hate Leduc and take her back. Who could say what went on in women's minds? Only a fool would even try to guess.

Yes, but suppose Leduc had managed to get Valerie's knickers off and felt these plump lips Pierre-Raymond was now fingering. He knew about the little oval mole on her belly – logic said he had plunged his ugly *thing* into her and spurted his desire.

Then in his mind Pierre-Raymond shrugged. If Roland Leduc had been allowed to lie on Valerie's belly, then she must have been badly disappointed – she was accustomed to the daily attentions of Monsieur Ten-times. The outcome was obvious, she had given herself back to Pierre-Raymond.

There was no awkward complication of being in love with her – he had an affection for her which was based on free access to her sumptuous body. Only the present mattered, not the past. In the present, as his fingers on her warm *joujou* assured him, her beautiful well-fleshed body was his to enjoy.

That was an end to philosophising – there was no more to say. Inspired by this useful conclusion, he pulled her down onto the bed beside him and rolled her onto her back. He trailed his wet tongue over her sweet-scented skin, starting with her breasts, ending at her knees.

Valerie found it highly satisfactory. She put her hands under her head on the pillow and lay comfortably – her bountiful body fully exposed for his admiration. Her legs were well parted now to reveal the delicate pale hollows of her groin and the long fleshy groove of her *joujou*.

'You must make up your mind, Pierre-Raymond,' she said lazily, 'do you want me to stay with you or not?'

No doubt of it, Valerie was superbly well made for the act of love. If he compared her with Liliane, for example – Liliane had pert little spiky breasts and a waist small enough to span with your hands. If he compared her with Joelle, her body was dieted and exercised thin, with elegant small breasts and narrow hips.

In fashion they had the clear advantage, in bed they couldn't equal Valerie. Roland Leduc had told Liliane that Valerie was a real woman. with proper-sized breasts. He was absolutely right, of course – but it did not necessarily follow he'd seen Valerie naked. Or had his unwelcome hands on her breasts. Or so Pierre-Raymond hastily said to himself.

'But of course you must stay, Valerie,' he murmured as he was kissing the satin skin inside her thighs, 'I adore you.'

His fingers caressed the brown-haired delight that was fully exposed to him by the way her legs lay open.

'You like the feel of me,' she said, 'I know that well enough – but is your confidence in me restored, Pierre-Raymond – or do you still believe I plotted against you with a stranger?'

'I never really doubted you,' he said, with a total disregard for the truth, 'I let myself be confused for a moment, that was stupid of me. But in my heart I always knew I could rely on you completely. Forgive my imbecility, I adore you.'

If at that moment Pierre-Raymond had been less concerned

with her enticing breasts and belly and parted thighs, he would have noticed a gleam in her velvet-brown eyes, a corner of her mouth turning up in a half-grin.

'I adore you also, Pierre-Raymond,' she assured him, 'and you can prove how completely you trust me by doubling my salary.'

He couldn't decide whether she meant what she said or whether she was making a joke. He raised his head to grin at her and at once she pushed him over to lie on his back. For a large woman she moved surprisingly fast – she was on her knees over him and had his uprearing part in her clenched fist – holding it poised between her straddling thighs.

'You agree my idea is a good one, to prove that confidence is fully restored between us?' she said, fist jerking up and down his throbbing length. 'Surely you meant what you said?'

He could see down in between their naked bodies – her breasts hung touching his chest, her plump belly was five centimetres from his, the tip of his cherished shaft was only a centimetre from the pink open lips between her legs. He moaned and lunged upward in urgent need to get inside her. But her hand held him prisoner while its jerky rhythm was carrying him ever nearer to the moment of no return.

'*Je t'adore*, Valerie' he gasped, 'fifty per cent more, yes?'

'Double,' she said firmly and she put her face down to his to lick his mouth.

'Sixty per cent more,' he babbled.

She was rubbing the head of his straining part against smooth slippery flesh – he was being held back at the very entrance to Paradise. A hard push would take him in. But Valerie's hand was wrapped around his long stiff shaft and she prevented him.

'Double,' she said simply.

'All right then – double!' he shrieked.

She chuckled and guided him into her – he felt the smooth and slippery cling of her *joujou* as it engulfed him completely. But lying there on his back beneath a woman, he was reminded of the occasion when Joelle came to his apartment one Saturday morning and this gave him an uneasy fear that he was being exploited.

That would be intolerable. He was Pierre-Raymond Becquet, the very superior lover, not a gigolo, not a plaything for women.

But he realised it was different this time with Valerie. She wasn't kneeling over him as Joelle had, she wasn't bouncing up and down on him as if he were an upright post to impale herself on. Valerie was lying on him, her belly on his, her big breasts flattened on his chest. She held his head between her hands and kissed him while she let him take the full weight of her body.

'Valerie, *chérie*,' he murmured, certain that this was entirely different from the Saturday morning when Joelle ravaged him for her own pleasure. Valerie was making love to him, not using him for her own gratification – she was using her body to pleasure him. She truly adored him, he thought in a haze of affectionate desire and sensation.

Her bottom was moving rhythmically, only a few centimetres at each stroke, but enough to massage his deeply embedded part and cause him sensations of delight. He panted and squirmed beneath her – the sudden thought that he was being made love to in just the way he himself made love to women – even this couldn't stop the tremors of pleasure that shook him.

His hands were on the soft round cheeks of her bottom to

urge her on. In another moment he knew he would fountain his passion into her and the foreknowledge added to his excitement.

Her broad and smiling face was just above his, her hands were on either side of his head, compelling him to stare up at her.

'Now that we adore each other again I shall take good care of you,' she said.

'Ah . . .' he wailed as he felt the starburst in his belly.

Ecstasy was overwhelming him, he saw her smile but was unable to discern the mockery in it.

Uneasy Dispositions

Two nights after the understanding with Valerie, Pierre-Raymond was in his bed asleep and dreaming pleasantly, when he was woken by the sound of the doorbell ringing.

It was not of plump-breasted Valerie that he was dreaming, it was of Marie-Rose Fabien. More precisely, of her long string of black pearls. And the day in his studio-office when she'd wound that long strand of pearls around his most cherished part.

What a marvel of a sight it was – his fifteen centimetres of stiff flesh wrapped in black pearls, from its dark-curled root to its red-purple head. And the sensations – the pressure on his flesh of round smooth pearls! At almost the first movement of Marie-Rose's hand on him he had spurted wildly.

The doorbell was ringing and ringing. He sat up in bed in the dark. *Grandjean* was standing fiercely hard between his thighs – sticking out of his pyjama trousers without shame. Half asleep, half awake, Pierre-Raymond slipped his hand down inside the bed and clasped his stiff part to check if it was wrapped in pearls or not – the dream had been vivid. And very exciting.

He felt no pearls, only warm flesh. He sighed and looked at the luminous dial of his bedside clock – the time was twenty past two. In the morning. Who the devil came calling at such an unlikely time?

He switched on the light and climbed out of bed with another sigh. Twenty past two, he'd been asleep for an hour and half – it was atrocious to be disturbed like this. He struggled into his crimson silk dressing gown and went to answer the door – he didn't trouble to put on his beautiful maroc leather slippers – he had to stop the unwanted caller ringing that confounded bell before everybody in the entire building woke up. Or there would complaints in the morning.

He opened the door enough to put his head out and look around it. Between bed and door a dreadful thought had occurred to him – Roland Leduc could be outside, waiting to smash his fist into Pierre-Raymond's handsome face the instant he saw it.

After a night at Pierre-Raymond's apartment, Liliane had expected to stay almost permanently. But that was much too inconvenient. Far too restricting an arrangement. Besides that, if an enraged Leduc arrived, bent on revenge, and found Liliane in residence, *bon Dieu*! The outcome could be catastrophic.

With all this in mind, Pierre-Raymond had persuaded her to go to stay with her mother. That was out in the suburbs, somewhere beyond Boissy. Liliane had only a few francs so he gave her all the cash he had in the apartment – about as much as she used to earn in a month with him.

'I can't bear to leave you,' she insisted.

'Only until Roland calms down,' he answered, 'a month perhaps will do. Unless he is the resentful type who bears a grudge for a long time. But when it's safe you can come back to Paris.'

Naturally, she understood that to mean she would move back in with Pierre-Raymond. Which was not at all what he intended – as ever, female logic was different.

Pierre-Raymond stared with apprehension round his door, ready to dart back in very quickly if a fist came at his head. But it was not a fuming Roland Leduc standing there with murder in his heart. It was Claudia Deneuve at his door. Beautiful Claudia.

'Ah, another lovers' quarrel,' he said, opening the door wide for her, 'you need a place to stay tonight. I understand – what a time to arrive! But come in, *chérie.*'

He was stupefied when she flung herself into his arms sobbing and clung to him desperately. His proud part was still long and stiff under his dressing gown, the dream of Marie-Rose's pearls was having an enduring effect. The feel of Claudia pressing her body against him in her grief increased his nervous excitement.

She was in a thin white summer frock and a little jacket with patch pockets. The jacket was open and as she wore nothing much under her frock Pierre-Raymond knew there could be only a layer or two of silk between her beautiful girlish belly and his hard upstanding part. It was a thought to bring delight.

'What on earth is the matter?' he asked, stroking her back.

'I am so unhappy,' she said between sobs.

He prised her loose and, with an arm around her waist, took her to his sitting room and poured her a glass of cognac. He sat on the grey sofa with her and put an arm about her shoulders while he encouraged her to drink. She sipped and sobbed and gradually became calm.

'I have left Janine forever,' she said dramatically.

'That I guessed. What caused it this time, another lover from her past?'

'The same one,' Claudia said miserably, 'Lucienne Boucher – I told you about her before.'

'Ah yes, the dark-haired beanpole, I remember now. How sad.'

'Tonight I saw them making love – *ah quelle horreur*!'

'Really?' said Pierre-Raymond, very interested to hear more. 'Where – how?'

'Janine is in a new play. I wasn't there tonight because I've seen it twice. And that dreadful Lucienne was there both times. When Janine wasn't home by midnight I knew somehow she was with Lucienne. I went to her apartment.'

'Lucienne's? How did you know where she lives?'

'It wasn't difficult – I found it in Janine's address book by the phone. With her number and her birthday. She lives near the Place Port Royal.'

'You went there to confirm your fears? My poor Claudia.'

'Her room is on the second floor of an old building. There is a fire escape – I went up and saw them through the window. They were making love – I thought I would die when I saw it.'

'Making love,' Pierre-Raymond said very thoughtfully, 'Janine and the tall thin Lucienne. But how? Can you explain it to me, a mere man with no understanding of these delicate moments.'

Claudia sniffled for a moment and took another sip of cognac.

'Janine was sitting on the edge of a divan bed with her skirt pulled right up her legs and her knees well apart,' she said at last. 'Lucienne was on her knees in front of her – with a hand between her legs. They were kissing – and then Janine fell back on the divan and shrieked, the way she always does.'

'Ah,' Pierre-Raymond said softly, visualising the fascinating scene, 'a dreadful moment for you, my poor darling. Did you run away then?'

'I wanted to, but I was so dumbfounded I couldn't move. I saw Janine pull the beanpole down on the divan and tear her clothes off – Janine who tells me a thousand times a day she adores me. What lies it all was!'

'You saw her making love to the thin woman?'

'She stripped her and had her on her back and forced her legs wide open. She's painfully thin, Lucienne, she has breasts like two boiled eggs and thighs like broom sticks – and yet Janine's hands were all over her. And her tongue too. It was more than I could bear! I stumbled down the fire escape and ran away along the street sobbing my heart out. Janine has destroyed me.'

Pierre-Raymond spoke words of comfort and poured another cognac for them both and stroked Claudia's back in consolation. Half an hour of that and the drama had reached its natural end. She said she was weary and she needed to lie down and sleep. He gave her the bedroom and tried to settle on the sofa.

There was not the least chance of sleep for him. His mind was full of the scenes Claudia had described to him – Janine on her back in orgasm on a divan bed while the thin woman on her knees attended to her pleasure. To be truthful, Pierre-Raymond's male part had never gone limp again after his dream of black pearls. He was hoping Claudia would recovered from her miseries by the next morning to let him get into bed with her.

He was holding *Grandjean* in his hand to feel his aggressively strong twitching – and a natural train of thought reminded him of the morning when he persuaded Liliane to go to stay with her mother out in the far suburbs. She'd been reluctant, but agreed eventually – though she was determined to make him miss her and want her to come back soon.

It happened here in the sitting room, her suitcase packed and waiting by the apartment door for him to carry down to a taxi. They stood embracing, mouths locked in a fond kiss, arms around each other – Liliane pushed at him to make him walk backward to the sofa. The pressure of her belly and thighs against him gave him sensations so delicious that there was an instant bulge in his trousers.

He let her press him down on the sofa, thinking she was going to straddle him. But she knelt between his feet and flicked his zip open – his hard-risen part jerked out like Jack-in-the-Box. Liliane stared into his flushed face, her eyes gleaming and the tip of her tongue showing between her lips.

'You'll miss me when I'm away,' she murmured.

She bowed her head and took the plum-purple head of *Grandjean* into her wet mouth.

'Lili, Lili,' Pierre-Raymond moaned to the flick of her agile tongue. His ecstasy came fast and he spurted into her mouth in shuddering spasms.

That was only thirty-six hours ago – now he lay in frustration on his sofa, dying to make love to Claudia. Or Liliane. Or Valerie. Or Joelle, or Monique. Or any woman he knew. And very certainly to Janine Bonnard, though there was no chance of that.

But suppose a miracle had occurred the day she posed naked in his studio? Impossible, of course, but suppose Janine had been overcome by his natural charm – and intrigued by his reputation as Monsieur Ten-times. To the point where her views on men were set aside temporarily. Her sexual preferences put into abeyance for the time being . . . ?

Sitting on the wickerwork settee, one foot on the floor, one foot up on the seat and her knees splayed wide. Her plump dark-haired *lapin* beautifully displayed between her strong thighs. A picture to give to her intimate friends – but it was also meant as a taunt for Pierre-Raymond. But it had become an invitation. Janine was asking to be shown what men do to women.

Pierre-Raymond would be on his knees in an instant, his hands on those strong thighs of hers while he kissed her *lapin* with a fervour that flattered her and made her gasp in unexpected joy. He'd pull her down from the settee and turn her right around to present her broad back to him. And the firm round cheeks of her bottom – *ah Dieu*, what rapture!

Janine on her knees, arms on the cushioned seat, superb round bare bottom revealed to him. His proud length jerked stiffly as he edged close behind her and felt those cheeks. Her knees were apart on the floor – Janine was offering him all he desired. He was sighing continuously, in near ecstasy already. Between her magnificent thighs he saw her dark-haired mound and the pouting lips – he stroked them with light, quick touches. Janine's head turned sideways to see him over her shoulder – her eyes shining in surprise and pleasure.

He bent down to kiss her round bottom, but he was too aroused to delay any longer. He gripped her by the hips while he thrust his loins forward and pressed the head of his fifteen centimetres to soft lips. Slowly and carefully he started to push into her wet warmth.

Was he the first man to slide into Janine? Was *Grandjean* the first proud male part to penetrate her? Presumably the

271

answer was yes, but it was impossible ever to be certain. She may have opened her legs for a man when she was a girl – and hadn't much liked what he did, therefore deciding never to risk it again. With other women she knew where she was.

But Janine had surrendered to the charm of Monsieur Tentimes and his beloved friend was inside her and his arms were around her waist to hold her while he rode her in a stately rhythm. It did not last very long, his self-control – the occasion was too overwhelming. The feel of her soft flesh holding his hard flesh was too exciting – he started to butt at her like a wild goat.

She was completely open to him, she was yielding and willing. She braced herself to withstand his hard thrusting, moaning and sighing all the while. He stabbed faster into her slipperiness, he gave a great gasp as he spurted, his belly smacking against her bare bottom, his hands beneath her to squeeze her breasts.

Janine's head jerked up and she shrieked shrilly – she always did that in her moments of orgasm. He knew because Claudia told him so.

Naturally, this intensity of yearning and imagining could not endure for long. Under his blanket on the sofa Pierre-Raymond's beloved part bucked in his clasping hand and jetted his essence into his silk pyjamas. *Ah Janine, you bitch* he sighed brokenly, *that's what you should have let me do to you in my studio.*

Sometimes Fate deals with us even more ironically than usual. Pierre-Raymond's desire was assuaged by fantasies of Janine and he was able to compose himself for sleep at last. But before he dropped off, pyjamas sticking wetly to him, the door opened and into the sitting room came Claudia.

She moved cautiously across the room in the dark and sat down on the edge of the sofa.

'Are you awake?' she asked.

It wasn't pitch-dark, the curtains were open and enough light came in from the street for him to make out she was wearing her bra and knickers. Like the last time she slept in his apartment – and on that memorable occasion he'd been able to talk her out of her underwear. He'd taken her knickers off with his teeth.

'I'm awake,' he answered, 'can't you sleep, *chérie* '

'There's something I haven't told you yet,' she said. 'I know I was a fool to believe Janine when she said she loved me.'

Pierre-Raymond said nothing. He took her hand and held it to comfort her.

'She never told me you'd been her lover,' Claudia said with a tremor in her voice, 'she kept that a secret from me.'

'Did Janine tell you we were lovers?' he asked – he was very puzzled by all this.

'She showed me the pictures you took of her – when I saw them I knew straight away. Till then I'd been completely taken in by her – she insisted she despised men and wouldn't allow one near her. That's what she tells everybody – and I believed her. Then she showed me the photos with your name in the corner.'

'But did she *say* we'd been lovers?' he asked curiously.

'She denied it, naturally – but anyone can see from the poses that she was crazy about the photographer and ready for him to make love to her.'

Pierre-Raymond remembered very well how Janine posed that day she came to his studio for nude pictures. Lying on her side on a fur rug with her legs together. Very provocative. The best of them – the most deliberately erotic one – was when she sat upon the wicker settee with one foot up on it, legs well splayed and hands holding her shin. A perfect view of the plump dark-haired *lapin* between her thighs.

The reason he recalled it so well was because of what he'd done after Claudia admitted she was in love with Janine Bonnard. The very next day in the studio he took the negatives from the file and made enlargements. He was tormented by jealousy and haunted by images in his mind of Claudia with Janine.

Janine undressing in the changing room before the long mirror and asking if Claudia thought her breasts were starting to sag. Pressing Claudia to the wall with a hand up her skirt while kissing her. And in bed together the first time, Janine's hands stroking Claudia's body. Over her breasts and between her legs.

Claudia lying on her back with legs wide apart, Janine's head between her thighs, tongue busy with her pretty blonde *joujou* – that darling soft peach Pierre-Raymond adored. And then Claudia playing with something he'd been allowed to see but could never touch, Janine's dark-haired *lapin*. This was why he'd made large prints of the photo where she sat naked on the wicker settee.

He'd stared at the print for the longest time – he was trying to imagine what it was like to kiss those plump lips. *Grandjean* rose to his full height of fifteen centimetres and throbbed with hot passion – he knew exactly what he'd do if he was ever permitted to penetrate that forbidden delight. He'd ravage it into total submission.

But in the end, naked bodies were only bodies. Pierre-

Raymond had seen many, many naked female bodies. One thing he knew for sure was that the facial expression of the sitter made pictures interesting or boring. After all, everyone had seen breasts and bellies and patches of curls.

The emotions on the model's face made photos exciting or not. And Janine's expression during the session had been disdainful, haughty, proud – the expression that said *look at me but don't imagine you can touch me*.

He'd understood it perfectly – Janine was telling him that he was a miserable and insensitive male creature beneath contempt, especially that length of stiff flesh twitching in his trousers at the sight of her naked body. She flaunted herself to let him see that never in a thousand years would he enjoy the privilege of sliding his nasty male thing into her beautiful *joujou*.

It was amusing that Claudia had misread that look on Janine's face and assumed she and he had been lovers. He wanted to laugh sarcastically, but then he'd have to explain – and he certainly wasn't going to do Janine a favour. Claudia might have a change of heart if he told her he'd never been between Janine's legs.

'It was a long time ago,' he said judiciously, 'before I knew you, *chérie*. I'd forgotten I took those pictures.'

A total lie, of course, but it served his purpose very well.

'I know it was before we met,' she said and squeezed his hand, 'I found the date you always put on the back of your portraits. But that didn't change anything. I realised Janine was false at that moment. When I saw her tonight with Lucienne it wasn't the complete shock it might have been.'

Pierre-Raymond's hands were above the blanket, but beneath it his beloved part was hard and throbbing. Especially when in the half-dark he made out Claudia reaching behind her to unhook her bra. She stood up beside the sofa, her long thighs a pale gleam in the darkness as she slipped her little knickers off.

Hastily he got his silk pyjama jacket off and flicked them over the sofa back onto the floor – it would be embarrassing for Claudia to find a wet patch and realise what had happened. Then she was under the blanket with him, kissing him. He stroked her smooth sides and back, he cupped her breasts in his eager hands.

'What an idiot I was to be taken in so easily by that woman,' she said. 'I ought to have listened to you, Pierre-Raymond, you were absolutely right about her the night I was here. You told me she envied my body and wanted to exploit me.'

Feeling and caressing Claudia's naked body had thrown Pierre-Raymond into such rapture that he hardly heard what she said to him. But it seemed appropriate to murmur *je t'adore* as he slid his hand between her long thighs to touch her blonde beauty.

'I know,' she murmured back, 'you never let me down, *chéri*. If you can forgive me and take me back, I promise to listen to you in future. I'll never hurt you or disappoint you again.'

Such words were immensely pleasing to him, though he reminded himself that darling Claudia was eighteen years old – and *never* was a much longer time than she imagined. But what of it?

She was holding his long throbbing part through the thin silk of his pyjama trousers and massaging it very lightly.

'I forgive you,' he sighed, desperate to get into her.

'*Je t'aime*, Pierre-Raymond,' she said, turning onto her back. 'I want you to exploit me. Brutalise me, crush me under you and ravage me!'

The words were Janine's – Claudia was turning her expressions of loathing for male desire into an invitation. He accepted at once and slid onto her belly. Her legs parted as she pulled his hardness out of his pyjamas and guided it into her soft warmth. He slid inside with a strong push and felt the warm wet cling of her *joujou* about his shaft.

He was trembling on the very brink of ecstasy, without even a single thrust. She felt the shaking of his body on hers and she guessed his condition and whispered, '*Yes, yes, yes . . .*' He pushed further in, moving slowly, almost holding his breath. But there was no way to hold back the oncoming explosion – the sensations were prodigious and he spurted frantically into her.

Claudia raised her long slender legs and wound them about his waist to hold him. She sighed in ecstasy to his urgent thrusts. She squirmed under him, uttering little cries of delight.

Five minutes later, when they had both recovered a little, he carried her into the bedroom. In the morning he would phone the studio and say he wouldn't be in that day. Or the day after. He would have to think of an excuse for Valerie. It was impossible to tell her he had Claudia back and he was going to stay close, very close, until they needed a rest.

Valerie could reschedule the bookings. Then a slightly uneasy thought intruded into Pierre-Raymond's happiness for a moment – it would require all his skill and cunning to stop dear Claudia from becoming jealous of Valerie. He didn't want to give up his mornings and afternoons feeling and playing with Valerie's big beautiful breasts. And doing other things to her.

And another tiny problem – Liliane would eventually come back and hope to work for him and move into his apartment. Which was obviously impossible because of Claudia and Valerie. He adored them both. On the other hand, he also adored Liliane. It would be tragic to lose her – he had the fondest memory of sitting on the sofa while she took his long heavy shaft in her mouth.

It was absurd to imagine he'd risk losing a woman who adored him as Liliane did. Arrangements must be made to keep her happy and adoring him. And to keep her away from Claudia and Valerie. But awkward little problems like those could be solved when the event demanded. No sensible man borrows trouble from tomorrow.

He laid Claudia down gently on the bed. She smiled at him and slid her hands under her blonde head, a charming little gesture of welcome. His heart was bursting with male pride as he stared at her upstanding breasts and her smooth belly.

'Pierre-Raymond, do you truly adore me?' she murmured.

He lay on the bed between her long shapely legs.

'*Je t'adore*, Claudia *chérie*,' he sighed, his beloved part was stiff as he kissed her between her slender young thighs.

He knew Janine had kissed her here. Touched the delicate lips of Claudia's *joujou* with her tongue. Opened them with a lover's fingers and put the tip of her tongue inside to lick the secret little bud. Had made Claudia jerk and cry out in ecstasy.

That was all she had done – all that she could do. She lacked the necessary fifteen centimetres of strong flesh to thrust up into darling Claudia. Games with fingers and tongue

– yes, all right as far as they went. But for real love making it was essential to have what he had. And know how to use it.

He was Pierre-Raymond Becquet. He was Monsieur Tentimes. And he was going to do enchanting things to Claudia.

Headline Delta Erotic Survey

In order to provide the kind of books you like to read – and to qualify for a free erotic novel of the Editor's choice – we would appreciate it if you would complete the following survey and send your answers, together with any further comments, to:

Headline Book Publishing
FREEPOST (WD 4984)
London
NW1 0YR

1. Are you male or female?
2. Age? Under 20 / 20 to 30 / 30 to 40 / 40 to 50 / 50 to 60 / 60 to 70 / over
3. At what age did you leave full-time education?
4. Where do you live? (Main geographical area)
5. Are you a regular erotic book buyer / a regular book buyer in general / both?
6. How much approximately do you spend a year on erotic books / on books in general?
7. How did you come by this book?
7a. If you bought it, did you purchase from: a national bookchain / a high street store / a newsagent / a motorway station / an airport / a railway station / other . . .
8. Do you find erotic books easy / hard to come by?
8a. Do you find Headline Delta erotic books easy / hard to come by?
9. Which are the best / worst erotic books you have ever read?
9a. Which are the best / worst Headline Delta erotic books you have ever read?
10. Within the erotic genre there are many periods, subjects and literary styles. Which of the following do you prefer:
10a. (period) historical / Victorian / C20th / contemporary / future?
10b. (subject) nuns / whores & whorehouses / Continental frolics / s&m / vampires / modern realism / escapist fantasy / science fiction?

10c. (styles) hardboiled / humorous / hardcore / ironic / romantic / realistic?

10d. Are there any other ingredients that particularly appeal to you?

11. We try to create a cover appearance that is suitable for each title. Do you consider them to be successful?

12. Would you prefer them to be less explicit / more explicit?

13. We would be interested to hear of your other reading habits. What other types of books do you read?

14. Who are your favourite authors?

15. Which newspapers do you read?

16. Which magazines?

17 Do you have any other comments or suggestions to make?